The de Bercy Affair

A Winter and Furneaux Mystery

By Louis Tracy

Writing As

Gordon Holmes

Originally published in 1910

BIN TRAVELER FORM

Cut By: _Georgello Ispure #4_ Qty _32_ Date _07-13-26_

Scanned By: _____ Qty _____ Date _____

Scanned Batch ID's

_____

Notes / Exceptions

_____

The de Bercy Affair

© 2016 Resurrected Press
www.ResurrectedPress.com

Published by Resurrected Press

This classic book was handcrafted by Resurrected Press. Resurrected Press is dedicated to bringing high quality classic books back to the readers who enjoy them. These are not scanned versions of the originals, but, rather, quality checked and edited books meant to be enjoyed!

Please visit ResurrectedPress.com to view our entire catalogue!

For updates on future releases, LIKE us on Facebook:
http://www.Facebook.com/ResurrectedPress

ISBN 13: 978-1-943403-17-2

Printed in the United States of America

Resurrected Press books in A. E. Fielding's *The Chief Inspector Pointer Mystery* Series

The Eames-Erskine Case (1924)
The Charteris Mystery (1925)
The Footsteps that Stopped (1926)
The Clifford Affair (1927)
The Cluny Problem (1928)
The Net Around Joan Ingilby (1928)
The Murder at the Nook (1929)
The Mysterious Partner (1929)
The Craig Poisoning Mystery (1930)
The Wedding Chest Mystery (1930)
The Upfold Farm Mystery (1931)
Death of John Tait (1932)
The Westwood Mystery (1932)
The Tall House Mystery (1933)
The Cautley Conundrum (1934)
The Paper-Chase (1934)
The Case of the Missing Diary (1935)
Tragedy at Beechcroft (1935)
The Case of the Two Pearl Necklaces (1935)
Mystery at the Rectory (1936)
Black Cats Are Lucky (1937)
Scarecrow (1937)
Pointer to a Crime (1944)

RESURRECTED PRESS CLASSIC MYSTERY CATALOGUE

Journeys into Mystery
Travel and Mystery in a More Elegant Time

The Edwardian Detectives
Literary Sleuths of the Edwardian Era

Gems of Mystery
Lost Jewels from a More Elegant Age

Anne Austin
One Drop of Blood
The Black Pigeon
Murder at Bridge
Murder Backstairs

E. C. Bentley
Trent's Last Case: The Woman in Black

Ernest Bramah
Max Carrados Resurrected:
The Detective Stories of Max Carrados

Agatha Christie
The Secret Adversary
The Mysterious Affair at Styles

Octavus Roy Cohen
Midnight

Freeman Wills Croft
The Ponson Case
The Pit Prop Syndicate

J. S. Fletcher

The Herapath Property
The Rayner-Slade Amalgamation
The Chestermarke Instinct
The Paradise Mystery
Dead Men's Money
The Middle of Things
Ravensdene Court
Scarhaven Keep
The Orange-Yellow Diamond
The Middle Temple Murder
The Tallyrand Maxim
The Borough Treasurer
In the Mayor's Parlour
The Saftey Pin

R. Austin Freeman

The Mystery of 31 New Inn from the Dr. Thorndyke Series
John Thorndyke's Cases from the Dr. Thorndyke Series
The Red Thumb Mark from The Dr. Thorndyke Series
The Eye of Osiris from The Dr. Thorndyke Series
A Silent Witness from the Dr. John Thorndyke Series
The Cat's Eye from the Dr. John Thorndyke Series
Helen Vardon's Confession: A Dr. John Thorndyke Story
As a Thief in the Night: A Dr. John Thorndyke Story
Mr. Pottermack's Oversight: A Dr. John Thorndyke Story
Dr. Thorndyke Intervenes: A Dr. John Thorndyke Story
The Singing Bone: The Adventures of Dr. Thorndyke
The Stoneware Monkey: A Dr. John Thorndyke Story
The Great Portrait Mystery, and Other Stories: A Collection of Dr. John Thorndyke and Other Stories
The Penrose Mystery: A Dr. John Thorndyke Story

The Uttermost Farthing: A Savant's Vendetta

Arthur Griffiths
The Passenger From Calais
The Rome Express

Fergus Hume
The Mystery of a Hansom Cab
The Green Mummy
The Silent House
The Secret Passage

Edgar Jepson
The Loudwater Mystery

A. E. W. Mason
At the Villa Rose

A. A. Milne
The Red House Mystery

Baroness Emma Orczy
The Old Man in the Corner

Edgar Allan Poe
The Detective Stories of Edgar Allan Poe

Arthur J. Rees
The Hampstead Mystery
The Shrieking Pit
The Hand In The Dark
The Moon Rock
The Mystery of the Downs

Mary Roberts Rinehart
Sight Unseen and The Confession

Dorothy L. Sayers

Whose Body?

Sir William Magnay
The Hunt Ball Mystery

Mabel and Paul Thorne
The Sheridan Road Mystery

Louis Tracy
The Strange Case of Mortimer Fenley
The Albert Gate Mystery
The Bartlett Mystery
The Postmaster's Daughter
The House of Peril
The Sandling Case: What Would You Have Done?

Charles Edmonds Walk
The Paternoster Ruby

John R. Watson
The Mystery of the Downs
The Hampstead Mystery

Edgar Wallace
The Daffodil Mystery
The Crimson Circle

Carolyn Wells
Vicky Van
The Man Who Fell Through the Earth
In the Onyx Lobby
Raspberry Jam
The Clue
The Room with the Tassels
The Vanishing of Betty Varian
The Mystery Girl
The White Alley
The Curved Blades

FOREWORD

Chief Inspector (later Superintendent) Winter and Detective Inspector Furneaux may well have been the original "Odd Couple" of detection. The pair, the creation of Louis Tracy, a British journalist and author, could not have been more different. Winter, a tall, beefy Englishman who looked more like a country squire than a policeman, and the small, dark, wiry Furneaux, a native of the island of Jersey and more Gallic than British both in his manner and the way he thought. Yet this pair were to collaborate on a series of mysteries stretching from the pre-World War I era into the 1920's.

Though Chief Inspector was technically Furneaux's superior, their working relationship was one of equals, with each bringing certain strengths to the partnership, Furneaux, intuition and a talent for disguises and undercover work, and Winter, dogged British determination and an instinct for solving crimes. Despite their different personalities, the two are fast friends, though their conversations while on the hunt often exhibit wit at the other's expense, and professionally their differences allow them to look at the same problem from different angles, something which accounts for their success.

Yet, despite this closeness, *The de Bercy Affair* sees the two detectives working at loggerheads. The case involves the murder of a French actress, Rose de Bercy, who has been killed in a particularly brutal manner, stabbed through the eye and then mutilated about the face. Furneaux, who usually works in close partnership with his superior, seems to be operating with his own agenda, so much so, that Winter begins to suspect his old friend of having a role in the crime!

Tracy's career can be hard to follow at times. He wrote under several pen-names as well as his own,

Gordon Holmes and Robert Fraser. To further complicate matters, he shared the pseudonym Gordon Holmes with the writer M. P. Shiel, sometimes in collaboration and sometimes in solo efforts, with the Winter and Furneaux mysteries appearing as by Tracy and Holmes. To even further complicate things, at least one mystery appeared in two forms, *The Park Lane Mystery*, and the earlier *The House of Peril* in which Winter and Furneaux have been transformed into New York city detectives with Furneaux being a French-Canadian. In addition to his mysteries, Tracy also wrote adventure, science-fiction, and supernatural works.

The Winter and Furneaux mysteries are prime examples of British detective fiction just before the Golden Age of the period between the wars. They are written with a certain sense of style and personality that is missing from many of the mysteries of the period. It is with pleasure that Resurrected Press presents this new edition of *The de Bercy Affair*.

About the Author

Louis Tracy (1863-1928) was a British journalist and author. He wrote numerous books both under his own name and using the pseudonyms Gordon Holmes and Robert Fraser. He shared these pseudonyms and collaborated with P.M. Shiel on a number of works. Among his books are *The Wings of Morning* (1903), *The Stowmarket Mystery* (1904), and *Number Seventeen* (1916).

Greg Fowlkes
Editor-In-Chief
Resurrected Press
www.ResurrectedPress.com

TABLE OF CONTENTS

I. SOME PHASES OF THE PROBLEM 1

II. DARKNESS...13

III. A CHANGE OF ADDRESS... 25

IV. THE NEW LIFE.. 41

V. THE MISSING BLADE..53

VI. TO TORMOUTH 69

VII. AT TORMOUTH..85

VIII. AT THE SUN-DIAL 101

IX. THE LETTER 119

X. THE DIARY, AND ROSALIND..135

XI. ENTRAPPED!...151

XII. THE SARACEN DAGGER.. 165

XIII. OSBORNE MAKES A VOW 179

XIV: THE ARRESTS 195

XV. CLEARING THE AIR..211

XVI. WHEREIN TWO WOMEN TAKE THE FIELD...........................227

XVII. THE CLOSING SCENE.. 241

I. Some Phases Of The Problem

Chief Inspector Winter sat in his private office at New Scotland Yard, while a constable in uniform, bare-headed, stood near the door in the alert attitude of one who awaits the nod of a superior. Nevertheless, Mr. Winter, half-turning from a desk littered with documents, eyed the man as though he had just said something outrageous, something so opposed to the tenets of the Police Manual that the Chief Commissioner alone could deal with the offense.

"Have you been to Mr. Furneaux's residence?" he snapped, nibbling one end of a mustache already clipped or chewed so short that his strong white teeth could barely seize one refractory bristle.

"Yes, sir."

"Have you telephoned to any of the district stations?"

"Oh, yes, sir--to Vine Street, Marlborough Street, Cannon Row, Tottenham Court Road, and half-a-dozen others."

"No news of Mr. Furneaux anywhere? The earth must have opened and swallowed him!"

"The station-sergeant at Finchley Road thought he saw Mr. Furneaux jump on to a 'bus at St. John's Wood about six o'clock yesterday evening, sir; but he could not be sure."

"No, he wouldn't. I know that station-sergeant. He is a fat-head.... When did you telegraph to Kenterstone?"

"At 6.30, sir."

Mr. Winter whisked a pink telegraphic slip from off the blotting-pad, and read:

Inspector Furneaux not here to my knowledge.

Police Superintendent,
KENTERSTONE.

"Another legal quibbler—fat, too, I'll be bound," he growled. Then he laughed a little in a vein of irritated perplexity, and said:

"Thank you, Johnson. You, at least, seem to have done everything possible. Try again in the morning. I *must* see Mr. Furneaux at the earliest moment! Kindly bring me the latest editions of the evening papers, and, by the way, help yourself to a cigar."

The gift of a cigar was a sign of the great man's favor, and it was always an extraordinarily good one, of which none but himself knew the exact brand. Left alone for a few minutes, he glanced through a written telephone message which he had thrust under the blotting-pad when Police Constable Johnson had entered. It was from Paris, and announced that two notorious Anarchists were en route to England by the afternoon train, due at Charing Cross at 9.15 p.m.

"Anarchists!" growled the Chief Inspector—"Pooh! Antoine Descartes and Émile Janoc—Soho for them— absinthe and French cigarettes—green and black poison. Poor devils! they will do themselves more harm than his Imperial Majesty. Now, where the deuce *is* Furneaux? This Feldisham Mansions affair is just in his line— Clarke will ruin it."

Johnson came back with a batch of evening papers. Understanding his duties—above all, understanding Mr. Winter—he placed them on the table, saluted, and withdrew without a word. Soon the floor was littered with discarded news-sheets, those quick-moving eyes ever seeking one definite item—"The Murder in the West End—Latest"—or some such headline, and once only was his attention held by a double-leaded paragraph at the top of a column:

A correspondent writes:—"I saw the deceased lady

in company with a certain popular American millionaire at the International Horse Show in June, and was struck by her remarkable resemblance to a girl of great beauty resident in Jersey some eight years ago. The then village maid was elected Rose Queen at a rural *fête*, I photographed her, and comparison of the photograph with the portrait of Mademoiselle de Bercy exhibited in this year's Academy served to confirm me in my opinion that she and the Jersey Rose Queen were one and the same person. I may add that my accidental discovery was made long before the commission of the shocking crime of yesterday."

Under present circumstances, of course, we withhold from publication the name of the Jersey Rose Queen, but the line of inquiry thus indicated may prove illuminative should there be any doubt as to the earlier history of the hapless lady whose lively wit and personal charm have brought London society to her feet since she left the Paris stage last year.

Winter did not hurry. Tucking the cigar comfortably into a corner of his mouth, he read each sentence with a quiet deliberation; then he sought a telephone number among the editorial announcements, and soon was speaking into a transmitter.

"Is that the *Daily Gazette*?... Put me on to the editorial department, please.... That you, Arbuthnot? Well, I'm Winter, of Scotland Yard. Your evening edition, referring to the Feldisham Mansions tragedy, contains an item.... Oh, you expected to hear from me, did you? Well, what is the lady's name, and who is your correspondent?... What? Spell it. A-r-m-a-u-d. All right; if you feel you *must* write to the man first, save time by asking him to send me the photograph. I will pass it on to you exclusively, of course. Thanks. Good-by."

Before the receiver was on its hook, the Chief Inspector was taking a notebook from his breast pocket, and he made the following entry:

Mirabel Armaud, Rose Queen, village near St. Heliers, summer of 1900.

A knock sounded on the door.

"Oh, if this could only be Furneaux!" groaned Winter. "Come in! Ah! Glad to see you, Mr. Clarke. I was hoping you would turn up. Any news?"

"Nothing much, sir—that is to say, nothing really definite. The maid-servant is still delirious, and keeps on screaming out that Mr. Osborne killed her mistress. I am beginning to believe there is something in it—"

Winter's prominent steel blue eyes dwelt on Clarke musingly.

"But haven't we the clearest testimony as to Osborne's movements?" he asked.

"He quitted Miss de Bercy's flat at 6.25, drove in his motor to the Ritz, attended a committee meeting of the International Polo Club at 6.30, occupied the chair, dined with the committee, and they all went to the Empire at nine o'clock. Unless a chauffeur, a hall-porter, a head-waiter, two under-waiters, five polo celebrities, a box-office clerk, and several other persons, are mixed up in an amazing conspiracy to shield Mr. Rupert Osborne, he certainly could not have murdered a woman who was alive in Feldisham Mansions at half-past seven."

Clarke pursed his lips sagely. As a study in opposites, no two men could manifest more contrasts. Clarke might have had the words "Detective Inspector" branded on his forehead: his features sharp, cadaverous, eyes deep-set and suspicious, his nose and chin inquisitive, his lips fixed as a rat-trap. Wide cheek-bones, low-placed ears, and narrow brows gave him a sinister aspect. In his own special department, the hunting out of "confidence men," card-sharpers, and similar hawklike pluckers of the provincial pigeon fluttering through London's streets, he was unrivaled. But Winter more resembled an intellectual prizefighter than the typical detective of fiction. His round head, cropped hair, wide-open eyes, joined to a powerful physique and singular alertness of glance and movement, suggested that he varied the healthy monotony of a gentleman farmer's life by attendance at the National Sporting Club and other haunts of pugilism. A terror to wrongdoers, he was never disliked by them, whereas Clarke was hated. In a word, Winter was a sharp brain, Clarke a sharp nose, and that is why Winter groaned inwardly at being compelled to intrust the Feldisham Mansions crime to Clarke.

"What is your theory of this affair?" he said, rather by way of making conversation than from any hope of being enlightened.

"It is simple enough," said Clarke, his solemn glance resting for a moment on the box of cigars. Winter nodded in the same direction. His cigars were sometimes burnt offerings as well as rewards.

"Light up," he said, "and tell me what you think."

"Mademoiselle de Bercy was killed by either a disappointed lover or a discarded husband. All these foreign actresses marry early, but grow tired of matrimony within a year. If, then, there is no chance of upsetting Mr. Osborne's alibi, we must get the Paris police to look into Miss de Bercy's history. Her husband will probably turn out to be some third-rate actor or broken-down manager. Let us find *him*, and see if *he* is as sure of his whereabouts last evening as Mr. Rupert Osborne professes to be."

"You seem to harp on Osborne's connection with the affair?"

"And why not, sir? A man like him, with all his money, ought to know better than to go gadding about with actresses."

"But he is interested in the theater—he is quite an authority on French comedy."

"He can tackle French tragedy now—he is up to the neck in this one."

"You still cling to the shrieking housemaid—to her

ravings, I mean?"

"Perhaps I should have mentioned it sooner, sir, but I have come across a taxicab driver who picked up a gentleman uncommonly like Mr. Osborne at 7.20 p.m. on Tuesday, and drove him from the corner of Berkeley Street to Knightsbridge, waited there nearly fifteen minutes, and brought him back again to Berkeley Street."

The Chief Inspector came as near being startled as is permissible in Scotland Yard.

"That is a very serious statement," he said quietly, wheeling round in his chair and scrutinizing his subordinate's lean face with eyes more wide-open than ever, if that were possible. "It is tantamount to saying that some person resembling Mr. Osborne hired a cab outside the Ritz Hotel, was taken to Feldisham Mansions at the very hour Miss de Bercy was murdered, and returned to the Ritz in the same vehicle."

"Exactly so," and Clarke pursed his thin lips meaningly.

"So, then, you *have* discovered something?"

Mr. Winter's tone had suddenly become dryly official, and the other man, fearing a reprimand, added:

"I admit, sir, I ought to have told you sooner, but I don't want to make too much of the incident. The taxicab chauffeur does not know Mr. Rupert Osborne by sight, and I took good care not to mention the name. The unknown was dressed like Mr. Osborne, and looked like him—that is all."

"Who is the driver?"

"William Campbell—cab number X L 4001. I have hired him to-morrow morning from ten o'clock, and then he will have an opportunity of seeing Mr. Osborne—"

"Meet me here at 9.30, and I will keep the appointment for you. Until—until I make other arrangements, I intend to take this Feldisham Mansions affair into my own hands. Of course, I should have been delighted to leave it in your charge, but during the past hour something of vastly greater importance has turned up, and I want you to tackle it immediately."

"Something more important than a society murder?" Clarke could not help saying.

"Yes. You know that the Tsar comes to London from Windsor to-morrow? Well, read this," and Winter, with the impressive air of one who communicates a state secret, handed the Paris message.

"Ah!" muttered Clarke, gloating over the word "Anarchists."

"Now you understand," murmured Winter darkly. "Unfortunately these men are far too well acquainted with me to render it advisable that I should shadow them. So I shall accompany you to Charing Cross, point them out, and leave them to you. A live monarch is of more account than a dead actress, so you see now what confidence I have in you, Mr. Clarke."

Clarke's sallow cheeks flushed a little. Winter might be a genial chief, but he seldom praised so openly.

"I quite recognize that, sir," he said. "Of course, I am sorry to drop out of this murder case. It has points, first-rate points. I haven't told you yet about the stone."

"Why—what stone?"

"The stone that did for Miss de Bercy. The flat was not thoroughly searched last night, but this morning I examined every inch of it, and under the piano I found—this."

He produced from a pocket something wrapped in a handkerchief. Unfolding the linen, he rose and placed on the blotting-pad, under the strong light of a shaded lamp, one of those flat stones which the archeologist calls "celts," or "flint ax-heads." Indeed, no expert eye was needed to determine its character. The cutting edge formed a perfect curve; two deep indentations showed how it had been bound on to a handle of bone or wood. At the broadest part it measured fully four inches, its length the same, thickness about three-quarters of an inch. That it was a genuine neolithic flint could not be questioned. A modern lapidary might contrive to chip a flint into the same shape, but could not impart that curious bloom which apparently exudes from the heart of the stone during its thousands of centuries of rest in prehistoric cave or village mound. This specimen showed the gloss of antiquity on each smooth facet.

But it showed more. When used in war or the chase by the fearsome being who first fashioned it to serve his savage needs, it must often have borne a grisly tint, and now *again* each side of the strangely sharp edge was smeared with grewsome daubs, while some black hairs clung to the dried clots which clustered on the irregular surfaces.

Sentiment finds little room in the retreat of a Chief Inspector, so Winter whistled softly when he set eyes on this weird token of a crime.

"By gad!" he cried, "in my time at the Yard I've seen many queer instruments of butchery—ranging from a crusader's mace to the strings of a bass fiddle—but this beats the lot."

"It must have come out of some museum," said the other.

"It suggests a tragedy of the British Association," mused Winter aloud.

"It ought to supply a first-rate clew, anyhow," said Clarke.

"Oh, it does; it must. If only—"

Winter checked himself on the very lip of indiscretion, for Clarke detested Furneaux. He consulted his watch.

"We must be off now," he said briskly. "Leave the stone with me, and while we are walking to Charing Cross I can give you a few pointers about these Anarchist pests. Once they are comfortably boxed up in some café in Old Compton Street you can come away safely for the night, and pick them up again about midday to-morrow. They are absolutely harm—I mean they cannot do any harm until the Tsar arrives. From that moment you must stick to them like a limpet to a rock; I will arrange for a man to relieve you in the evening, nor shall I forget to give your name to the Embassy people when they begin to scatter diamond pins around."

When he meant to act a part, Winter was an excellent comedian, and soon Clarke was prowling at the heels of those redoubtables, Antoine Descartes and Émile Janoc.

Once Clarke was safely shelved, Winter called the first taxicab he met and was driven to Feldisham Mansions. An unerring instinct had warned him at once that the murder of the actress was no ordinary crime; but Clarke had happened to be on duty when the report of it reached the Yard a few minutes after eight o'clock the previous evening, and Winter had bewailed the mischance which deprived him of the services of Furneaux, the one man to whom he could have left the inquiry with confidence.

The very simplicity of the affair was baffling. Mademoiselle Rose de Bercy was the leading lady in a company of artistes, largely recruited from the *Comédie Française*, which had played a short season in London during September of the past year. She did not accompany the others when they returned to Paris, but remained, to become a popular figure in London society, and was soon in great demand for her *contes drôles* at private parties. She was now often to be seen in the company of Mr. Rupert Osborne, a young American millionaire, whose tastes ordinarily followed a less frivolous bent than he showed in seeking the society of an undeniably chic and sprightly Frenchwoman. It had been rumored that the two would be married before the close of the summer, and color was lent to the statement by the lady's withdrawal from professional engagements.

So far as Winter's information went, this was the position of affairs until a quarter to eight on the night of the first Tuesday in July. At that hour, Mademoiselle de Bercy's housemaid either entered or peered into her mistress's drawing-room, and saw her lifeless body stretched on the floor. Shrieking, the girl fled out into the lobby and down a flight of stairs to the hall-porter's little office, which adjoined the elevator. By chance, the man had just collected the letters from the boxes on each of the six floors of the block of flats, and had gone to the post; Mademoiselle de Bercy's personal maid and her cook, having obtained permission to visit an open-air exhibition, had, it seemed, been absent since six o'clock; the opposite flat on the same story was closed, the tenants being at the seaside; and the distraught housemaid, pursued by phantoms, forthwith yielded to the strain, so that the hall-porter, on his return, found her lying across the threshold of his den.

He summoned his wife from the basement, and the frenzied girl soon regained a partial consciousness. It was difficult to understand her broken words, but, such as they were, they sent the man in hot haste to the flat on the first floor. The outer and inner doors were wide open, as was the door of the drawing-room, and sufficient daylight streamed in through two lofty windows to reveal something of the horror that had robbed the housemaid of her wits.

The unfortunate Frenchwoman was lying on her back in the center of the room, and the hall-porter's hurried scrutiny found that she had been done to death with a brutal ferocity, her face almost unrecognizable.

Not until the return of the French maid, Pauline, from the exhibition, could it be determined beyond doubt that robbery was not the motive of the crime, for she was able to assure the police that her mistress's jewels were untouched. A gold purse was found on a table close to the body, a bracelet sparkled on a wrist cruelly bruised, and a brooch fastened at the neck the loose wrap worn as a preliminary to dressing for the evening.

Owing to the breakdown of the only servant actually present in the flat at the time of the murder, it was impossible to learn anything intelligible beyond the girl's raving cry that "Mr. Osborne did it." Still, there was apparently little difficulty in realizing what had happened. The housemaid had been startled while at supper, either by a shriek or some noise of moving furniture, had gone to the drawing-room, given one glance at the terrifying spectacle that met her eyes, and was straightway bereft of her wits.

The Chief Inspector was turning over in his mind the puzzling features of the affair when his automobile swept swiftly out of the traffic and glare of Knightsbridge into the quiet street in which stood Feldisham Mansions. A policeman had just strolled along the pavement to disperse a group of curious people gathered near the entrance, so Winter stopped his cab at a little distance and alighted unobserved.

He walked rapidly inside and found the hall-porter at his post. When the man learnt the visitor's identity he seemed surprised.

"Mr. Clarke has bin here all day, sir," he said, "and, as soon as he left, another gentleman kem, though I must say he hasn't bothered *me* much—" this with a touch of resentment, for the hall-porter's self-importance was enhanced by his connection with the tragedy.

"Another gentleman!"—this was incomprehensible, since Clarke would surely place a constable in charge of the flat. "What name did he give?"

"He's up there at this minnit, sir, an' here's his card."

Winter read: "Mr. Charles Furneaux, Criminal Investigation Department, Scotland Yard."

"Well, I'm jiggered!" he muttered, and he added fuel to the fire of the hall-porter's annoyance by disregarding the elevator and rushing up the stairs, three steps at a time.

II. Darkness

Winter felt at once relieved and displeased. Twice during the hour had his authority been disregarded. He was willing to ignore Clarke's method of doling out important facts because such was the man's secretive nature. But Furneaux! The urgent messages sent to every place where they might reach him, each and all summoned him to Scotland Yard without the slightest reference to the Feldisham Mansions crime. It was with a stiff upper lip, therefore, that the Chief Inspector acknowledged the salute of the constable who admitted him to the ill-fated Frenchwoman's abode. Furneaux was his friend, Furneaux might be admirable, Furneaux was the right man in the right place, but Furneaux must first receive an official reminder of the claims of discipline.

The subdued electric lights in the hall revealed within a vista of Oriental color blended with Western ideals of comfort. Two exquisitely fashioned lamps of hammered iron, rifled from a Pekin temple, softened by their dragons and lotus leaves the glare of the high-powered globes within them. Praying carpets, frayed by the deserts of Araby, covered the geometric design of a parquet floor, and bright-hued draperies of Mirzapur hid the rigid outlines of British carpentry. A perfume of joss-sticks still clung to the air: it suggested the apartments of a Sultana rather than the bower of a fashionable lady in the West End of London.

First impressions are powerful, and Winter acknowledged the spell of the unusual here, but his impassive face showed no sign of this when he asked the constable the whereabouts of Mr. Furneaux.

"In there, sir," said the man, pointing to a door.

Winter noted instantly that the floor creaked beneath his light tread. The rugs deadened his footsteps, but the parquetry complained of his weight. It was, he perceived, almost impossible for anyone to traverse an old flooring of that type without revealing the fact to ordinarily acute ears. Once when his heel fell on the bare wood, it rang with a sharp yet hollow note. It seemed, somehow, that the place was empty—that it missed its presiding spirit.

Oddly enough, as he remembered afterwards, he hesitated with outstretched hand in front of the closed door. He was doubtful whether or not to knock. As a matter of fact, he did tap slightly on a panel before turning the handle. Then he received his second vague impression of a new and strange element in the history of a crime. The room was in complete darkness.

Though Winter never admitted the existence of nerves, he did not even try to conceal from his own consciousness that he started distinctly when he looked into a blackness rendered all the more striking by the glimpse of a few feet of floor revealed by the off-shine from the hall-light.

"Are you here, Furneaux?" he forced himself to say quickly.

"Ah, that you, Winter!" came a voice from the interior. "Yes, I was dreaming in the dusk, I think. Let me give you a light."

"Dusk, you call it? Gad, it's like a vault!"

Winter's right hand had found the electric switches, and two clusters of lamps on wall-brackets leaped alight. Furneaux was standing, his hands behind his back, almost in the center, but the Chief Inspector gathered that the room's silent occupant had been seated in a corner farthest removed from the windows, and that his head had been propped on his clenched hands, for the dull red marks of his knuckles were still visible on both cheeks.

Each was aware of a whiff of surprise.

"Queer trick, sitting in the dark," Furneaux remarked, his eyes on the floor. "I—find I collect my wits better that way—sometimes. Sometimes, one cannot have light enough: for instance, the moment I saw fear in Lady Holt's face I knew that her diamonds had been stolen by herself—"

Winter reflected that light was equally unkind to Furneaux as to "Lady Holt," for the dapper little man looked pallid and ill at ease in this flood of electric brilliancy.

There was a silence. Then Furneaux volunteered the remark: "In this instance, thought is needed, not observation. One might gaze at that for twenty years, but it would not reveal the cause of Mademoiselle de Bercy's murder."

"*That*" was a dark stain near the center of the golden-brown carpet. Winter bent a professional eye on it, but his mind was assimilating two new ideas. In the first place, Furneaux was not the cheery colleague whose perky chatterings were his most deadly weapons when lulling a rogue into fancied security. In the second, he himself had not been prepared for the transit from a hall of Eastern gorgeousness to a room fastidiously correct in its reproduction of the period labeled by connoisseurs "after Louis XV."

The moment was not ripe for an inquiry anent Furneaux's object in hastening to Feldisham Mansions without first reporting himself. Winter somehow felt that the question would jar just then and there, and though not forgotten, it was waived; still, there was a hint of it in his next comment.

"I must confess I am glad to find you here," he said. "Clarke has cleared the ground somewhat, but—er—he has a heavy hand, and I have turned him on to a new job—Anarchists."

He half expected an answering gleam of fun in the dark eyes lifted to his, for these two were close friends at all seasons; but Furneaux seemed not even to hear! His lips muttered:

"I—wonder."

"Wonder what?"

"What purpose could be served by this girl's death. Who bore her such a bitter grudge that not even her death would sate their hatred, but they must try also to destroy her beauty?"

Now, the Chief Inspector had learnt that everyone who had seen the dead woman expressed this same sentiment, yet it came unexpectedly from Furneaux's lips; because Furneaux never said the obvious thing.

"Clarke believes,"—Winter loathed the necessity for this constant reference to Clarke—"Clarke believes that she was killed by one of two people, either a jealous husband or a dissatisfied lover."

"As usual, Clarke is wrong."

"He may be."

"He is."

In spite of his prior agreement with Furneaux's estimate of their colleague's intelligence, Winter felt nettled at this omniscience. From the outset, his clear brain had been puzzled by this crime, and Furneaux's extraordinary pose was not the least bewildering feature about it.

"Oh, come now," he said, "you cannot have been here many minutes, and it is early days to speak so positively. I have been hunting you the whole afternoon—in fact, ever since I saw what a ticklish business this was likely to prove—and I don't suppose you have managed to gather all the threads of it into your fingers so rapidly."

"There are so few," muttered Furneaux, looking down on the carpet with the morbid eyes of one who saw a terrible vision there.

"Well, it is a good deal to have discovered the instrument with which the crime was committed."

Furneaux's mobile face instantly became alive with excitement.

"It was a long, thin dagger," he cried. "Something in the surgical line, I imagine. Who found it, and where?"

Some men in Winter's shoes might have smiled in a superior way. He did not. He knew Furneaux, profoundly distrusted Clarke.

"There is some mistake," he contented himself with saying. "Miss de Bercy was killed by a piece of flint, shaped like an ax-head—one of those queer objects of the stone age which is ticketed carefully after it is found in an ancient cave, and then put away in a glass case. Clarke searched the room this morning, and found it there—tucked away underneath," and he turned round to point to the foot of the boudoir grand piano, embellished with Watteaux panels on its rosewood, that stood in the angle between the door and the nearest window.

The animation died out of Furneaux's features as quickly as it had appeared there.

"Useful, of course" he murmured. "Did you bring it?"

"No; it is in my office."

"But Mi—Mademoiselle de Bercy was not killed in that way. She was supple, active, lithe. She would have struggled, screamed, probably overpowered her adversary. No; the doctor admits that after a hasty examination he jumped to conclusions, for not one of the external cuts and bruises could have produced unconsciousness—not all of them death. Miss de Bercy was stabbed through the right eye by something strong and pointed—something with a thin, blunt-edged blade. I urged a thorough examination of the head, and the post mortem proved the correctness of my theory."

Winter, one of the shrewdest officials who had ever won distinction in Scotland Yard, did not fail to notice that curious slip of a syllable before "Mademoiselle," but it was explained a moment later when Furneaux used the English prefix "Miss" before the name. It was more natural for Furneaux to use the French word, however. Winter spoke French fluently—like an educated Englishman—but Furneaux spoke it like a native of Paris. The difference between the two was clearly shown by their pronunciation of "de Bercy." Winter sounded three distinct syllables—Furneaux practically two, with a slurred "r" that Winter could not have uttered to save his life.

Moreover, he was considerably taken aback by the discovery that Furneaux had evidently been working on the case during several hours.

"You have gone into the affair thoroughly, then," he blurted out.

"Oh, yes. I read of the murder this morning, just as I was leaving Kenterstone on my way to report at the Yard."

"Kenterstone!"

He was almost minded to inquire if the local superintendent was a fat man.

"Sir Peter and Lady Holt left town early in the day, so I went to Kenterstone from Brighton late last night.... The pawnbroker who held Lady Holt's diamonds was treating himself to a long weekend by the sea, and I thought it advisable to see him in person and explain matters."

A memory of the Finchley Road station-sergeant who thought that he had seen Furneaux get on a 'bus at 6 p.m. in North London the previous evening shot through Winter's mind; but he kept to the main line of their talk.

"Do you know who this Rose de Bercy really is?" he suddenly demanded.

For a second Furneaux seemed to hesitate, but the reply came in an even tone.

"I have reason to believe that she was born in Jersey, and that her maiden name was Mirabel Armaud," he said.

"The Rose Queen of a village fête eight years ago?"

Perhaps it was Furneaux's turn to be surprised, but he showed no sign. "May I ask how you ascertained that fact?" he asked quietly.

"It is published in one of the evening papers. A man who happened to photograph her in Jersey recognized the likeness when he saw the Academy portrait of Rose de Bercy. But if you have not seen his statement already, how did *you* come to know that Miss de Bercy was

Mirabel Armaud?"

"I am a Jersey man by birth, and, although I quitted the island early in life, I often go back there. Indeed, I was present at the very *fête* you mention."

"I suppose the young lady was in a carriage and surrounded by a crowd? It would be an odd thing if you figured in the photograph," laughed Winter.

"There have been more unlikely coincidences, but my early sight of the remarkable woman who was killed in this room last night explains my intense desire to track her murderer before Clarke had time to baffle my efforts. It forms, too, a sort of excuse for my departure from official routine. Of course, I would have reported myself this evening, but, up to the present, I have been working hard to try and dispel the fog of motive that blocks the way."

"You have heard of Rupert Osborne, then?"

Furneaux was certainly not the man whom Winter was accustomed to meet at other times. Usually quick as lightning to grasp or discard a point, to-night he appeared to experience no little difficulty in focusing his attention on the topic of the moment. The mention of Rupert Osborne's name did not evoke the characteristically vigorous repudiation that Winter looked for. Instead, there was a marked pause, and, when the reply came, it was with an effort.

"Yes. I suppose Clarke wants to arrest him?"

"He has thought of it!"

"But Osborne's movements last night are so clearly defined?"

"So one would imagine, but Clarke still doubts."

"Why?"

Winter told of the taxicab driver, and the significant journey taken by his fare. Furneaux shook his head.

"Strange, if true," he said; "why should Osborne kill the woman he meant to marry?"

"She may have jilted him."

"No, oh, no. It was—it must have been—the aim of

her life to secure a rich husband. She was beautiful, but cold—she had the eye that weighs and measures. Have you ever seen the Monna Lisa in the Louvre?"

Winter did not answer, conscious of a subtle suspicion that Furneaux really knew far more of the inner history of this tragedy than had appeared hitherto. Clarke, in his own peculiar way, was absurdly secretive, but that Furneaux should want to remain silent was certainly baffling.

"By the way," said Winter with seeming irrelevance, "if you were in Brighton and Kenterstone yesterday afternoon and evening, you had not much time to spare in London?"

"No."

"Then the station-sergeant at Finchley Road was mistaken in thinking that he saw you in that locality about six o'clock—'jumping on to a 'bus' was his precise description of your movements."

"I was there at that time."

"How did you manage it? St. John's Wood is far away from either Victoria or Charing Cross, and I suppose you reached Kenterstone by way of Charing Cross?"

"I returned from Brighton at three o'clock, and did not visit Sir Peter Holt until half-past nine at Kenterstone. Had I disturbed him before dinner the consequence might have been serious for her ladyship. Besides, I wished to avoid the local police at Kenterstone."

Both men smiled constrainedly. There was a barrier between them, and Furneaux, apparently, was not inclined to remove it; as for Winter, he could not conquer the impression that, thus far, their conversation was of a nature that might be looked for between a police official and a reluctant witness—assuredly not between colleagues who were also on the best of terms as comrades. Furneaux was obviously on guard, controlling his face, his words, his very gestures. That so outspoken a man should deem it necessary to adopt such a rôle with his close friend was annoying, but long years of forced self-repression had taught Winter the wisdom of throttling back utterances which might be regretted afterwards. Indeed, he tried valiantly to repair the fast-widening breach.

"Have a cigar," he said, proffering a well-filled case. "Suppose we just sit down and go through the affair from A to Z. Much of our alphabet is missing, but we may be able to guess a few additional letters."

Furneaux smiled again. This time there was the faintest ripple of amusement in his eyes.

"Now, you know how you hate to see me maltreat a good Havana," he protested.

"This time I forgive you before the offense—anything to jolt you into your usual rut. Why, man alive, here have I been hunting you all day, yet no sooner are you engaged on the very job for which I wanted you, than I find myself cross-examining you as though—as though you had committed some flagrant error."

The Chief Inspector did not often flounder in his speech as he had done twice that night. He was about to say "as though I suspected you of killing Rose de Bercy yourself"; but his brain generally worked in front of his voice, and he realized that the hypothesis would have sounded absurd, almost insane.

Furneaux took the cigar. He did not light it, but deliberately crushed the wrapper between thumb and forefinger, and then smelled it with the air of one who dallies with a full-scented rose, passing it to and fro under his nostrils. Winter, meantime, was darting several small rings of smoke through one wide and slowly dissipating circle, both being now seated, Winter's bulk, genially aggressive, well thrust forward—but Furneaux, small, compact, a bundle of nerves under rigid control, was sunk back into the depths of a large and deep-seated chair, and seemed to shirk the new task imposed on his powers of endurance. Winter was so conscious of this singularly unexpected behavior on his friend's part that his conscience smote him.

"I say, old man," he said, "you look thoroughly done up. I hardly realized that you had been hard at work all day. Have you eaten anything?"

"Had all I wanted," said Furneaux, thawing a little under this solicitude.

"Perhaps you didn't want enough. Come, own up. Have you dined?"

"No—I was not hungry."

"Where did you lunch?"

"I ate a good breakfast."

Winter sprang to his feet again.

"By Jove!" he cried, "this affair seems to have taken hold of you—I meant to send for the hall-porter and the French maid—Pauline is her name, I think; she ought to be able to throw some light on her mistress's earlier life— but we can leave all that till to-morrow. Come to my club. A cutlet and a glass of wine will make a new man of you."

Furneaux rose at once. Anyone might have believed that he was glad to postpone the proposed examination of the servants.

"That will be splendid," he said with an air of relief that compared markedly with his reticent mood of the past few minutes. "The mere mention of food has given me an appetite. I suppose I am fagged out, or as near it as I have ever been. Moreover, I can tell you everything that any person in these Mansions knows of what took place here between six and eight o'clock last night—a good deal more, by the way, than Clarke has found out, though he scored a point over that stone. Where is it?—in the office, you said. I should like to see it—in the morning."

"You will see more than that. Clarke has arranged to meet the taxicab driver at ten o'clock. He meant to confront him with Rupert Osborne, but we must manage things differently. Of course the man's testimony may be important. Alibi or no alibi, it will be awkward for Osborne if a credible witness swears that he was in this locality for nearly a quarter of an hour about the very time that this poor young lady was killed."

Furneaux, holding the broken cigar under his nose, offered no comment, but, as they entered the hall, he said, glancing at its quaint decoration:

"If opportunity makes the thief, so, I imagine, does it sometimes inspire the murderer. Given the clear moment, the wish, the fury, can't you picture the effect these bizarre surroundings would exercise on a mind already strung to the madness of crime? For every willful slayer of a fellow human being is mad—mad.... Ah, there was the genius of a maniac in the choice of that flint ax to rend Mirabel Armaud's smooth skin—yet she had the right to live—perhaps—"

He stopped; and Winter anew felt that this musing Furneaux of to-day was a different personality from the Furneaux of his intimate knowledge.

And how compellingly strange it was that he should choose to describe Rose de Bercy by the name which she had ceased to bear during many years! Winter dispelled the scent of the joss-sticks by a mighty puff of honest tobacco smoke.

"Oh, come along," he growled, "let us eat—we are both in need of it. The flat is untenanted, of course. Very well, lock the door," he added, addressing the policeman. "Leave the key with the hall-porter, and tell him not to admit anybody, on any pretext whatsoever, until Mr. Furneaux and I come here in the morning."

III. A Change Of Address

On the morning after the inquest on Rose de Bercy, the most miserable young man in London, in his own estimation, was Mr. Rupert Glendinning Osborne. Though utterly downcast and disconsolate, he was in excellent health, and might have eaten well of the good things on his breakfast table had he not thoughtlessly opened a newspaper while stirring his coffee.

Under other circumstances, he might have laughed at the atrocious photograph which depicted "Mr. Rupert Osborne arriving at the coroner's court." The camera had foreshortened an arm, deprived him of his right leg below the knee, discredited his tailor, and given him the hang-dog aspect of a convicted pickpocket, for he had been "snapped" at the moment of descent from his automobile, when a strong wind was blowing, and he had been annoyed by the presence of a gaping crowd.

The camera had lied, of course. In reality, he was a good-looking man of thirty, not tall or muscular, but of well-knit figure, elegant though by no means effeminate. For a millionaire, and a young one, he was by way of being a phenomenon. He cared little for society; drove his own horses, but was hardly ever seen in the Park; rode boldly to hounds, yet refused to patronize a racing stable. He seldom visited a theater, though he wrote well-informed articles on the modern French stage for the *New Review*; he preferred a pleasant dinner with a couple of friends to a banquet with hundreds of acquaintances; in a word, he conducted himself as a staid citizen whether in New York, or London, or Paris. Never had a breath of scandal or notoriety attached itself to his name until he was dragged into lurid prominence by the stupefying event of that fatal Tuesday evening.

Those who knew him best had expressed sheer

incredulity when they first heard of his contemplated marriage with the French actress. But a man's friends, as a rule, are the worst judges of his probable choice of a partner for life: and Rupert Osborne was drawn to Rose de Bercy because she possessed in superabundance those lively qualities and volatile charms in which he was himself deficient.

There could be no manner of doubt, however, that some part of his quivering nervous system had been seared by statements made about her during the inquest. It was not soothing for a distraught lover to learn that Mademoiselle de Bercy's reminiscences of her youth were singularly inaccurate. She could not well have been born in a patrician château on the Loire, and yet be the daughter of a Jersey potato-grower. Her father, Jean Armaud, was stated to be still living on a small farm near St. Heliers, whereas her own version of the family history was that Monsieur le Comte de Bercy did not survive the crash of the family fortunes in the Panama swindle. Other discrepancies were not lacking between official fact and romantic narrative. They gave Osborne the first glimpse of the abyss into which he had almost plunged. A loyal-hearted fellow, he shrank from the hateful consciousness that the hapless girl's tragic end had rescued him in all likelihood from another tragedy, bitter and long drawn out. But because he had been so foolish as to fall in love with a beautiful adventuress there was no reason why he should be blind and deaf when tardy common sense began to assert itself.

To a man who habitually shrank from the public eye, it was bad enough to be dragged into the fierce light that beats on the witness-box in an inquiry such as this, but it was far worse to feel in his inmost heart that he was now looked upon with suspicion by millions of people in England and America.

He could not shirk the meaning of the recorded evidence. The newspapers, it is true, had carefully avoided the ugly word alibi; but ninety per cent. of their readers could not fail to see that Rupert Osborne had escaped arrest solely by reason of the solid phalanx of testimony as to his movements on the Tuesday evening before and after the hour of the murder; the remaining ten per cent. reviled the police, and protested, with more or less forceful adjectives, that "there was one law for the rich and another for the poor."

At the inquest itself, Osborne was too sorrow-laden and stunned to realize the significance of certain questions which now seemed to leap at him viciously from out the printed page.

"How were you dressed when you visited Miss de Bercy that afternoon?" the coroner had asked him.

"I wore a dark gray morning suit and black silk hat," he had answered.

"You did not change your clothing before going to the Ritz Hotel?"

"No. I drove straight there from Feldisham Mansions."

"Did you dress for dinner?"

"No. My friends and I discussed certain new regulations as to the proposed international polo tournament, and it was nearly eight o'clock before we concluded the business of the meeting, so we arranged to dine in the grill-room and go to a Vaudeville entertainment afterwards."

That statement had puzzled the coroner. He referred to his notes.

"To the Vaudeville?" he queried. "I thought you went to the Empire Theater?" and Osborne explained that Americans spoke of "vaudeville" in the same sense as Englishmen use the word "music-hall" or "variety."

"You were with your friends during the whole time between 6.30 p.m. and midnight?"

"Practically. I left them for a few minutes before dinner, but only to go to the writing-room, where I wrote two short letters."

"At what hour, as nearly as you can recollect?"

"About ten minutes to eight. I glanced at the clock when the letters were posted, as I wished to be sure of catching the American mail."

"Were both letters addressed to correspondents in America?"

"No, one only. The other was to a man about a dog."

A slight titter relieved the gray monotony of the court at this explanation, but the coroner frowned it down, and Rupert added that he was buying a retriever in readiness for the shooting season.

But the coroner's questions suddenly assumed a sinister import when William Campbell, driver of taxicab number X L 4001, stated that on the Tuesday evening, at 7.20, he had taken a gentleman dressed in a dark gray suit and a tall hat from the corner of Berkeley Street (opposite the Ritz Hotel) to the end of the street in Knightsbridge in which Feldisham Mansions were situated, had waited there for him for about fifteen minutes, and had brought him back to Berkeley Street.

"I thought I might know him again, sir, an', as I said yesterday—-" the man continued, glancing at Rupert, but he was stopped peremptorily.

"Never mind what you said yesterday," broke in the coroner. "You will have another opportunity of telling the jury what happened subsequently. At present I want you to answer my questions only."

An ominous hush in the court betrayed the public appreciation of the issues that might lurk behind this deferred evidence. Rupert remembered looking at the driver with a certain vague astonishment, and feeling that countless eyes were piercing him without cause.

The hall-porter, too, Simmonds by name, introduced a further element of mystery by saying that at least two gentlemen had gone up the stairs after Mr. Osborne's departure in his automobile, and that one of them bore some resemblance to the young millionaire.

"Are you sure it was not Mr. Osborne?" said the coroner.

"Yes, sir—leastways, I'm nearly positive."

"Why do you say that?"

"Because Mr. Osborne, like all American gentlemen, uses the lift, sir."

"Can any stranger enter the Mansions without telling you their business?"

"Not as a rule, sir. But it does so happen that between seven an' eight o'clock I have a lot of things to attend to, and I often have to run round the corner to get a taxi for ladies and gentlemen goin' out to dinner or the theater."

So, there was a doubt, and Rupert Osborne had not realized its deadly application to himself until he read question and answer in cold type while he toyed with his breakfast on the day after the inquest, which, by request of Mr. Winter, had been adjourned for a fortnight.

It was well for such shreds of stoicism as remained in his tortured brain that the housemaid was still unable to give evidence, and that no mention was made of the stone ax-head found in Rose de Bercy's drawing-room. The only official witnesses called were the constable first summoned by the hall-porter, and the doctor who made the autopsy. The latter—who was positive that Mademoiselle de Bercy had not been dead many minutes when he was brought to her flat at ten minutes to eight— ascribed the cause of death to "injuries inflicted with a sharp instrument," and the coroner, who knew the trend of the inquiry, would not sate public curiosity by putting, or permitting the jury to put, any additional questions until the adjourned inquest. Neither Clarke nor Furneaux was present in court. To all seeming, Chief Inspector Winter was in charge of the proceedings on behalf of the police.

Rupert ultimately abandoned the effort to eat, shoved his chair away from the table, and determined to reperuse with some show of calmness and criticism, the practically verbatim report of the coroner's inquiry.

Then he saw clearly two things—Rose de Bercy had willfully misled him as to her past life, and he was now regarded by the public as her probable betrayer and certain murderer. There was no blinking the facts. He had almost committed the imprudence of marrying a woman unworthy of an honorable man's love, and, as if such folly called for condign punishment, he must rest under the gravest suspicion until her slayer was discovered and brought to justice.

Rupert Osborne's lot had hitherto been cast in pleasant places, but now he was face to face with a crisis, and it remained to be seen if the force that had kept three generations of ancestors in the forefront of the strenuous commercial warfare of Wall Street had weakened or wholly vanished in the person of their dilettante descendant.

At any rate, he did not flinch from the drab reality of fact. He read on, striving to be candid as to meanings and impartial in weighing them.

At the end of the evidence were two paragraphs setting forth the newspaper's own researches. The first of these ran:

Our correspondent at St. Heliers has ascertained that the father and sister of the deceased will leave the island by to-day's mail steamer for the double purpose of identifying their relative and attending the funeral. There can be no question that their first sad task will be in the nature of a formality. They both admit that Rose de Bercy was none other than Mirabel Armaud. Mademoiselle Marguerite Armaud, indeed, bears a striking resemblance to her wayward sister, while Monsieur Armaud, though crippled with toil and rheumatism, shows the same facial characteristics that are so marked in his two daughters. The family never revealed to their neighbors in the village any knowledge of Mirabel's whereabouts. After her disappearance eight years ago her name was seldom, if ever, mentioned to any of their friends, and their obvious wishes in the matter soon came to be respected by would-be sympathizers. It is certain, however, that Marguerite, on one occasion, dared her father's anger and went to Paris to plead with her sister and endeavor to bring her home. She failed, as might be expected, since Rose de Bercy was then attaining the summit of her ambition by playing a small part in a play at the Gymnase, though at that period no one in Paris was able to foresee the remarkable success she was destined to achieve on the stage.

Each word cut like a knife. The printed statements were cruel, but the inferences were far worse. Rupert felt sick at heart; nevertheless he compelled himself to gather the sense of the next item:

It was a favorite pose of Mademoiselle de Bercy— using the name by which the dead actress was best known—to describe herself as an Anarchist. It is certain that she attended several Anarchist meetings in Paris, probably for amusement or for professional study of an interesting type, and in this connection it is a somewhat singular coincidence that Detective-Inspector Clarke, who was mentioned on Wednesday as being in charge of the police investigations into the murder, should have arrested two notorious Anarchists on the Thames Embankment yesterday shortly before the Tsar passed that way *en route* to the Guildhall. The two men, who refused to give any information as to their identity, were said to be none other than Emile Janoc and Antoine Descartes, both well-known French revolutionaries. They were brought before the Extradition Court, and ordered to be deported, the specific charge against them being the carrying of fire-arms without a license. It was stated that on each man was found an unloaded revolver.

So far as Rupert could judge, the newspaper was merely pandering to the craze for sensationalism in bracketing Rose de Bercy with a couple of unwashed scoundrels from Montmartre. On one occasion, indeed, she had mentioned to him her visits to an Anarchist club; but their object was patent when she exhibited a collection of photographs and laudatory press notices of herself in the stage part of a Russian lady of high rank who masqueraded as a Terrorist in order to save her lover from assassination.

"It would have been only fair," he growled savagely, "if the fellow who is raking up her past so assiduously had placed on record her appearance on the stage as *Marie Dukarovna*. And who is this detective who made the arrests? Clarke was not the name of the man I met yesterday."

Then he groaned. His glance had just caught a detailed description of himself, his tastes, his family history, and his wealth. It was reasonably accurate, and not unkindly in tone, but it grated terribly at the moment, and in sheer desperation of spirit he crushed the newspaper in his clenched hands.

At that instant his man entered. Even the quiet-voiced and impenetrable-faced Jenkins spoke in an awed tone when he announced:

"Chief Inspector Winter, of Scotland Yard, wishes to see you, sir."

"Very well, show him in; and don't be scared, Jenkins. He will not arrest *you*."

Rupert must have been stung beyond endurance before he would fling such a taunt at his faithful servitor. Jenkins, at a loss for a disclaimer, glanced reproachfully at the table.

"You have hardly eaten a morsel, sir," he said. "Shall I bring some fresh coffee and an egg?"

Then Rupert laughed grimly.

"Wait till I have seen Mr. Winter," he said. "Perhaps he may join me. If he refuses, Jenkins, be prepared for the worst."

But the Chief Inspector did not refuse. He admitted that coffee-drinking and smoking were his pet vices, and his breezy cheerfulness at once established him on good terms with his host.

"I want you to understand, Mr. Osborne, that my presence here this morning is entirely in your interests," he said when they were seated, and Rupert was tackling a belated meal. "The more fully we clear up any doubtful points as to your proceedings on Tuesday the more easy it will be for the police to drop you practically out of the inquiry except as an unimportant witness."

Rupert's heart warmed to this genial-mannered official.

"It is very kind of you to put things in that light when every newspaper in the country is prepared to announce my arrest at any moment," he replied.

Winter was astonished. His face showed it; his big blue eyes positively bulged with surprise.

"Arrest!" he cried. "Why should I arrest you, sir?"

"Well, after the chauffeur's evidence—"

"That is exactly what brings me here. Personally, I have no doubt whatsoever that you did not leave the Ritz Hotel between half-past six and nine o'clock on the evening of the murder. Two of your friends on the committee saw you writing those letters, and the clerk at the inquiry desk remembers supplying you with stamps. Just as a matter of form, you might give me the names of your correspondents?"

Rupert supplied the desired information, which Winter duly scribbled in a notebook, but it did not escape the American's usually quick perception that his visitor had already verified the statement made before the coroner. That being so, some other motive lay behind this visit. What was it?

Winter, at the moment, seemed to be fascinated by the leaf-color and aroma of the cigar which Jenkins had brought with the coffee. He puffed, smelled, pinched, and scrutinized—was completely absorbed, in fact.

"Don't you like it?" asked Osborne, smiling. The suggestion was almost staggering to the Chief Inspector.

"Why, of course I do," he cried. "This is a prize cigar.

You young gentlemen who are lucky enough to command practically unlimited money can generally obtain anything you want, but I am bound to say, Mr. Osborne, that you could not buy a thousand cigars like this in London to-day, no matter what price you paid."

"I imagine you are right," said Rupert. "The estate on which that tobacco was grown is one of the smallest in Cuba, but it is on the old rich belt. My manager is a scientist. He knows to half an ounce per acre how much sulphate of potash to add each year."

"Sulphate of potash?" questioned Winter, ever ready to assimilate fresh lore on the subject of the weed.

"Yes, that is the secret of the flavor, plus the requisite conditions of soil and climate, of course. The tobacco plant is a great consumer of mineral constituents. A rusty nail, a pinch of salt, and a small lump of lime, placed respectively near the roots of three plants in the same row, will produce three absolutely different varieties of tobacco, but all three will be inferior to the plants removed from such influences."

"Dear me!" said Winter, "how very interesting!"

But to his own mind he was saying: "Why in the world did Furneaux refuse to meet this nice young fellow? Really, this affair grows more complex every hour."

Osborne momentarily forgot his troubles in the company of this affable official. It was comforting, too, that his hospitality should be accepted. Somehow, he felt certain that Winter would have declined it if any particle of suspicion had been attached to the giver, and therein his knowledge of men did not deceive him. With a lighter heart, therefore, than he would have thought possible a few minutes earlier, he, too, lit a cigar.

Winter saw that Rupert was waiting for him to resume the conversation momentarily broken. He began with a straightforward question.

"Now, Mr. Osborne," he said, "will you kindly tell me if it is true that you were about to marry Mademoiselle de Bercy?"

"It is quite true."

"How long have you known her?"

"Since she came to London last fall."

"I suppose you made no inquiries as to her past life?"

"No, none. I never gave a thought to such a thing."

"I suppose you see now that it would have been wiser had you done something of the kind?"

"Wisdom and love seldom go hand in hand."

The Chief Inspector nodded agreement. His profession had failed utterly to oust sentiment from his nature.

"At any rate," he said, "her life during the past nine months has been an open book to you?"

"We soon became friends. Since early in the spring I think I could tell you of every engagement Mademoiselle de Bercy fulfilled, and name almost every person she met, barring such trivialities as shopping fixtures and the rest."

"Ah; then you would know if she had an enemy?"

"I—think so. I have never heard of one. She had hosts of friends—all sympathetic."

"What was the precise object of your visit on Tuesday?"

"I took her a book on Sicily. We—we had practically decided on Taormina for our honeymoon. As I would be occupied until a late hour, she arranged to dine with Lady Knox-Florestan and go to the opera to hear *Pagliacci*. It was played after *Philémon et Baucis*, so the dinner was fixed for half-past eight."

"Would anyone except yourself and Lady Knox-Florestan be aware of that arrangement?"

"I think not."

"Why did she telephone to Lady Knox-Florestan at 7.30 and plead illness as an excuse for not coming to the dinner?"

Rupert looked thoroughly astounded. "That is the first I have heard of it," he cried.

"Could she have had any powerful reason for changing her plans?"

"I cannot say. Not to *my* knowledge, most certainly."

"Did she expect any visitor after your departure?"

"No. Two of her servants were out for the evening, and the housemaid would help her to dress."

Winter looked at the American with a gleam of curiosity when the housemaid was mentioned.

"Did this girl, the housemaid, open the door when you left?" he asked.

"No. I just rushed away. She admitted me, but I did not see her afterwards."

"Then she may have fancied that you took your departure much later?"

"Possibly, though hardly likely, since her room adjoins the entrance, and, as it happened, I banged the door accidentally in closing it."

Winter was glad that a man whom he firmly believed to be innocent of any share in the crime had made an admission that might have told against him under hostile examination.

"Suppose—just suppose—" he said, "that the housemaid, being hysterical with fright, gave evidence that you were in Feldisham Mansions at half-past seven—how would you explain it?"

"Your own words 'hysterical with fright' might serve as her excuse. At half-past seven I was arguing against the ever-increasing height of polo ponies, with the rest of the committee against me. Does the girl say any such thing?"

"Girls are queer sometimes," commented Winter airily. "But let that pass. I understand, Mr. Osborne, that you have given instructions to the undertaker?"

Rupert flinched a little.

"What choice had I in the matter?" he demanded. "I thought that Mademoiselle de Bercy was an orphan—that all her relatives were dead."

"Ah, yes. Even now, I fancy, you mean to attend the funeral to-morrow?"

"Of course. Do you imagine I would desert my

promised wife at such an hour—no matter what was revealed—"

"No, Mr. Osborne, I did not think it for one instant. And that brings me to the main object of my visit. Please be advised by me—don't go to the funeral. Better still, leave London for a few days. Lose yourself till the day before the adjourned inquest."

"But why—in Heaven's name?"

"Because appearances are against you. The public mind—I had better be quite candid. The man in the street is a marvelous detective, in his own opinion. Being an idler, he will turn up in his thousands at Feldisham Mansions and Kensal Green Cemetery to-morrow afternoon, and, if you are present, there may be a regrettable scene. Moreover, you will meet a warped old peasant named Jean Armaud and a narrow-souled village girl in his daughter Marguerite. Take my advice—pack a kit-bag, jump into a cab, and bury yourself in some seaside town. Let me know where you are—as I may want to communicate with you— and—er—when you send your address, don't forget to sign your letter in the same way as you sign the hotel register."

Rupert rose and looked out of the window. He could not endure that another man should see the agony in his face.

"Are you in earnest?" he said, when he felt that his voice might be trusted.

"Dead in earnest, Mr. Osborne," came the quiet answer.

"You even advise me to adopt an alias?"

"Call it a *nom de voyage*," said Winter.

"I shall be horribly lonely. May I not take my valet?"

"Take no one. I suppose you can leave some person in charge of your affairs?"

"I have a secretary. But she and my servants will think my conduct very strange."

"I shall call here to-morrow and tell your secretary you have left London for a few days at my request. What is her name?"

"Prout—Miss Hylda Prout. She comes here at 11 a.m. and again at 3 p.m."

"I see. Then I may regard that matter as settled?"

Again there was silence for a time. Oddly enough, Rupert was conscious of a distinct feeling of relief.

"Very well," he said at last. "I shall obey you to the letter."

"Thank you. I am sure you are acting for the best."

Winter, whose eyes had noted every detail of the room while Rupert's back was turned, rose as if his mission were accomplished.

"Won't you have another cigar?" said Rupert.

"Well, yes. It is a sin to smoke these cigars so early in the day—"

"Let me send you a hundred."

"Oh, no. I am very much obliged, but—"

"Please allow me to do this. Don't you see?—if I tell Jenkins, in your presence, to pack and forward them, it will stifle a good deal of the gossip which must be going on even in my own household."

"Well—from that point of view, Mr. Osborne—"

"Ah, I cannot express my gratitude, but, when all this wretched business is ended, we must meet under happier conditions."

He touched a bell, and Jenkins appeared.

"Send a box of cigars to Chief Inspector Winter, at Scotland Yard, by special messenger," said Rupert, with as careless an air as he could assume.

Jenkins gurgled something that sounded like "Yes, sir," and went out hastily. Rupert spread his hands with a gesture of utmost weariness.

"You are right about the man in the street," he sighed. "Even my own valet feared that you had come to arrest me."

"Ha, ha!" laughed Winter.

But when Jenkins, discreetly cheerful, murmured "Good-day, sir," and the outer door was closed behind him, Winter's strong face wore its prizefighter aspect.

"Clarke *would* have arrested him," he said to himself. "But that man did not kill Mirabel Armaud. Then who did kill her? *I* don't know, yet I believe that Furneaux guesses. *Who* did it? Damme, it beats me, and the greatest puzzle of all is to read the riddle of Furneaux."

IV. The New Life

No sooner did Rupert begin to consider ways and means of adopting Winter's suggestion than he encountered difficulties. "Pack a kit-bag, jump into a cab, and bury yourself in some seaside town" might be the best of counsel; but it was administered in tabloid form; when analyzed, the ingredients became formidable. For instance, the Chief Inspector had apparently not allowed for the fact that a man in Osborne's station would certainly carry his name or initials on his clothing, linen, and portmanteaux, and on every article in his dressing-case.

Despite his other troubles—which were real enough to a man who loathed publicity—Rupert found himself smiling in perplexity when he endeavored to plan some means of hoodwinking Jenkins. Moreover, he could not help feeling that his identity would be proclaimed instantly when a sharp-eyed hotel valet or inquisitive chambermaid examined his belongings. He was sure that some of the newspapers would unearth a better portrait of himself than the libelous snapshot reproduced that day, in which event no very acute intelligence would be needed to connect "Osborne" or "R. G. O." with the half-tone picture. Of course, he could buy ready-made apparel, but the notion was displeasing; ultimately, he abandoned the task and summoned Jenkins.

Jenkins was one of those admirable servants—bred to perfection in London only—worthy of a coat of arms with the blazoned motto: "Leave it to me." His sallow, almost ascetic, face brightened under the trust reposed in him.

"It is now half-past ten, sir," he said. "Will it meet your convenience if I have everything ready by two o'clock?"

"I suppose so," said his master ruefully.

"What station shall I bring your luggage to, sir?"

"Oh, any station. Let me see—say Waterloo, main line."

"And you will be absent ten days or thereabouts, sir."

"That is the proposition as it stands now."

"Very well, sir. I shall want some money—not more than twenty pounds—"

Rupert opened a door leading to the library. He rented a two-story maisonette in Mayfair, with the drawing-room, dining-room, library, billiard-room and domestic offices grouped round the hall, while the upper floor was given over to bedrooms and dressing-rooms. His secretary was not arrived as yet; but he had already glanced through a pile of letters with the practiced eye of one who receives daily a large and varied correspondence.

He wrote a check for a hundred pounds, and stuffed the book into a breast pocket.

"There," he said to Jenkins, "cash that, buy what you want, and bring me the balance in five-pound notes."

"Yes, sir, but will you please remember to pack the clothes you are now wearing into a parcel, and post them to me this evening?"

"By gad, Jenkins, I should have forgotten that my name is stitched on to the back of the coat I am wearing. How will you manage about my other things?"

"Rip off the tabs, sir, and get you some new linen, unmarked."

"Good. But I may as well leave my checkbook here."

"No, sir, take it with you. You may want it. If you do, the money will be of more importance than the name."

"Right again, Socrates. I wish I might take you along, too, but our Scotland Yard friend said 'No,' so you must remain and answer callers."

"I have sent away more than a dozen this morning, sir."

"Oh? Who were they?"

"Newspaper gentlemen, sir, every one of 'em, though

they tried various dodges to get in and have a word with you. If I were you, sir, I would drive openly in the motor to some big hotel, and let your car remain outside while you slip out by another door."

"Jenkins, you seem to be up to snuff in these matters."

"Well, sir, I had a good training with Lord Dunningham. His lordship was a very free and easy sort of gentleman, and I never did meet his equal at slipping a writter. They gave it up at last, and went in for what they call substitooted service."

A bell rang, and they heard a servant crossing the hall.

"That will be Miss Prout, sir," said Jenkins. "What shall I tell her?"

"Nothing. Mr. Winter will see her in the morning. Now, let us be off out of this before she comes in."

Rupert was most unwilling to frame any subterfuge that might help to explain his absence to his secretary. She had been so manifestly distressed in his behalf the previous day, that he decided to avoid her now, being anxious not to hurt her feelings by any display of reticence as to his movements. As soon as the library door closed behind the newcomer, he went to his dressing-room and remained there until his automobile was in readiness. He was spoken to twice and snapshotted three times while he ran down the steps and crossed the pavement; but he gave no heed to his tormentors, and his chauffeur, quick to appreciate the fact that a couple of taxicabs were following, ran into Hyde Park by the nearest gate, thus shaking off pursuit, since vehicles licensed to ply for hire are not allowed to enter London's chief pleasure-ground.

"Yes," said Rupert to himself, "Winter is right. The solitary cliff and the deserted village for me during the next fortnight. But where are they to be found? England, with August approaching, is full to the brim."

He decided to trust to chance, and therein lay the germ of complications which might well have given him pause, could he have peered into the future.

Having successfully performed the trick of the cab "bilker" by leaving his motor outside a hotel, Rupert hurried away from the main stream of fashion along several narrow streets until his attention was caught by a tiny restaurant on which the day's eatables were scrawled in French. It was in Soho; an open-air market promised diversion; and he was wondering how winkles tasted, extracted from their shells with a pin, when some commotion arose at the end of an alley. A four-wheeled cab had wormed its way through a swarm of picturesque loafers, and was drawn up close to the kerb. Pavement and street were pullulating with child life, and the appearance from the interior of the cab of a couple of strongly-built, square-shouldered men seemed to send an electric wave through adults and children alike.

Instantly there was a rush, and Rupert was pinned in the crowd between a stout Frenchwoman and a young Italian who reeked of the kitchen.

"What is it, then?" he asked, addressing madame in her own language.

"They are police agents, those men there," she answered.

"Have they come to make an arrest?"

"But no, monsieur. Two miserables who call themselves Anarchists have been sent back to France, and the police are taking their luggage. A nice thing, chasing such scarecrows and letting that bad American who killed Mademoiselle de Bercy go free. Poor lady! I saw her many times. Ah, *mon Dieu*, how I wept when I read of her terrible end!"

Rupert caught his breath. So he was judged and found guilty even in the gutter!

"Perhaps the police know that Monsieur Osborne did not kill her," he managed to say in a muffled tone.

"Oh, là, là!" cried the woman. "He has money, *ce vilain* Osborne!"

The ironic phrase was pitiless. It denounced,

condemned, explained. Rupert forced a laugh.

"Truly, money can do almost anything," he said.

A detective came out of the passage, laden with dilapidated packages. The woman smiled broadly, saying:

"My faith, they do not prosper, those Anarchists."

Rupert edged his way through the crowd. On the opposite side of the street the contents bills of the early editions of the evening newspapers glared at him: "West End murder—Relatives sail from Jersey." "Portrait sketch of Osborne"; "Paris Life of Rose de Bercy"; the horror of it all suddenly stifled his finer impulses: from that hour Rupert squared his shoulders and meant to scowl at the jeering multitude.

Probably because he was very rich, he cultivated simple tastes in the matter of food. At one o'clock he ate some fruit and a cake or two, drank a glass of milk, and noticed that the girl in the cashier's desk was actually looking at his own "portrait sketch" when he tendered her a shilling. About half-past one he took a hansom to Waterloo Station, where he bought a map and railway guide at the bookstall, and soon decided that Tormouth on the coast of Dorset offered some prospect of a quiet anchorage.

So, when Jenkins came with a couple of new leather bags, Rupert bought a third-class ticket. Traveling in a corridor compartment, he heard the Feldisham Mansions crime discussed twice during the afternoon. Once he was described as a "reel bad lot—one of them fellers 'oo 'ad too little to do an' too much to do it on." When, at Winchester, these critics alighted, their places were taken by a couple of young women; and the train had hardly started again before the prettier of the two called her companion's attention to a page in an illustrated paper.

"Poor thing! Wasn't she a beauty?" she asked, pointing to a print of the Academy portrait of Mademoiselle de Bercy.

"You can never tell—them photographs are so touched up," was the reply.

"There's no touching up of Osborne, is there?" giggled the other, looking at the motor-car photograph.

"No, indeed. He looks as if he had just done it," said the friend.

A lumbering omnibus took him to Tormouth. At the Swan Hotel he haggled about the terms, and chose a room at ten shillings per diem instead of the plutocratic apartment first offered at twelve and six. In the register he signed "R. Glyn, London," and at once wrote to Winter. He almost laughed when he found that Jenkins's address on the label was some street in North London, where that excellent man's sister dwelt.

He found that Tormouth possessed one great merit— an abundance of sea air. It was a quiet old place, a town of another century, cut off from the rush of modern life by the frenzied opposition to railways displayed by its local magnates fifty years earlier. Rupert could not have selected a better retreat. He dined, slept, ate three hearty meals next day, and slept again with a soundness that argued him free from care.

But newspapers reached even Tormouth, and, on the second morning after his arrival, Osborne's bitter mood returned when he read an account of Rose de Bercy's funeral. The crowds anticipated by Winter were there, the reporters duly chronicled Rupert's absence, and there could be no gainsaying the eagerness of the press to drag in his name on the slightest pretext.

But the arrows of outrageous fortune seemed to be less barbed when he found himself on a lonely path that led westward along the cliffs, and his eyes dwelt on the far-flung loveliness of a sapphire sea reflecting the tint of a turquoise sky. A pleasant breeze that just sufficed to chisel the surface of the water into tiny facets flowed lazily from the south. From the beach, some twenty feet or less beneath the low cliff, came the murmur of a listless tide. On the swelling uplands of Dorset shone glorious patches of gold and green, with here and there a hamlet or many-ricked farm, while in front, a mile away,

the cliff climbed with a gentle curve to a fine headland
that jutted out from the shore-line like some great pier
built by a genie for the caravels of giants. It was a
morning to dispel shadows, and the cloud lifted from
Rupert's heart under its cheery influence. He stopped to
light a cigar, and from that moment Rupert's
regeneration was complete.

"It is a shame to defile this wonderful atmosphere
with tobacco smoke," he mused, "so I must salve my
conscience by burning incense to the spirit of the place.
That sort of spirit is invariably of the female gender.
Where is the lady? Invisible, of course."

Without the least expectation of discovering either fay
or mortal on the yellow sands that spread their broad
highway between sea and cliff, Rupert stepped off the
path on to the narrow strip of turf that separated it from
the edge and looked down at the beach. Greatly to his
surprise, a girl sat there, painting. She had rigged a big
Japanese umbrella to shield herself and her easel from
the sun. Its green-hued paper cover, gay with pink
dragons and blue butterflies, brought a startling note of
color into the placid foreground. The girl, or young
woman, wore a very smart hat, but her dress was a
grayish brown costume, sufficiently indeterminate in tint
to conceal the stains of rough usage in climbing over
rocks, or forcing a way through rank vegetation. Indeed,
it was chosen, in the first instance, so that a dropped
brush or a blob of paint would not show too vivid traces;
and this was well, for some telepathic action caused the
wearer to lift her eyes to the cliff the very instant after
Rupert's figure broke the sky-line above the long grasses
nodding on the verge. The result was lamentable. She
squeezed half a tube of crimson lake over her skirt in a
movement of surprise at the apparition.

She was annoyed, and, of course, blamed the man.

"What do you want?" she demanded. "Why creep up in
that stealthy fashion?"

"I didn't," said Rupert.

"But you did." This with a pout, while she scraped the paint off her dress with a palette knife.

"I am very sorry that you should have cause to think so," he said. "Will you allow me to explain—"

As he stepped forward, lifting his hat, the girl cried a warning, but too late; a square yard of dry earth crumbled into dust beneath him, and he fell headlong. Luckily, the strata of shale and marl which formed the coast-line at that point had been scooped by the sea into a concavity, with a ledge, which Rupert reached before he had dropped half-way. Some experience of Alpine climbing had made him quick to decide how best to rectify a slip, and he endeavored now to spring rather than roll downward to the beach, since he had a fleeting vision of a row of black rocks that guarded the foot of the treacherous cliff. He just managed to clear an ugly boulder that would have taken cruel toll of bruised skin, if no worse, had he struck it, but he landed on a smooth rock coated with seaweed. Exactly what next befell neither he nor the girl ever knew. He performed some wild gyration, and was brought up forcibly by the bamboo shaft of the umbrella, to which he found himself clinging in a sitting posture. His trousers were split across both knees, his coat was ripped open under the left arm, and he felt badly bruised; nevertheless, he looked up into the girl's frightened face, and laughed, on which the fright vanished from her eyes, and she, too, laughed, with such ready merriment and display of white teeth, that Rupert laughed again. He picked himself up and stretched his arms slowly, for something had given him a tremendous thump in the ribs.

"Are you hurt?" cried the girl, anxiety again chasing the mirth from her expressive features.

"No," he said, after a deep breath had convinced him that no bones were broken. "I only wished to explain that your word 'stealthy' was undeserved."

"I withdraw it, then.... I saw you were a stranger, so it is my fault that you fell. I ought to have told you about that dangerous cliff instead of pitching into you because you startled me."

"I can't agree with you there," smiled Rupert. "We were both taken by surprise, but I might have known better than to stand so near the edge. Good job I was not a mile farther west," and he nodded in the direction of the distant headland.

"Oh, please don't think of it, or I shall dream to-night of somebody falling over the Tor."

"Is that the Tor?" he asked.

"Yes; don't you know? You are visiting Tormouth, I suppose?"

"I have been here since the day before yesterday, but

my local knowledge is nil."

"Well, if I were you, I should go home and change my clothes. How did your coat get torn? Are you sure you are not injured?"

He turned to survey the rock on which his feet had slipped. Between it and the umbrella the top of a buried boulder showed through the deep sand, ever white and soft at highwater mark.

"I am inclined to believe that I butted into that fellow during the hurricane," he said. Then, feeling that an excuse must be forthcoming, if he wished to hear more of this girl's voice, and look for a little while longer into her face, he threw a plaintive note into a request.

"Would you mind if I sat down for a minute or so?" he asked. "I feel a bit shaken. After the briefest sort of rest I shall be off to the Swan."

"Sit down at once," she said with ready sympathy. "Here, take this," and she made to give him the canvas chair from which she had risen at the first alarm.

He dropped to the sand with suspicious ease.

"I shall be quite comfortable here," he said. "Please go on with your painting. I always find it soothing to watch an artist at work."

"I must be going home now," she answered. "I obtain this effect only at a certain stage of tide, and early in the day. You see, the Tor changes his appearance so rapidly when the sun travels round to the south."

"Do you live at Tormouth?" he ventured to ask.

"Half a mile out."

"Will you allow me to carry something for you? I find that I have broken two ribs—of your umbrella," he added instantly, seeing that those radiant eyes of hers had turned on him with quick solicitude.

"Pity," she murmured, "bamboo is so much harder to mend than bone. No—you will not carry anything. I think, if you are staying at the Swan, you will find a path up a little hollow in the cliff about a hundred yards from here."

"Yes, and if you, too, are going—"

"In the opposite direction."

"Ah, well," he said, "I am a useless person, it seems. Good-by. May I fall at your feet again to-morrow?"

The absurd question brought half a smile to her lips. She began to reply: "Worship so headlong—"

Then she saw that which caused her face to blanch.

"Why, your right hand is smothered in blood— something has happened—"

He glanced at his hand, which a pebble had cut on one of the knuckles; and he valiantly resisted the temptation that presented itself, and stood upright.

"It is a mere scratch," he assured her. "If I wash it in salt water it will be healed before I reach Tormouth. Good-by—mermaid. I believe you live in a cavern— out there—beneath the Tor. Some day soon I shall swim out among the rocks and look for you."

With that he stooped to recover his hat, walked seaward to find a pool, and held his hand in the water until the wound was cauterized. Then he lit another cigar, and saw out of the tail of his eye that the girl was now on the top of the cliff at some distance to the west.

"I wonder who she is," he murmured. "A lady, at any rate, and a very charming one."

And the girl was saying:

"Who is he?—A gentleman, I see. American? Something in the accent, perhaps. Or perhaps not. Americans don't come to torpid old Tormouth."

V. The Missing Blade

On that same morning of the meeting on the sands at Tormouth, Inspector Clarke, walking southward down St. Martin's Lane toward Scotland Yard, had a shock. Clarke was hardly at the moment in his best mood, for to the natural vinegar of his temperament a drop of lemon, or of gall, had been added within the last few days. That morning at breakfast he had explained matters with a sour mouth to Mrs. Clarke.

"Oh, it was all a made-up job between Winter and Furneaux, and I was only put on to the Anarchists to make room for Furneaux—that was it. The two Anarchists weren't up to any mischief—'Anarchists' was all a blind, that's what '*Anarchists*' was. But that's the way things are run now in the Yard, and there's no fair play going any more. Furneaux must have Feldisham Mansions, of course; Furneaux this, and Furneaux that—of course. But wait: he hasn't solved it yet! and he isn't going to; no, and I haven't done with it yet, not by a long way.... Now, where do you buy these eggs? Just look at this one."

The fact was, now that the two Anarchists, Descartes and Janoc, had been deported by the Court, and were gone, Clarke suddenly woke to find himself disillusioned, dull, excluded from the fun of the chase. But, as he passed down St. Martin's Lane that morning, his underlooking eyes, ever on the prowl for the "confidence men" who haunt the West End, saw a sight that made him doubt if he was awake. There, in a little by-street to the east, under the three balls of a pawnbroker's, he saw, or dreamt that he saw—Émile Janoc!—Janoc, whom he *knew* to be in Holland, and Janoc was so deep, so lost, in talk with a girl, that he could not see Clarke standing there, looking at him.

And Clarke knew the girl, too! It was Bertha Seward, the late cook of the murdered actress, Rose de Bercy.

Could he be mistaken as to Janoc? he asked himself. Could *two* men be so striking to the eye, and so alike—the lank figure, stooping; the long wavering legs, the clothes hanging loose on him; the scraggy throat with the bone in it; the hair, black and plenteous as the raven's breast, draping the sallow-dark face; the eyes so haggard, hungry, unresting. Few men were so picturesque: few so greasy, repellent. And there could be no mistake as to Bertha Seward—a small, thin creature, with whitish hair, and little Chinese eyes that seemed to twinkle with fun—it was she!

And how earnest was the talk!

Clarke saw Janoc clasp his two long hands together, and turn up his eyes to the sky, seeming to beseech the girl or, through her, the heavens. Then he offered her money, which she refused; but, when he cajoled and insisted, she took it, smiling. Shaking hands, they parted, and Janoc looked after Bertha Seward as she hurried, with a sort of stealthy haste, towards the Strand. Then he turned, and found himself face to face with Clarke.

For a full half-minute they looked contemplatively, eye to eye, at one another.

"Janoc?" said Clarke.

"That is my name for one moment, sare," said Janoc politely in a very peculiar though fluent English: "and the yours, sare?"

"Unless you have a very bad memory you know mine! How on earth come you to be here, Émile Janoc?"

"England is free country, sare," said Janoc with a shrug; "I see not the why I must render you account of movement. Only I tell you this time, because you are so singular familiarly with my name of family, you deceive yourself as to my little name. I have, it is true, a brother named Émile—"

Clarke looked with a hard eye at him. The resemblance, if they were two, was certainly very strong. Since it seemed all but impossible that Émile Janoc should be in England, he accepted the statement grudgingly.

"Perhaps you wouldn't mind letting me see your papers?" he asked.

Janoc bowed.

"That I will do with big pleasure, sare," he said, and produced a passport recently viséd in Holland, by which it appeared that his name was not Émile, but Gaston.

They parted with a bow on Janoc's side and a nod on Clarke's; but Clarke was puzzled.

"Something queer about this," he thought. "I'll keep my eye on *him*.... What was he doing talking like that—*so earnest*—to the actress's cook? Suppose she was murdered by Anarchists? It is certain that she was more or less mixed up with them—more, perhaps, than is known. Why did those two come over the night after her murder?—for it's clear that they had no design against the Tsar. I'll look into it on my own. Easy, now, Clarke, my boy, and may be you'll come out ahead of Furneaux, Winter, and all the lot in the end."

When he arrived at his Chief's office in the Yard, he mentioned to Winter his curious encounter with the other Janoc, but said not a word of Bertha Seward, since the affair of the murder was no longer his business, officially.

Winter paid little heed to Janoc, whether Émile or Gaston, for Furneaux was there with him, and the two were head to head, discussing the murder, and the second sitting of the inquest was soon to come. Indeed, Clarke heard Winter say to Furneaux:

"I promised Mr. Osborne to give some sort of excuse to his servants for his flight from home. I was so busy that I forgot it. Perhaps you will see to that, too, for me."

"Glad you mentioned it. I intended going there at

once," Furneaux said in that subdued tone which seemed to have all at once come upon him since Rose de Bercy was found lying dead in Feldisham Mansions.

"Well, then, from henceforth everything is in your hands," said Winter. "Here I hand you over our dumb witness"—and he held out to Furneaux the blood-soiled ax-head of flint that had battered Rose de Bercy's face.

He was not sure—he wondered afterwards whether it was positively a fact—but he fancied that for the tenth part of a second Furneaux shrank from taking, from touching, that object of horror—a notion so odd and fantastic that it affected Winter as if he had fancied that the poker had lifted its head for the tenth part of a second. But almost before the conceit took form, Furneaux was coolly placing the celt in his breast-pocket, and standing up to go.

Furneaux drove straight, as he had said, to Mayfair, and soon was being ushered into Osborne's library, where he found Miss Prout, the secretary, with her hat on, busy opening and sorting the morning's correspondence.

He introduced himself, sat beside her, and, while she continued with her work, told her what had happened— how Osborne had been advised to disappear till the popular gale of ill-will got stilled a little.

"Ah, that's how it was," the girl said, lifting interested eyes to his. "I was wondering," and she pinned two letters together with the neatness of method and order.

Furneaux sat lingeringly with her, listening to an aviary of linnets that prattled to the bright sunlight that flooded the library, and asking himself whether he had ever seen hair so glaringly red as the lady secretary's—a great mass of it that wrapped her head like a flame.

"And where has Mr. Osborne gone to?" she murmured, making a note in shorthand on the back of one little bundle of correspondence.

"Somewhere by the coast—I think," said Furneaux.

"West coast? East coast?"

"He didn't write to me: he wrote to my Chief"—for,

though Furneaux well knew where Osborne was, his retreat was a secret.

The girl went on with her work, plying the paper-knife, now jotting down a memorandum, now placing two or more kindred letters together: for every hospital and institution wrote to Osborne, everyone who wanted money for a new flying machine, or had a dog or a hunter to sell, or intended to dine and speechify, and send round the hat.

"It's quite a large batch of correspondence," Furneaux remarked.

"Half of these," the girl said, "are letters of abuse from people who never heard Mr. Osborne's name till the day after that poor woman was killed. All England has convicted him before he is tried. It seems unfair."

"Yes, no doubt. But 'to understand is to pardon,' as the proverb says. They have to think something, and when there is only one thing for them to think, they think it—meaning well. It will blow over in time. Don't you worry."

"Oh, I!—What do I care what forty millions of vermin choose to say or think?"

She pouted her pretty lips saucily.

"Forty—millions—of vermin," cried Furneaux; "that's worse than Carlyle."

Hylda Prout's swift hands plied among her papers. She made no answer; and Furneaux suddenly stood up.

"Well, you will mention to the valet and the others how the matter stands as to Mr. Osborne. He is simply avoiding the crowd—that is all. Good-day."

Hylda Prout rose, too, and Furneaux saw now how tall she was, well-formed and lithe, with a somewhat small face framed in that nest of red hair. Her complexion was spoiled and splashed with freckles, but otherwise she was dainty-featured and pretty—mouth, nose, chin, tiny, all except the wide-open eyes.

"So," she said to Furneaux as she put out her hand, "you won't let me know where Mr. Osborne is? I may want to write to him on business."

"Why, didn't I tell you that he didn't write to me?"

"That was only a blind."

"Dear me! A blind.... It is the truth, Miss Prout."

"Tell that to someone else."

"What, don't you like the truth?"

"All right, keep the information to yourself, then."

"Good-by—I mustn't allow myself to dally in this charming room with the linnets, the sunlight, and the lady."

For a few seconds she seemed to hesitate. Then she said suddenly: "Yes, it's very nice in here. That door there leads into the morning room, and that one yonder, at the side— "

Her voice dropped and stopped; Furneaux appeared hardly to have heard, or, if hearing, to be merely making conversation.

"Yes, it leads where?" he asked, looking at her. Now, her eyes, too, dropped, and she murmured:

"Into the museum."

"The—! Well, naturally, Mr. Osborne is a connoisseur—quite so, only I rather expected you to say 'a picture gallery.' Is it—open to inspection? Can one—?"

"It is open, certainly: the door is not locked, But there's nothing much—"

"Oh, do let me have a look around, and come with me, if it will not take long. No one is more interested in curios than I."

"I—will, if you like," said the girl with a strange note of confidence in her voice, and led the way into the museum.

Furneaux found himself in a room, small, but full of riches. On a central table were several illuminated missals and old Hoch-Deutsch MSS., some ancient timepieces, and a collection of enameled watches of Limoges. Around the walls, open or in cabinets, were arms, blades of Toledo, minerals arranged on narrow shelves, an embalmed chieftain's head from Mexico, and many other bizarre objects.

Hylda Prout knew the name and history of every one, and murmured an explanation as Furneaux bent in scrutiny.

"Those are what are called 'celts,'" she said; "they are not very uncommon, and are found in every country— made of flint, mostly, and used as ax-heads by the ancients. These rough ones on this side are called Palæolithic—five hundred thousand years old, some of them; and these finer ones on this side are Neolithic, not quite so old—though there isn't much to choose in antiquity when it comes to hundreds of thousands! Strange to say, one of the Neolithic ones has been missing for some days—I don't know whether Mr. Osborne has given it away or not?"

The fact that one *was* missing was, indeed, quite obvious, for the celts stood in a row, stuck in holes drilled in the shelf; and right in the midst of the rank gaped one empty hole, a dumb little mouth that yet spoke.

"Yes, curious things," said Furneaux, bending meditatively over them. "I remember seeing pictures of them in books. Every one of these stones is stained with blood."

"Blood!" cried the girl in a startled way.

"Well, they were used in war and the chase, weren't they? Every one of them has given agony, every one would be red, if we saw it in its true color."

Red was also the color of Furneaux's cheek-bones at the moment—red as hectic; and he was conscious of it, as he was conscious also that his eyes were wildly alight. Hence, he continued a long time bending over the "celts" so that Miss Prout might not see his face. His voice, however, was calm, since he habitually spoke in jerky, clipped syllables that betrayed either no emotion or too much.

When he turned round, it was to move straight to a little rack on the left, in which glittered a fine array of daggers—Japanese kokatanas, punals of Salamanca, cangiars of Morocco, bowie-knives of old California, some with squat blades, coming quickly to a point, some long and thin to transfix the body, others meant to cut and gash, each with its label of minute writing.

Furneaux's eye had duly noted them before, but he had passed them without stopping. Now, after seeing the celts, he went back to them.

To his surprise, Miss Prout did not come with him. She stood looking on the ground, her lower lip somewhat protruded, silent, obviously distrait.

"And these, Miss Prout?" chirped he, "are they of high value?"

She neither answered nor moved.

"Perhaps you haven't studied their history?" ventured Furneaux again.

Now, all at once, she moved to the rack of daggers, and without saying a word, tapped with the fore-finger of her right hand, and kept on tapping, a vacant hole in the rack, though her eyes peered deeply into Furneaux's face. And for the first time Furneaux made acquaintance with the real splendor of her eyes—eyes that lived in sleep, torpid like the dormouse; but when they woke, woke to such a lambency of passion that they fascinated and commanded like the basilisk's.

With eyes so alight she now kept peering at Furneaux, standing tall above him, tapping at the empty hole.

"Oh, I see," muttered Furneaux, *his* eyes, too, alight like live coals, "there's an article missing here, also—one from the celts, one from the daggers."

"He is innocent!" suddenly cried Hylda Prout, in a tempest of passionate reproach.

"She loves him," thought Furneaux.

And the girl thought: "He knew before now that these things were missing. His acting would deceive every man, but not every woman. How glad I am that I drew him on!"

Now, though the fact of the discovery of the celt by Inspector Clarke under the dead actress's piano had not been published in the papers, the fact that she had been stabbed through the eye by a long blade with blunt edges was known to all the world. There was nothing strange in this fierce outburst of Osborne's trusted secretary, nor that tears should spring to her eyes.

"Mr. Furneaux, he is innocent," she wailed in a frenzy. "Oh, he is! You noticed me hesitate just now to bring you in here: well, *this* was the reason—this, this, this—" she tapped with her forefinger on the empty hole—"for I knew that you would see this, and I knew that you would be jumping to some terrible conclusion as to Mr. Osborne."

"Conclusion, no," murmured Furneaux comfortingly— "I avoid conclusions as traps for the unwary. Interesting, of course, that's all. Tell me what you know, and fear nothing. Conclusion, you say! I don't jump to conclusions. Tell me what was the shape of the dagger that has disappeared."

She was silent again for many seconds. She was wrung with doubt, whether to speak or not to speak.

At last she voiced her agony.

"Either I must refuse to say, or I must tell the truth— and if I tell the truth, you will think—"

She stopped again, all her repose of manner fled.

"You don't know what I will think," put in Furneaux. "Sometimes I think the most unexpected things. The best way is to give me the plain facts. The question is, whether the blade that has gone from there was shaped like the one supposed to have committed the crime in the flat?"

"It was labeled 'Saracen Stiletto: about 1150,'" muttered the girl brokenly, looking Furneaux straight in the face, though the fire was now dead in her eyes. "It had a square bone handle, with a crescent carved on one of the four faces—a longish, thin blade, like a skewer, only not round—with blunt-edged corners to it."

Furneaux took up a little tube containing radium from a table at his hand, looked at it, and put it down again.

Hylda Prout was too distraught to see that his hand

shook a little. It was half a minute before he spoke.

"Well, all that proves nothing, though it is of interest, of course," he said nonchalantly. "How long has that stiletto been lying there?"

"Since—since I entered Mr. Osborne's employment, twelve months ago."

"And you first noticed that it was gone—when?"

"On the second afternoon after the murder, when I noticed that the celt, too, was gone."

"The second—I see."

"I wondered what had become of them! I could imagine that Mr. Osborne might have given the celt to some friend. But the stiletto was so rare a thing—I couldn't think that he would give that. I assumed—I assume—that they were stolen. But, then, by whom?"

"That's the question," said Furneaux.

"Was it this same stiletto that I have described to you that the murder was done with?" asked Hylda.

"Now, how can I tell that?" said Furneaux. "*I* wasn't there, you know."

"Was not the weapon, then, found in the unfortunate woman's flat?"

"No—no weapon."

"Well, but that is excessively odd," she said in a low voice.

"Why so excessively odd?" demanded Furneaux.

"Why? Because—don't you see?—the weapon would be blood-stained—of course; and I should expect that after committing his horrid deed, the murderer would be only too glad to get rid of it, and would leave it—"

"Oh, come, that is hardly a good guess, Miss Prout. I shall never make a lady detective of you. Murderers don't leave their weapons about behind them, for weapons are clews, you see."

He was well aware that if the fact of the discovery of the celt had been published in the papers, Hylda might justly have answered: "But *this* murderer did leave *one* of his weapons behind, namely the celt; and it is excessively odd that, since he left one, the smaller one, he did not leave the other, the larger one."

As it was, the girl took thought, and her comment was shrewd enough:

"All murderers do not act in the same way, for some are a world more cunning and alert than others. I say that it *is* odd' that the murderer did not leave behind the weapon that pierced the woman's eye, and I will prove it to you. If the stiletto was stolen from Mr. Osborne—and it really must have been stolen—and if that was the same stiletto that the deed was done with, then, the motive of the thief in stealing it was to kill Mademoiselle de Bercy with it. But why should one steal a weapon to commit a murder? And why should the murderer have chosen *Mr. Osborne* to steal his weapon from? Obviously, because he wanted to throw the suspicion upon him—in which case he would *naturally* leave the weapon behind as proof of Mr. Osborne's guilt. Now, then, have I proved my point?"

Though she spoke almost in italics, and was pale and flurried, she looked jauntily at Furneaux, with her head tossed back; and he, with half a smile, answered:

"I withdraw my remark as to your detective qualifications, Miss Prout. Yes, I think you reason well. If there was a thief, and the thief was the murderer, he would very likely have acted as you say."

"Then, why was the stiletto not found in the flat?" she asked.

"The fact that it was not found would seem to show that there was *not* a thief," he said; and he added quickly: "Perhaps Mr. Osborne gave it, as well as the celt, to someone. I suppose you asked him?"

"He was gone away an hour before I missed them," Hylda answered. She hesitated again. When next she spoke it was with a smile that would have won a stone.

"Tell me where he is," she pleaded, "and I will write to him about it. You may safely tell *me*, you know, for Mr. Osborne has no secrets from *me*."

"I wish I could tell you.... Oh, but he will soon be back

again, and then you will see him and speak to him once
more."

Some tone of badinage in these jerky sentences
brought a flush to her face, but she tried to ward off his
scrutiny with a commonplace remark.

"Well, that's some consolation. I must wait in patience
till the mob finds a new sensation."

Furneaux took a turn through the room, silently
meditating.

"Thanks so much for your courtesy, Miss Prout," he
said at last. "Our conversation has been—fruitful."

"Yes, fruitful in throwing still more suspicion upon an
innocent man, if that is what you mean. Are not the
police *quite* convinced yet of Mr. Osborne's innocence,
Inspector Furneaux?"

"Oh, quite, quite," said he hastily, somewhat taken
aback by her candor.

"Two 'quites' make a 'not quite,' as two negatives
make an affirmative," said she coldly, fingering and
looking down at some wistaria in her bosom.

She added with sudden warmth: "Oh, but you should,
Inspector Furneaux! You should. He has suffered; his
honest and true heart has been wounded. And he has his
alibi, which, though in reality it may not be so good as
you think, is yet quite good enough. But I know what it is
that poisons your mind against him."

"You are full of statements, Miss Prout," said
Furneaux with an inclination of the head; "what is it,
now, that poisons my mind against that gentleman?"

"It is that taxicabman's delusion that he took him
from the Ritz Hotel to Feldisham Mansions and back,
added to the housekeeper's delusion that she saw him
here—"

Furneaux nearly gasped. Up to that moment he had
heard no word about a housekeeper's delusion, or of a
housekeeper's existence even. A long second passed before
he could answer.

"Well, she was no doubt mistaken. I have not yet

examined her personally, but I have every reason to believe that she is in error. At what hour, by the way, does she say that she thought she saw him here?"

"*She* says she thinks it was about five minutes to eight. But at that time, I take it from the evidence, he must have been writing those two letters at the Ritz. If she were right, that would make out that after doing the deed at about 7.40 or so, he would just have time to come back here by five to eight, and change his clothes. But he was at the Ritz—he was at the Ritz! And Mrs. Bates only saw his back an instant going up the stairs—his ghost's back, she means, his double's back, not his own. He was at the Ritz, Inspector Furneaux."

"Precisely." said Furneaux, with a voice that at last had a quiver in it. "If any fact is clear in a maze of doubt, that, at least, is established beyond cavil. And Mrs. Bates's other name—I—forget it?"

"Hester."

"That's it. Is she here now?"

"She is taking a holiday to-day. She was dreadfully upset."

"Thanks. Good-by."

He held out his hand a second time, quite affably. Hylda Prout followed him out to the library and, when the street door had closed behind him, peeped through the curtains at his alert, natty figure as he hastened away.

Furneaux took a motor-bus to Whitehall, and, what was very odd, the 'bus carried him beyond his destination, over Westminster Bridge, indeed, he was so lost in meditation.

His object now was to see Winter and fling at his chief's head some of the amazing things he had just learned.

But when he arrived at Scotland Yard, Winter was not there. At that moment, in fact, Winter was at Osborne's house in Mayfair, whither he had rushed to meet Furneaux in order to whisper to Furneaux without a moment's delay some news just gleaned by the merest chance—the news that Pauline Dessaulx, Rose de Bercy's maid, had quarreled with her mistress on the morning of the murder, and had been given notice to quit Miss de Bercy's service.

When Winter arrived at Osborne's house Furneaux, of course, was gone. To his question at the door, "Is Mr. Furneaux here?" the parlor-maid answered: "I am not sure, sir—I'll see."

"Perhaps you don't know Mr. Furneaux," said Winter, "a small-built gentleman—"

"Oh, yes, sir, I know him," the girl answered. "I let him in this morning, as well as when he called some days ago."

No words in the English tongue could have more astonished Winter, for Furneaux had not mentioned to him that he had even been to Osborne's. What Furneaux could have been doing there "some days ago" was beyond his guessing. Before his wonderment could get out another question, the girl was leading the way towards the library.

In the library were Miss Prout, writing, and Jenkins handing her a letter.

"I came to see if Inspector Furneaux was here," Winter said; "but evidently he has gone."

"Only about three minutes," said Hylda Prout, throwing a quick look round at him.

"Thanks—I am sorry to have troubled you," he said. Then he added, to Jenkins: "Much obliged for the cigars!"

"Do not mention it, sir," said Jenkins.

Winter had reached the library door, when he stopped short.

"By the way, Jenkins, is this Mr. Furneaux's first visit here?—or don't you remember?"

"Mr. Furneaux came here once before, sir," said Jenkins in his staid official way.

"Ah, I thought perhaps—when was that?"

"Let me see, sir. It was—yes—on the third, the

afternoon of the murder, I remember."

The third—the afternoon of the murder. Those words ate their way into Winter's very brain. They might have been fired from a pistol rather than uttered by the placid Jenkins.

"The afternoon, you say," repeated Winter. "Yes— quite so; he wished to see Mr. Osborne. At what exact *hour* about would that be?"

Jenkins again meditated. Then he said: "Mr. Furneaux called, sir, about 5.45, as far as I can recollect. He wished to see my master, who was out, but was expected to return. So Mr. Furneaux was shown in here to await him, and he waited a quarter of an hour, if I am right in saying that he came at 5.45, because Mr. Osborne telephoned me from Feldisham Mansions that he would not be returning, and as I entered the museum there, where Mr. Furneaux then was, to tell him, I heard the clock strike six, I remember."

At this Hylda Prout whirled round in her chair.

"The museum!" she cried. "How odd, how exceedingly odd! Just now Mr. Furneaux seemed to be rather surprised when I told him that there was a museum!"

"He doubtless forgot, miss," said Jenkins, "for he had certainly gone in there when I entered the library."

"Thanks, thanks," said Winter lightly, "that's how it was—good-day"; and he went out with the vacant air of a man who has lost something, but knows not what.

He drove straight to Scotland Yard. There in the office sat Furneaux.

For a long time they conferred—Winter with hardly a word, one hand on his thigh, the other at his mustache, looking at Furneaux with a frown, with curious musing eyes, meditating, silent. And Furneaux told how the celt and the stiletto were missing from Osborne's museum.

"And the inference?" said Winter, speaking at last, his round eyes staring widely at Furneaux.

"The inference, on the face of it, is that Osborne is guilty," said Furneaux quietly.

"An innocent man, Furneaux?" said Winter almost with a groan of reproach—"an innocent man?"

Furneaux's eyes flashed angrily an instant, and some word leapt to his lips, but it was not uttered. He stood up.

"Well, that's how it stands for the moment. Time will show—I must be away," he said.

And when he had gone out, Winter rose wearily, and paced with slow steps a long time through the room, his head bent quite down, staring. Presently he came upon a broken cigar, such as Furneaux delighted in smelling. Then a fierce cry broke from him.

"Furneaux, my friend! Why, this is madness! Oh, d—n everything!"

VI. To Tormouth

"An absinthe!"

"A packet of Caporal!"

"Un bock pour vous, m'sieur?"

"A vodka!"

A frowsy waiter was hurrying through some such jangle of loud voices from the "comrades" scattered among the tables set in a back room in a very back street of Soho. The hour was two in the morning, and the light in that Anarchist Club was murky and blurred. Only one gas-jet on the wall lit the room, and that struggled but feebly through the cigarette smoke that choked the air like a fog—air that was foul and close as well as dim, for some thirty persons, mostly men but some few women, were crowded in there as if there was no place else on earth for them.

One heard the rattle of dice, the whirr of cards being shuffled against the thumbs, the grating of glass tumblers against imitation granite. Two poor girls, cramped in a corner, were attempting to dance to the rhythm of an Italian song. They were laughing with wide mouths, their heads thrown back, weary unto death, yet alive with make-believe mirth.

At one of the tables sat Gaston Janoc, the man who had been seen by Inspector Clarke talking in St. Martin's Lane to Bertha Seward, one-time cook in the Feldisham Mansions flat. Playing vingt-et-un with him was a burly Russian-looking man, all red beard and eyebrows; also a small Frenchman with an imperial and a crooked nose; while a colored man of Martinique made the fourth of a queer quartette. But somehow Janoc and the rough, red Russian seemed not to be able to agree in the game. They were antagonistic as cat and dog, and three times one or other threw down his cards and looked at his adversary, as who should say:

"A little more of you, and my knife talks!"

"Who are you, then, Ruski?" cried Janoc at last, speaking French, since the Russian only glared at him when he swore in his quaint English.

Yet the Russian grumbled in English in his beard: "No French."

"And no Italian, and no Spanish, and no German, and very, very small English," growled Janoc in English, frowning at him; "Well, then, shall we converse, sare?"

"What is that—'*converse*'?" asked the Russian.

Janoc shrugged disgustedly, while the little Frenchman, whose eyes twinkled at every tiff between the pair, said politely in French:

"We await your play, m'sieurs."

Twice, on the very edge of the precipice of open hostilities, Janoc and the Russian stopped short; but a little after two o'clock, when much absinthe and vodka had been drunk, an outbreak took place: for the Russian then cried out loudly above the hubbub of tongues:

"Oh, you—how you call it?—*tcheeeet*!"

"Who? I—me?" cried Janoc sharply, pale, half-standing—"cheat?"

"Yes—*tcheeet*, you *tcheeet*!" insisted the bearded Slav. And now the little Frenchman with the crooked nose, who foreknew that the table was about to be upset, stood up quickly, picked up his thimbleful of anisette, and holding it in hand, awaited with merry eyes the outcome.

Instantly Janoc, who was dealing, sent the pack of cards like an assault of birds into the Russian's face, the Russian closed with Janoc, and forthwith the room reeled into chaos. The struggle need not be described. Suffice it to say, that it lasted longer than the Russian had probably expected, for Janoc proved to have sinews of steel, though thin steel. His lank arms embraced the Russian, squeezing like a cable that is being tighter and tighter wound. However, he was overcome by mere weight, thumping to the floor among a tumbled dance of tables, chairs, and foreign drinks, while the women shrieked, the men bellowed, and the scared manager of the den added to the uproar by yelling:

"M'sieurs! M'sieurs! Je vous prie! The police will come!"

Only one soul in the room remained calm, and that was the diminutive Frenchman, who kept dodging through the legs and arms of the flood of humanity that surged around the two on the floor.

He alone of them all saw that the Russian, in the thick of the struggle, was slipping his hand into pocket after pocket of Janoc under him, and was very deftly drawing out any papers that he might find there.

In two minutes the row was ended, and the gaming and drinking recommenced as if nothing had happened. The Russian had been half led, half hustled to the front door, and was gone. Immediately after him had slipped out the bright-eyed Frenchman.

The Russian, after pacing down an alley, turned into Old Compton Street, twice peering about and behind him, as if disturbed by some instinct that he was being shadowed. And this was so—but with a skill so nimble, so expert, so inbred, did the Frenchman follow, that in this pursuit the true meaning of the word "shadowing" was realized. The Russian did not see his follower for the excellent reason that the Frenchman made himself an invisibility. He might have put on those magic shoes that shadows shoot and dash and slink in, so airily did he glide on the trail. Nor could mere genius have accomplished such a feat, and with such ease—were it not for the expertness that was wedded to genius.

When the Russian emerged into the wide thoroughfare close to the Palace Theater, he stood under a lamp to look at one of the papers picked from Janoc's pockets; and only then did he become aware of the Frenchman, who rose up out of the ground under his elbow with that pert ease with which a cork bobs to the surface of water.

"Got anything of importance?" asked the Frenchman, his twinkling eyes radiant with the humor of the chase.

The Russian stared at him half a minute with the hung jaw of astonishment. Then, all at once remembering his rôle, he cried hoarsely:

"No English!"

"Oh, chuck it!" remarked the other.

Again the Russian gazed at the unexpected little phenomenon, and his voice rumbled:

"What is that—'chuck it'?"

Suddenly the Frenchman snatched Janoc's paper neatly with thumb and finger out of the Russian's hand, and ran chuckling across Charing Cross Road eastward. The Russian, with a grunt of rage, made after him with his long legs. But, from the first, he saw that he was being left behind by the nimble pace set up by a good runner. He seemed to understand that a miracle was needed, and lo, it occurred, for, as the two crossed the road in front of the Palace Theater, the Russian lifted his voice into:

"Stop him! Stop thief! Police! Police!"

Not only did he yell in most lucid English, but he also plucked a police whistle from his coat and blew it loudly.

No policeman happened to be near, however, and the deep sleep of London echoed their pelting steps eastward, until the Russian saw the paper-snatcher vanish from sight in the congeries of streets that converge on the top of St. Martin's Lane.

He lost hope then, and slackened a little, panting but swearing in a language that would be appreciated by any London cabman. Nevertheless, when he, too, ran into St. Martin's Lane, there was the small Frenchman, standing, wiping his forehead, awaiting him.

The Russian sprang at him.

"You little whelp!" he roared. "I arrest you—"

"Oh, what's the good, Clarke? You are slow this evening. I just thought I'd wake you up."

"Furneaux!"

"Fancy not knowing me!"

"It was *you*!"

"Who else? Here's your Janocy document. You might let me have a look at it. Share and share alike."

Clarke tried to retrieve lost prestige, though his hand shook as he took the paper.

"Well—I—could have sworn it was you!" he said.

"Of course you could—and did, no doubt. Let's have a glimpse at those documents."

"But what were *you* doing in the Fraternal Club, anyhow? Something on in that line?"

"No. An idle hour. Chance of picking up a stray clew. I sometimes do dive into those depths without special object. You managed that to a T with Janoc. Where are the other papers? Hand them over."

"With pleasure," said Clarke, but there was no pleasure in his surly Russian face, in which rage shone notwithstanding a marvelous make-up. Still, he opened the paper under the lamp—a sheet of notepaper with some lines of writing on the first page; and on the top of it, printed, the name of a hotel, "The Swan, Tormouth."

The two detectives peered over it. To the illimitable surprise of both, this letter, stolen by Clarke from Janoc's pocket, was addressed to Clarke himself—a letter from Rupert Osborne, the millionaire.

And Osborne said in it:

DEAR INSPECTOR CLARKE:—Yours of the 7th duly to hand. In reply to your inquiry, I am not aware that the late Mlle. Rose de Bercy had any relations with Anarchists, either in London or in Paris, other than those which have been mentioned in the papers—i.e., a purely professional interest for stage purposes. I think it unlikely that her connection with them extended further.

I am,

Sincerely yours,
    RUPERT OSBORNE.

Furneaux and Clarke looked at each other in a blank bewilderment that was not assumed by either man.

"*Did* you write to Mr. Osborne, asking that question?" asked Furneaux.

"No," said Clarke—"never. I didn't even know where Osborne was."

"So Janoc must have written to him in your name?" said Furneaux. "Janoc, then, wishes to know how much information Osborne can give you as to Mademoiselle de Bercy's association with Anarchists. That seems clear. But why should Janoc think that *you* particularly are interested in knowing?

Clarke flushed hotly under the paint, being conscious that he was investigating the case on his own private account and in a secret way. As a matter of fact, he was by this time fully convinced that Rose de Bercy's murder was the work of Anarchist hands, but he was so vexed with Furneaux's tricking him, and so fearful of official reprimand from Winter that he only answered:

"Why Janoc should think that I am interested, I can't imagine. It beats me."

"And how can Janoc know where Osborne is, or his assumed name, to write to him?" muttered Furneaux. "I thought that that was a secret between Osborne, Winter, and myself."

Clarke, equally puzzled, scratched his head under his wig, which had been insufferably hot in that stifling room.

"Janoc and his crew must be keeping an eye on Osborne, it seems—for some reason," he exclaimed. "Heaven knows why—I don't. I am out of the de Bercy case, of course. My interest in the Janoc crowd is—political."

"Let me see the letter again," said Furneaux; and he read it carefully once more. Then he opened the sheet, as if seeking additional information from the blank pages, turned it over, looked at the back—and there at the back he saw something else that was astounding, for, written backwards, near the bottom of the page, in Osborne's handwriting, was the word "Rosalind."

"Who is 'Rosalind'?" asked Furneaux—"see here, an impression from some other letter written at the same time."

"Don't know, I'm sure," said Clarke. "A sister, perhaps."

"A sister. Why, though, should his sister's name appear at the back of a note written to Janoc, or to Inspector Clarke, as he thought?" said Furneaux to himself, deep in meditation. He suddenly added brightly: "Now, Clarke, there's a puzzle for   ... her walk has the undulating smoothness that one looks for in some untamed creature of the wild.... You are a painter, and a poet, and a student of the laws of Beauty. Well, knowing all that, I still feel sure that you would be conscious of a you!"

"I don't see it, see any puzzle, I mean. It might have appeared on any other letter, say to his bankers, or to a friend. It was a mere accident. There is nothing in that."

"Quite right," grinned Furneaux. "And it was a sister's name, of course. 'Rosalind.' A pretty name. Poor girl, she will be anxious about her fond and doting brother."

"It may be another woman's name," said Clarke sagely—"though, for that matter, he'd hardly be on with a new love before the other one is cold in her grave, as the saying is."

Furneaux laughed a low, mysterious laugh in his throat. It had a peculiar sound, and rang hard and bitter in the ears of the other.

"I'll keep this, if you don't mind," he said, lapsing into the detective again.

Meantime, Furneaux knew that there were other papers of Janoc's in Clarke's pocket, and he lingered a little to give his colleague a chance of exhibiting them.

Clarke made no move, however, so he put out his hand, saying, "Well, good luck," and disappeared southward, while Clarke walked northward toward his residence, Hampstead way. But in Southampton Row an overwhelming impatience to see the other Janoc papers overcame him, and he commenced to examine them as he went.

Two were bills. A third was a newspaper cutting from the *Matin* commenting on the murder in Feldisham Mansions. The fourth had power to arrest Clarke's steps. It was a letter of three closely-written pages—in French; and though Clarke's French, self-taught, was not fluent, it could walk, if it could not fly. In ten minutes he had read and understood....

St. Petersburg says that since the secret meeting, a steady growth of courage in the rank-and-file is observable. As for the Nevski funds, an individual highly placed, whose name is in three syllables, is said to be willing to come to the rescue. Lastly, as to the traitress, you will see to it that she to whose hands vengeance has been intrusted shall fall on the 3rd.

This was in the letter; and as Inspector Clarke's eyes fell on the date, "the 3d," his clenched hand rose triumphantly in air. It was on July *the 3d* that Rose de Bercy had been done to death!

When Clarke again walked onward his eyes were alight with a wild exultation. He was thinking:

"Now, Allah be praised, that I didn't show Furneaux this thing, as I nearly was doing!"

He reached his house with a sense of surprise—he had covered so much ground unconsciously, and the dominant thought in his mind was that the race was not always to the swift.

"Luck is the thing in a man's career," he said to himself, "not wit, or mere sharpness to grasp a point.

Slow, and steady, and lucky—that's the combination. The British are a race slower of thought than some of the others, just as *I* may be a slower man than Furneaux, but we Britons rule the world by luck, as we won the battle of Waterloo by luck. Luck and prime beef, they go together somehow, I do believe. And what I am to-day I owe to luck, for it's happened to me too often to doubt that I've got the gift of it in my marrow."

He put his latch-key into the door with something of a smile; and the next morning Mrs. Clarke cried delightedly to him:

"Well, something must have happened to put you in this good temper!"

At that same hour of the morning Furneaux, for his part, was at Osborne's house in Mayfair, where he had an appointment with Mrs. Hester Bates, Osborne's housekeeper. He was just being admitted into the house when the secretary, Miss Prout, walked up to the door—rather to his surprise, for it was somewhat before the hour of a secretary's attendance. They entered together and passed into the library, where Hylda Prout invited him to sit down for a minute.

"I am only here just to collect and answer the morning's letters," she explained pleasantly. "There's a tree which I know in Epping Forest—an old beech—where I'm taking a book to read. See my picnic basket?—tomato and cress sandwiches, half a bottle of Chianti, an aluminum folding cup to drink from. I'll send for Mrs. Bates in a moment, and leave her to your tender inquiries. But wouldn't you prefer Epping Forest on a day like this? Do you like solitude, Inspector Furneaux? Dreams?"

"Yes, I like solitude, as boys like piracy, because unattainable. I can only just find time to sleep, but not time enough to dream."

Hylda lifted her face beatifically.

"I *love* to dream!—to be with myself—alone: the world in one compartment, I in another, with myself; with silence to hear my heart beat in, and time to fathom a little what its beating is madly trying to say; an old tree overhead, and breezes breathing through it. Oh, *they* know how to soothe; *they* alone understand, Inspector Furneaux, and *they* forgive."

Furneaux said within himself: "Well, I seem to be in for some charming confidences"; and he added aloud: "Quite so; *they* understand—if it's a lady: for Nature is feminine; and only a lady can fathom a lady."

"Oh, women!" Hylda said, with her pretty pout of disdain,—"they are nothing, mostly shallow shoppers. Give me a man—if he is a man. And there have been a few women, too—in history. But, man or woman, what I believe is that for the greater part, we remain foreigners to ourselves through life—we never reach that depth in ourselves, 'deeper than ever plummet sounded,' where the real *I* within us lives, the real, bare-faced, rabid, savage, divine *I*, naked as an ape, contorted, sobbing, bawling what it cannot speak."

Furneaux, who had certainly not suspected this blend of philosopher and poet beneath that mass of red hair, listened in silence. For the second time he saw this strange girl's eyes take fire, glow, rage a moment like a building sweltering in conflagration, and then die down to utter dullness.

Though he knew just when to speak, his reply was rather tame.

"There's something in that, too—you are right."

She suddenly smiled, with a pretty air of confusion.

"Surely," she said. "And now to business: first, Mrs. Bates—"

"One moment," broke in Furneaux. "Something has caused me to wish to ask you—do you know Mr. Osborne's relatives?"

"I know *of* them. He has only a younger brother, Ralph, who is at Harvard University—and an aunt."

"Aunt's name Rosalind?"

"No—Priscilla—Priscilla Emptage."

"Who, then, may 'Rosalind' be?"

"No connection of *his*. You must have made some mistake."

Furneaux held out the note of Rupert Osborne to Janoc intended for Clarke, holding it so folded that the name of the hotel was not visible—only the transferred word "Rosalind."

And as Hylda Prout bent over it, perplexed at first by the seeming scrawl, Furneaux's eye was on her face. He was aware of the instant when she recognized the handwriting, the instant when reasoning and the putting of two-and-two together began to work in her mind, the instant when her stare began to widen, and her tight-pressed lips to relax, the rush of color to fade from her face, and the mask of freckles to stand out darkly in strong contrast with her ivory white flesh. When she had stared for a long minute, and had had enough, she did not say anything, but turned away silently to stand at a window, her back to Furneaux.

He looked at her, thinking: "She guesses, and suffers."

Suddenly she whirled round. "May I—see that letter?" she asked in a low voice.

"The whole note?" he said; "I'm afraid that it's private—not *my* secret—I regret it—an official document, you know."

"All right," she said quietly. "You may come to me for help yet"—and turned to the pile of letters on the desk.

"Anyway, Rosalind is not a relative, to your knowledge?" he persisted.

"No."

She stuffed the letters into a drawer, bowed, and was gone, leaving him sorry for her, for he saw a lump working in her throat.

Some minutes after her disappearance, a plump little woman came in—Mrs. Hester Bates, housekeeper in the Osborne *ménage*. Her hair lay in smooth curves on her brow as on the upturned bulge of a china bowl. There was an apprehensive look in her upward-looking eyes, so

Furneaux spoke comfortingly to her, after seating her near the window.

"Don't be afraid to speak," he said reassuringly. "What you have to say is not necessarily against Mr. Osborne's interests. Just state the facts simply—you did see him here on the murder night, didn't you?"

She muttered something, as a tear dropped on the ample bosom of her black dress.

"Just a little louder," Furneaux said.

"Yes," she sobbed, "I saw his back."

"You were—where?"

"Coming up the kitchen stairs to talk to Mr. Jenkins."

"Don't cry. And when you reached the top of the kitchen stairs you saw his back on the house stairs—at the bottom? at the top?"

"He was nearer the top. I only saw him a minute."

"A moment, you mean, I think. And in that one moment you became quite sure that it was Mr. Osborne? Though it was only his back you saw?"

"Yes, sir...."

"No, don't cry. It's nothing. Only are you certain sure—that's the point?"

"Yes, I am sure enough, but—"

"But what?"

"I thought he was the worse for drink, which was a mad thing."

"Oh, you thought that. Why so?"

"His feet seemed to reel from side to side—almost from under him."

"His feet—I see. From side to side.... Ever saw him the worse for drink before?"

"Never in all my life! I was amazed. Afterwards I had a feeling that it wasn't Mr. Osborne himself, but his spirit that I had seen. And it may have been his spirit! For my Aunt Pruie saw the spirit of her boy one Sunday afternoon when he was alive and well in his ship on the sea."

"But a spirit the worse for drink?" murmured

Furneaux; "a spirit whose feet seemed to reel?"

She dropped her eyes, and presently wept a theory.

"A spirit walks lighter-like than a Christian, sir."

"Did you, though," asked Furneaux, making shorthand signs in his notebook, "did you have the impression that it might be a spirit at the time, or was it only afterwards?"

"It was only afterwards when I thought matters over," said Mrs. Bates. "Even at the time it crossed my mind that there was something in it I didn't rightly understand."

"Now, what sort of something?—can't you say?"

"No, sir. I don't know."

"And when you saw Mr. Jenkins immediately afterwards, did you mention to him that you had seen Mr. Osborne?"

"No, I didn't say anything to him, nor him to me."

"Pity.... But the hour. You have said, I hear, that it was five minutes to eight. Now, the murder was committed between 7.30 and 7.45; and at five to eight Mr. Osborne is said by more than one person to have been at the Ritz Hotel. If he was there, he couldn't have been here. If he was here, he couldn't have been there. Are you sure of the hour—five to eight?"

As to that Mrs. Bates was positive. She had reason to remember, having looked at the clock *à propos* of the servants' supper. And Furneaux went away from her with eyes in which sparkled a light that some might have called wicked, and all would have called cruel, as when the cat hears a stirring, and crouches at the hole's rim with her soul crowded into an unblinking stare of expectation.

He looked at his watch, took a cab to Waterloo, and while in the vehicle again studied that scrawled "Rosalind" on Osborne's letter to Janoc.

"A trip to Tormouth should throw some light on it," he thought. "If it can be shown that he is actually in love— again—already—" and as he so thought, the cab ran out of St. James's Street into Pall Mall.

"Look! quick! There—in that cab!" hissed a man at that moment to a girl with whom he was lurking in a doorway deep under the shadow of an awning near the corner. "Look!"

"That's him!"

"Sure? Look well!"

"The very man!"

"Well, of all the fatalities!"

The cab dashed out of sight, and the man—Chief Inspector Winter—clapped his hand to his forehead in a spasm of sheer distraction and dismay. The woman with him was the murdered actress's cook, Bertha Seward, the same whom Inspector Clarke had one morning seen in earnest talk with Janoc under the pawnbroker's sign in St. Martin's Lane.

Winter walked away from her, looking on the ground, seeking his lost wits there. Then suddenly he turned and overtook her again.

"And you swear to me, Miss Seward," he said gravely, "that that very man was with your mistress in her flat on the evening of the murder?"

"I would know him anywhere," answered the slight girl, looking up into his face with her oblique Chinese eyes that were always half shut as if shy of light. "I thought to myself at the time what a queer, perky person he was, and what working eyes the little man had, and I wondered who he could be. That's the very man in that cab, I'm positive."

"And when you and Pauline went out to the Exhibition you left him with your mistress, you say?"

"Yes, sir. They were in the drawing-room together; and quarreling, too, for her voice was raised, and she laughed twice in an angry way."

"Quarreling—in French? You didn't catch—?"

"No, it was in French."

Inspector Winter leant his shoulder against the house-wall, and his head slowly sank, and then all at once dropped down with an air of utter abandonment, for Furneaux was his friend—he had looked on Furneaux as a brother.

Furneaux, meantime, at Waterloo was taking train to Tormouth, and his fixed stare boded no good will to Rupert Osborne.

VII. At Tormouth

Furneaux reached Tormouth about three in the afternoon, and went boldly to the Swan Hotel, since he was unknown by sight to Osborne. It was an old-fashioned place, with a bar opening out of the vestibule, and the first person that met his eye was of interest to him—a man sitting in the bar-parlor, who had "Neapolitan" written all over him—a face that Furneaux had already marked in Soho. He did not know the stranger's name, but he would have wagered a large sum that this queer visitor to Tormouth was a bird of the Janoc flock.

"What is he doing here?" Furneaux asked himself; and the only answer that suggested itself was: "Keeping an eye on Osborne. Perhaps that explains how Janoc got hold of the name 'Glyn.'"

When he was left alone in the bedroom which he took, he sat with his two hands between his knees, his head bent low, giving ten minutes' thought by the clock to the subject of Anarchists. Presently his lips muttered:

"Clarke is investigating the murder on his own account; he suspects that Anarchists were at the bottom of it; he has let them see that he suspects; and they have taken alarm, knowing that their ill repute can't bear any added load of suspicion. Probably she was more mixed up with them than is known; probably there was some quarrel between them and her; and so, seeing themselves suspected, they are uneasy. Hence Janoc wrote to Osborne in Clarke's name, asking how much Osborne knew of her connection with Anarchists. He must have managed somehow to have Osborne shadowed down here—must be eager to have Osborne proved guilty. Hence, perhaps, for some reason, the presence of that fellow below there in the parlor. But I, for my part, mustn't allow myself to be drawn off into proving *them* guilty. Another, another, is my prey!"

He stood up sharply, crept to his door, and listened. All the upper part of the house was as still as the tomb at that hour. Mr. Glyn—Osborne's name on the hotel register—was, Furneaux had been told, out of doors.

He passed out into a corridor, and, though he did not know which was Osborne's room, after peering through two doorways discovered it at the third, seeing in it a cane with a stag's head which Osborne often carried. He slipped within, and in a moment was everywhere at once in the room, filling it with his presence, ransacking it with a hundred eyes.

In one corner was an antiquated round table in mahogany, with a few books on it, and under the books a copper-covered writing-pad. In the writing-pad he found a letter—a long one, not yet finished, in Osborne's hand, written to "My dear Isadore."

The first words on which Furneaux's eyes fell were "her unstudied grace...."

certain astonishment on seeing her move, she moves so well. I confess I did not know, till I knew her, that our human flesh could express such music. Her waist is small, yet so willowy and sinuous that it cannot be trammeled in those unyielding ribs of steel and bone in which women love to girdle themselves. For her slimness she is tall, perhaps, what you might think a little too tall until you stood by her side and saw that her freedom of movement had deceived you. Nor is she what you would call a girl: her age can't be a day under twenty-three. But she does not make a motion of the foot that her waist does not answer to it in as exact a proportion as though the Angel of Grace was there with measuring-tape and rod. If her left foot moves, her waist sways by so much to the left; if her right, she sways to the right, as surely as a lily on a long stalk swings to the will of every wanton wind. But, after all, words cannot express the poetry of her being. With her every step, I am confident her toe in gliding forward touches the ground steadily, but so zephyr-lightly, that only a megaphone could report it to the ear. And not only is there a distinct forward bend of the body in walking, but with every step her whole being and soul walks—the mere physical movements are the least of it! And her walk, I repeat, has the security, the lissome elegance of a leopard's—her eyes, her mouth, her hair, her neck, those of a Naiad balanced on the crest of a curling wave....

"Ah-h-h!..." murmured Furneaux on a long-drawn breath, "'A Naiad'! Something more fairy-like than Rose de Bercy!"

He read on.

Soon I shall see her dance—dance with her! and then you shall hear. There's a certain Lord Spelding a little way from here whom I know through a local doctor, and he is giving a dance at his Abbey two evenings hence—she and her mother are to be there. She has promised me that she will dance, and I shall tell you how. But I expect nothing one whit more consummate in the way of charm from her dancing than from her ordinary motions. I know beforehand that her dancing will be to her walking what the singing of a lovely voice is to its talking—beauty moved to enthusiasm, but no increase of beauty; the moon in a halo, but still the moon. What, though, do you think of me in all this, my dear Isadore? I have asked myself whether words like "fickle," "flighty," "forgetful," will not be in your mind as you read. And if you are not tolerant, who will be? She, the other, is hardly cold yet in her untimely tomb, and here am I ... shall I say in love? say, at any rate, enraptured, down, down, on my two bended knees. Certainly, the other was bitter to me— she deceived, she pitilessly deceived; and I see now with the clearest eyes that love was never the name of what I felt for her, even if she had not deceived. But, oh, such a fountain of pity is in me for her—untimely gone, cut off, the cup of life in her hand, her lips purple with its wine— that I cannot help reproaching this wandering of my eye from her. It is rather shocking, rather horrible. And yet—I appeal to your sympathy—I am no more master of myself in this than of something that is now happening to the Emperor of China, or that once happened to his grandfather.

The corners of Furneaux's lips turned downward, and a lambent fire flamed in his eyes. He clutched the paper in his hand as if he would strangle its dumb eloquence. Still he glowered at the letter, and read.

But imagine, meanwhile, my false position here! I am known to her and to her mother as Mr. Glyn; and thrice has Osborne, the millionaire, the probable murderer of Rose de Bercy, been discussed between us. Think of it!— the misery, the falseness of it. If something were once to whisper to Mrs. Marsh, "this Mr. Glyn, to whom you are speaking in a tone of chilly censure of such men as Osborne, is Osborne himself; that translucent porcelain of your teacup has been made impure by his lips; you should smash your Venetian vases and Satsuma bowl of hollyhocks, since his not-too-immaculate hands have touched them: beware! a snake has stolen into your dainty and Puritan nest"—if some imp of unhappiness whispered that, what would she do? I can't exactly imagine those still lips uttering a scream, but I can see her lily fingers—like lilies just getting withered—lifted an instant in mild horror of the sacrilege! As it is, her admittance of me into the nest has been an unbending on her part, an unbending touched with informality, for it was only brought about through Richards, the doctor here, to whom I got Smythe, one of my bankers, who is likewise Richards' banker, to speak of a "Mr. Glyn." And if she now finds that being gracious to the stranger smirches her, compromises her in

the slightest, she will put her thin dry lips together a little,
and say "I am punished for my laxity in circumspection."
And then, ah! no more Rosalind for Osborne forever, if he
were ten times ten millionaires....

"'Rosalind,'" murmured Furneaux, "Rosalind Marsh.
That explains the scribble on the back of the Janoc letter.
He calls her Rosalind—breathes her name to the moon—
writes it! We shall see, though."

At that moment he heard a step outside, and stood
alert, ready to hide behind a curtain; but it was only some
hurrying housemaid who passed away. He then put back
the letter where he had found it; and instantly tackled
Osborne's portmanteaux. The larger he found locked, the
smaller, lying half under the bed, was fastened with
straps, but unlocked. He quickly ransacked the
knicknacks that it contained; and was soon holding up to
the light between thumb and finger a singular object
taken from the bottom of the bag—a scrap of lace about
six inches long, half of it stained with a brown smear that
was obviously the smear of—blood.

It was a peculiar lace, Spanish hand-made, and
Furneaux knew well, none better than he, that the
dressing-gown in which Rose de Bercy had been
murdered, which she had thrown on preparatory to
dressing that night, was trimmed with Spanish hand-
made lace. He looked at this amazing bit of evidence with
a long interest there in the light from the window,
holding it away from him, frowning, thinking his own
thoughts behind his brow, as shadow chases shadow. And
presently he muttered the peculiar words:

"Now, any detective would swear that this was a clew
against him."

He put it back into the bag, went out softly, walked
downstairs, and passed out into the little town. A
policeman told him where the house of Mrs. Marsh was to
be found, and he hastened half a mile out of Tormouth to
it.

The house, "St. Briavels," stood on a hillside behind walls and wrought-iron gates and leafage, through which peeped several gables rich in creepers and ivy. Of Osborne, so far, there was no sign.

Furneaux retraced his steps, came back to Tormouth, sauntered beyond the town over the cliffs, with the sea spread out in the sunlight, all sparkling with far-flung sprightliness. And all at once he was aware of a murmur of voices sounding out of Nowhere, like the hum of bumble-bees on a slumbrous afternoon. The ear could not catch if they were right or left, above or below. But they became louder; and suddenly there was a laugh, a delicious low cadence of a woman's contralto that seemed to roll up through an oboe in her throat. And now he realized that the speakers were just below him on the sands. He stepped nearer the edge of the cliff, and, craning and peering stealthily through its fringe of grasses, saw Osborne and a lady walking westward over the sands.

Osborne was carrying an easel and a Japanese umbrella. He was not looking where he was going, not seeing the sea, or the sands, or the sun, but seeing all things in the lady's face.

Furneaux watched them till they were out of sight behind a bend of the coast-line; he saw Osborne once stumble a little over a stone, and right himself without glancing at what he had stumbled on, without taking his gaze from the woman by his side.

A bitter groan hissed from Furneaux's lips.

"But how about this fair Rosalind?" he muttered half aloud. "Is this well for *her*? She should at least be told who her suitor is—his name—his true colors—the length and depth of his loves. There is a way of stopping this...."

He walked straight back to the hotel, and at once took pen and paper to write:

DEAR MISS PROUT:—It has occurred to me that possibly you may be putting yourself to the pains of discovering for me the identity of the friend of Mr. Osborne, the "Rosalind," as to whom I asked you—in which case, to save you any trouble, I am writing to tell you that I have now discovered who that lady is. I am, you see, at present here in Tormouth, a very agreeable little place.

Yours truly,
C. E. FURNEAUX.

And, as he directed the envelope, he said to himself with a curious crowing of triumph that Winter would have said was not to be expected from his friend:

"This should bring her here; and if it does—!"

Whereupon a singular glitter appeared an instant in his eyes.

Having posted the letter, he told the young woman in the bar, who also acted as bookkeeper, that, after all, he would not be able to stay the night. He paid, nevertheless, for the room, and walked away with his bag, no one knew whither, out of Tormouth. Two hours later he returned to the hotel, and for the second time that day took the same room, but not a soul suspected for a moment that it was the same Furneaux, since at present he had the look of a meek old civil servant living on a mite of pension, the color all washed out of his flabby cheeks and hanging wrinkles.

His very suit-case now had a different physiognomy. He bargained stingily for cheap terms, and then ensconced himself in his apartment with a senile chuckle, rubbing his palms together with satisfaction at having obtained such good quarters so cheaply.

The chambermaid, whom he had tipped well on leaving, sniffed at this new visitor. "Not much to be got out of him," she said to her friend, the boots.

The next afternoon at three o'clock an elderly lady arrived by the London train at Tormouth, and she, too, came to put up at the Swan.

Furneaux, at the moment of her arrival, was strolling

to and fro on the pavement in front of the hotel, very shaky and old, a man with feeble knees, threadbare coat, and shabby hat—so much so that the manager had told the young person in the bar to be sure and send in an account on Saturday.

Giving one near, clear, piercing glance into the newcomer's face, round which trembled a colonnade of iron-gray ringlets, Furneaux was satisfied.

"Marvelously well done!" he thought. "She has been on the stage in her time, and to some purpose, too."

The lady, without a glance at him, all a rustle of brown silk, passed into the hotel.

The same night the old skinflint and the lady of the iron-gray ringlets found themselves alone at a table, eating of the same dishes. It was impossible not to enter into conversation.

"Your first visit to Tormouth, I think?" began Furneaux.

The lady inclined her head.

"My name is Pugh, William Pugh," he told her. "I was in Tormouth some years ago, and know the place rather well. Charming little spot! I shall be most happy—if I may—if you will deign—"

"How long have you been here now?" she asked him in a rather mellow and subdued voice.

"I only came yesterday," he answered.

"Did you by chance meet here a certain Mr. Furneaux?" she asked.

"Let me see," said he—"Furneaux. I—stay—I believe I did! He was just departing at the time of my arrival—little man—sharp, unpleasant face—I—I—hope I do not speak of a friend or relative!—but I believe I did hear someone say 'Mr. Furneaux.'"

"At any rate, he is not here now?" she demanded, with an air of decision.

"No, he is gone."

"Ah!" she murmured, and something in the tone of that "Ah!" made Furneaux's eye linger doubtfully upon her an instant.

Then the elderly lady wished to know who else was in the hotel, if there was anyone of any interest, and "Mr. Pugh" was apparently eager to gossip.

"There is first of all a Mr. Glyn—a young man, an American, I think, of whom I have heard a whisper that he is enormously wealthy."

"Is he in the room?"

"No."

"Why is he—invisible?"

"I am told that he has made friends in Tormouth with a lady—a Mrs. Marsh—who resides at 'St. Briavels' some way out of town—not to mention *Miss* Marsh—Rosalind is her name—upon whom I hear he is more than a little sweet."

He bent forward, shading his lips with his palm to conceal the secret as it came out, and it was a strange thing that the newly-arrived visitor could not keep her ringlets from shaking with agitation.

"Well," she managed to say, "when young people meet—it is the old story. So he is probably at 'St. Briavels' now?"

"Highly probable—if all I hear be true."

The ringleted dame put her knife and fork together, rose, bowed with a gracious smile, and walked away. Five minutes later Furneaux followed her, went upstairs with soundless steps to his room, and within it stood some time listening at a crevice he had left between the door and the door-post.

Then he crept out, and spurting with swift suddenness, silent as a cat, to Osborne's room, sent the door open with a rush, and instantly was bowing profoundly, saying: "My dear madam! how *can* you pardon me?"

For the lady was also in Osborne's room, as Furneaux had known; and though there was no artificial light, enough moonlight flooded the room to show that even through her elaborate make-up a pallor was suggested in her face, as she stood there suspended, dumb.

Mr. Pugh seemed to be in a very pain of regret.

"I had no idea that it was your room!" he pleaded. "I—do forgive me—but I took it for my own!"

Oddly enough, the lady tittered, almost hysterically, though she was evidently much relieved to find who it was that had burst in so unceremoniously.

"The same accident has happened to me!" she cried. "I took it to be my room, but it doesn't seem—"

"Ah, then, we both.... By the way," he added, with a magnificent effort to escape an embarrassing situation, "what beautiful moonlight! And the Tormouth country under it is like a fairy place. It is a sin to be indoors. I am going for a stroll. May I hope to have the pleasure—?"

He wrung his palms wheedlingly together, and his attitude showed that he was hanging on her answer.

"Yes, I should like to take a walk—thank you," she answered. Together they made for the door; he fluttered to his room, she to hers, to prepare. Soon they were outside the hotel, walking slowly under the moon. Apparently without definite directive, they turned up the hill in the direction of "St. Briavels," nor was it many minutes before Mr. Pugh began to prove himself somewhat of a gallant, and gifted in the saying of those airy nothings which are supposed to be agreeable to the feminine ear. The lady, for her part, was not so thorny and hard of heart as one might have thought from the staidness of her air, and a good understanding was quickly established between the oddly-assorted pair.

"Rather an adventure, this, for people of our age...." she tittered, as they began to climb the winding road.

"But, madam, we are not old!" exclaimed the lively Mr. Pugh, who might be seventy from his decrepit semblance. "Look at that moon—are not our hearts still sensible to its seductive influences? You, for your part, may possibly be nearing that charming age of forty—"

"Oh, sir! you flatter me...."

"Madam, no, on my word!—not a day over forty would be given you by anyone! And if you have the heart of twenty, as I am sure that you have, what matters it if—"

"Hush!" she whispered, as a soft sound of the piano from "St. Briavels" reached them.

Before them on the roadway they saw several carriages drawn up near the great gates. The tinkle of the piano grew as they approached. Then they saw a few lantern lights in the grounds glimmering under the trees. Such signs spoke of a party in progress. For once, the English climate was gracious to its dupes.

The lady, without saying anything to her companion, stepped into the shadow of a yew-tree opposite the manor-close, and stood there, looking into the grounds over the bars of a small gate, beyond which a path ran through a shrubbery. On the path were three couples, ladies with light scarves draped over their décolleté dresses, men, bare-headed and smoking cigarettes. They were very dim to her vision, which must have been well preserved for one of her age, despite Mr. Pugh's gallantry. The overhanging foliage was dense, and only enough moonlight oozed through the canopy of leaves to toss moving patterns on the lawn and paths.

But the strange lady's eyes were now like gimlets, with the very fire of youth burning in them, and it was with the sure fleetness of youth that she suddenly ran in a moment of opportunity from the yew to the gate, pushed it a little open, and slipped aside into a footpath that ran parallel with the lawn on which the "St. Briavels" diners were now strolling.

With equal suddenness, or equal disregard of appearance, Mr. Pugh, too, became young again, as if both, like Philemon and Baucis, had all at once quaffed the elixir of youth; and he was soon by the young-old lady's side on the footpath. But her eyes, her ears, were so strained toward the lawn before her, that she seemed not to be aware of his presence.

"I did not guess that you were interested in the people

here," he whispered. "That man now coming nearer is Mr. Glyn himself, and with him is Miss Rosalind Marsh."

"*Sh-h-h*," came from her lips, a murmur long-drawn, absent-minded, her eyes peering keenly forward.

He nudged her.

"Is it fitting that we should be here? We place ourselves in a difficult position, if seen."

"Sh-h-h-h-h...."

Still he pestered her.

"Really it is a blunder.... We—we become—eavesdroppers—! Let us—I suggest to you—"

"Oh, *do* keep quiet," she whispered irritably; and in that instant the talk of Osborne and Rosalind became audible to her. She heard him say:

"Yes, I confess I have known Osborne, and I believe the man perfectly incapable of the act attributed to him by a hasty public opinion."

"Intimately known him?"

Rosalind turned her eyebrows upward in the moonlight. Seen thus, she was amazingly beautiful.

"Do we intimately know anyone? Do we intimately know ourselves?" asked Osborne as he passed within five yards of the two on the path. "I think I may say that I know Osborne about as well as I know anyone, and I am confident that he is horribly misjudged. He is a young man of—yes, I will say that for him—of good intentions; and he is found guilty, without trial, of a wrong which he never could have committed—and the wrong which he *has* committed he is not found guilty of."

"What wrong?" asked Rosalind.

"I have heard—I know, in fact—that in the short time that has passed since the murder of Miss de Bercy, Osborne, her acknowledged lover, has allowed himself to love another."

Rosalind laughed, with the quiet amusement of well-bred indifference.

"What a weird person!" she said.

And as their words passed beyond hearing, a hiss, like

a snake's in the grass, rose from the shrubbery behind them, a hiss of venom intensely low, and yet loud enough to be heard by Furneaux, who, standing a little behind the lady of the ringlets, rubbed his hands together in silent and almost mischievous self-congratulation.

The house end of the lawn was not far, the words of the returning pair were soon again within earshot. The fiery glance of the watching woman, ferreting, peering, dwelt on them—or rather on one of them, for she gave no heed to Osborne at all. Her very soul was centered on Rosalind, whose walk, whose lips, whose eyes, whose hair, whose voice, she ran over and estimated as an expert accountant reckons up a column of figures to ascertain their significance. She missed no item in that calculation. She noted the over-skirt of Chantilly, the wrap of Venetian lace on the girl's head, the white slippers, the roses disposed on her corsage with the harmless vanity of the artist's skill, all these that fixed stare ravenously devoured and digested while Rosalind took half a dozen slow steps.

"But seriously," she heard Osborne say, "what is your opinion of a love so apparently fickle and flighty as this of Osborne's?"

"Let me alone with your Osborne," Rosalind retorted with another little laugh. "A person of such a mood is merely uninteresting, and below being a topic. Let the dead lady's father or somebody horsewhip him—I cannot care, I'm afraid. Let us talk about—"

"*Ourselves?*"

"'Ourselves and our king.'"

"I have so much to say about ourselves! Where should I begin? And now that I have a few minutes, I am throwing them away. Do you know, I never seem to secure you free from interruption. Either yourself or someone else intervenes every time, and reduces me to silence and despair—"

Their words passed beyond earshot again in the other direction; and, as the lawn was wide between house and screen of shrubbery on the road front, it was some time before they were again heard. At last, though, they came, and then Rosalind's low tone of earnestness showed that this time, at least, Osborne had been listened to.

"I will, since you ask, since you wish"—her voice faltered—"to please you. You will be at the Abbey to-morrow evening. And, since you say that you so—desire it, I may then hear what you have to say. Now I'll go."

"But when—where—?"

"If the night is fine, I will stroll into the gardens during the evening. You will see me when I go. On the south terrace of the Abbey there is a sun-dial in the middle of a paved Italian garden. I'll pass that way, and give you half an hour."

"Rosalind!"

"Ah, no—not yet."

Her lips sighed. She looked at him with a lingering tenderness languishing in her eyes.

"Can I help it?" he murmured, and his voice quivered with passion.

"Are you glad now?"

"Glad!"

"Good-by."

She left him hurriedly and sped with inimitable grace of motion across the lawn toward the house, and, while he looked after her, with the rapt vision of a man who has communed with a spirit, the two listeners crept to the little gate, slipped out when a laughing couple turned their heads, and walked back to the hotel.

The lady said never a word. Mr. Pugh was full of chat and merriment, but no syllable fell from her tight-pressed lips.

The next day the lady was reported to have a headache—at any rate she kept to her room, and saw no one save the "boots" of the establishment, with whom during the afternoon she had a lengthy interview upstairs. At about seven in the evening she was writing these words:

MISS MARSH:—Are you aware that the "Mr. Glyn" whom you know here is no other than Mr. Rupert Osborne, who is in everyone's mouth in connection with the Feldisham Mansions Murder? You may take this as a positive fact from

"ONE WHO KNOWS."

She wrote it in a handwriting that was very different from her own, inclosed and directed it, and then, about half-past seven, sent for "boots" again.

Her instructions were quite explicit:

"Wait in the paved rose garden at the Abbey, the square sunken place with a sun-dial in the center," she said. "It is on the south terrace, and the lady I have described will surely come. The moment she appears hand the note to her, and be off—above all else, answer no questions."

So the youth, with a sovereign in his pocket, hurried away to do Hylda Prout's will—or was it Furneaux's? Who might tell?

VIII. At The Sun-Dial

The messenger of evil had waited twenty minutes by the side of the sun-dial, when he saw a lady come round the corner from the front of the house, and saunter towards him. Moonlight lay weltering on the white walks of the terrace, on the whiter slabs of stone, on the water of the basin, on the surface of the lake eastward where the lowest of the terraces curved into the parkland that the wavelets lapped on. It weltered, too, on the lady's hair, deftly coiled and twisted into the coiffure of a Greek statue. It shimmered on the powdered blue of her gown that made her coming a little ghostly in that light, on the rows of pearls around her throat, and on the satin gloss of her shoes. She made straight for the dial; and then, all at once, finding some unknown man keeping the tryst, half halted.

He ran out to her, touched his cap, saying "Miss Marsh," handed her the note, touched his cap again, and was going.

"From whom?" she called after him in some astonishment.

"Lady at the Swan, miss"—and he hurried off even more swiftly, for this was a question which he had answered against orders.

She stood a little, looking at the envelope, her breathing labored, an apprehension in her heart. Then, hearing the coming of footsteps which she knew, she broke it open, and ran her eye over the few words.

Bending slightly, with the flood of the moon on the paper, she could easily read the plainly written, message.

... The Mr. Glyn whom you know is no other than the Mr. Rupert Osborne who is in everyone's mouth in

connection with the Feldisham Mansions Murder....

Now she laughed with a sudden catch of the breath, gasping "Oh!" with a sharp impatience of all anonymous scandalizers. But as her head rather swam and span, she walked on quickly to the basin, and there found it necessary to sit down on the marble. The stab of pain passed in a few seconds, and again she sprang up and laughed as lightly as one of the little fountains in the basin that tossed its tinted drops to the moonbeams.

Not twenty yards away was Osborne coming to her.

She looked at him steadily—her marvelous eyes self-searching for sure remembrance of the earnestness with which he had pleaded in favor of the lover of Rose de Bercy—how he had said that Osborne had already loved again; and how she, Rosalind—oh, how blind and deaf!—heedlessly had brushed aside his words, saying that a man of that mood was below being a topic....

"Is it half an hour?" Osborne came whispering, with a bending of the body that was like an act of worship.

She smiled. In the moonlight he could not perceive how ethereally white was her face.

"It is one half-minute!... It was rather quixotic of you to have proposed, and of me to have accepted, such a meeting. But I felt sure that by this hour others would be strolling about the terraces. As it is, you see, we are pioneers without followers. So, till we meet again—"

She seemed to be about to hurry away without another word; he stood aghast.

"But, Rosalind—"

"What? How dare you call me Rosalind?"

Now her eyes flashed upon him like sudden lightning from a dark blue sky, and the scorn in her voice blighted him.

"I—I—don't understand," he stammered, trying to come nearer. She drew her skirts aside with a disdain that was terrifying.

Then she laughed softly again; and was gone.

He looked after her as after treasure that one sees sinking into the sea, flashing in its descent to the depths. For one mad instant he had an impulse to run in vain pursuit, but instead he gave way, sank down upon the edge of the marble basin, just where she had dropped a few brief seconds earlier, covered his face, and a groan that was half a sob broke so loudly from his throat that she heard it. She hesitated, nearly stopped, did not look round, scourged herself into resolution, and in another moment had turned the corner of the house and was lost to sight.

What had happened to change his Rosalind into this unapproachable empress Osborne was too stunned to ask himself explicitly. He knew he was banned, and that was enough. Deep in his subconsciousness he understood that somehow she had found out his wretched secret—found out that he was not the happy Glyn reeling through an insecure dream in fairyland, but the unhappy Osborne, heavily tangled in the sordid and the commonplace.

And, because he was unhappy and troubled, she left him without pity, turned her back eternally upon him. That hurt. As he stood up to walk away toward Tormouth, a fierce anger and a gush of self-pity battled in his eyes.

He had no more hope. He wandered on through the night, unseeing, stricken as never before. At last he reached the hotel, and, as soon as he could summon the energy, began to pack his portmanteau to go back to London. The day of the postponed inquest now loomed near, and he cared not a jot what became of him, only asking dumbly to be taken far from Tormouth.

As he was packing the smaller of the bags, he saw the scrap of blood-stained lace that Furneaux had already seen, had taken out, and had replaced. Osborne, with that same feeling of repulsion with which Furneaux had thrust it away from him, held it up to the light. What was it? How could it have got into his bag? he asked himself— a bit of lace stained with blood! His amazement knew no bounds—and would have been still more profound, if possible, had he seen Furneaux's singular act in replacing it in the bag after finding it.

He threw the horrible thing from him out of the window, and his very fingers tingled with disgust of it. But then came the disturbing thought—suppose it had been put into his bag as a trap? by the police, perhaps? And suppose any apparent eagerness of his to rid himself of it should be regarded as compromising? He was beginning to be circumspect now, timorous, ostentatious of that innocence in which a whole world disbelieved.

So he glanced out of the window, saw where the lace had dropped upon a sloping spread of turf in the hotel grounds, and ran down to get it. When he arrived at the spot where he had just seen it, the lace had disappeared.

He stood utterly mystified, looking down at the spot where the lace should be and was not; then looked around in a maze, to discover on a rustic seat that surrounded an oak tree an elderly lady and a bent old man sitting there in the shadow. Some distance off, lounging among the flower beds in the moonlight, was the figure of a tall man. Osborne was about to inquire of the two nearest him if they had seen the lace, when the old gentleman hurried nimbly forward out of the tree's shadow and asked if he was seeking a piece of something that had dropped from above.

"Yes," answered Osborne, "have you seen it?"

"That gentleman walking yonder was just under your window when it dropped, and I saw him stoop to pick it up," said the other.

Osborne thanked him, and made for "the gentleman," who turned out to be a jauntily-dressed Italian, bony-faced, square in the jaw, his hair clipped convict-short, but dandily brushed up at the corner of the forehead.

To the question: "Did you by chance pick up a bit of lace just now?" he at once bowed, and showing his teeth in a grin, said:

"He dropped right to my feet from the sky; here he is"—and he presented the lace with much ceremony.

"I am obliged," said Osborne.

"Do not say it," answered the other politely, and they parted, Osborne hurrying back to his room, with the intent to catch a midnight train from Tormouth.

As he entered the house again, the older man, incredibly quick on his uncertain feet, overtook him, and, touching him on the arm, asked if he intended to catch the train that night.

"That is my desire," answered Osborne.

"It is mine, too," said the other; "now, could you give me a seat in your conveyance?"

Osborne said, "With pleasure," and they entered the hotel to prepare to go.

At the same moment the Italian sauntered up to the oak tree beneath which sat Hylda Prout in her Tormouth make-up. Seating himself without seeking her permission, he lit a cigarette.

"Good-evening," he said, after enveloping himself in a cloud of smoke. She did not answer, but evidently he was not one to be rebuffed.

"Your friend, Mistare Pooh, he is sharp! My! he see all," he said affably.

This drew a reply.

"You are quite right," she said. "He sees all, or nearly all. Do you mean because he saw you pick up the lace?"

"Now—how *you* know it was *lace*?" asked the Italian, turning full upon her. "You sitting here, you couldn't see it was lace so far—no eyes could see that."

This frankness confused the lady a moment; then she laughed a little, for he had supplied her with a retort.

"Perhaps I see all, too, like my friend."

There was a silence, but the Italian was apparently waiting only to rehearse his English.

"You know Mr. Glyn—yes?" he said.

"No."

"Oh, don't say 'no'!" Reproach was in his ogle, his voice. His tone was almost wheedling.

"Why not?"

"The way I find you spying after him this morning tell me that you know him. And I know that you know him before that."

"What concern is it of *yours*?" she asked, looking at him with a lowering of the lids in a quick scrutiny that was almost startled. "What is *your* interest in Mr. Glyn?"

"Say 'Osborne' and be done," he said.

"Well, say 'Osborne,'" she responded.

"Good. We are going to understand the one the other,
I can see. But if you want to know what is 'my interest' in
the man, you on your part will tell me first if you are
friend or enemy of Osborne."

In one second she had reflected, and said: "Enemy."

His hand shot out in silence to her, and she shook it.
The mere action drew them closer on the seat.

"I believe you," he whispered, "and I knew it, too, for if
you had been a friend you would not be in a disguise from
him."

"How do you know that I am in a disguise?"

"Since yesterday morning I know," he answered,
"when I see you raise your blind yonder, not an old
woman, but a young and charming lady not yet fully
dressed, for I was here in the garden, looking out for what
I could see, and my poor heart was pierced by the vision
at the window."

He pressed his palm dramatically on his breast.

"Yes, of course, it is on the left, as usual," said Hylda
Prout saucily. "But let us confine ourselves to business for
the moment. I don't quite understand your object. As to
the bit of lace—"

"How you *know* it was lace?"

She looked cautiously all round before answering. "I
know because I searched Mr. Osborne's room, and saw it."

"Good! Before long we understand the one the other.
You be frank, I be frank. You spied into the bag, and *I* put
it in the bag."

"I know you did."

"Now, how you know?"

"There was no one else to do it!"

"No? Might not Osborne put it there himself? You
know where that bit of lace come from?"

"I guess."

"What you guess?"

"I guess that it is from the dress of the dead actress,
for it has blood on it."

"You guess good—very good. And Osborne killed her—

yes?"

She pondered a little. This attack had come on her from a moonlit sky.

"That I don't know. He may have, and he may not," she murmured.

"Which is more likely? That *he* killed her, or that *I* killed her?"

"I don't know. I should say it is more likely that you killed her."

"What! You pay me that compliment? Why so?"

"Well, you are in possession of a portion of the dress she wore when she was killed, and you put it into someone's belongings to make it seem that he killed her, an act which looks a little black against you."

"Ah, ma bella, now you jest," said the Italian, laughing. "The fact that I am so frank with you as to say you all this is proof that I not kill her."

"Yes, I see that," she agreed. "I was only joking. But since you did not kill her, how on earth did you get hold of that piece of her dress?"

"That you are going to know when I have received better proof that you are as much as I the enemy of Osborne. Did I not guess good, on seeing you yesterday morning at the window, that you are the same young lady who is Osborne's secretary in London, where I see you before?"

Hylda Prout admitted that she was the secretary.

"Good, then," said the Italian; "you staying in the house with him have every opportunity to find proof of his guilt of the murder; until which is proved, the necks of those I am working for are in danger."

With the impulsive gesture of his race he drew his forefinger in ghastly mimicry across his throat.

"So bad as that?" asked the woman coolly. "Unfortunately, I don't know who 'those' are you are working for. The—?"

"Yes."

"The Anarchists?"

"If you call them so."

"Did *they* kill her?"

"Not they!"

"Did they intend to?"

"Not they!"

"Then, where did you get that bit of lace? And where is the dagger?"

"Dagger! What about dagger now?"

He asked it with a guilty start. At last the talk was taking a turn which left Hylda Prout in command.

"If you have that lace, you have the dagger, too. And if you have the dagger, what help do you want from me? Produce that, and Osborne is done for."

Her voice sank to a whisper. If Furneaux could have been present he must have felt proud of her.

"Dagger!" muttered the Italian again in a hushed tone. "You seem to know much more—"

"Stay, let us get up and walk. It is not quite safe here.... There are too many trees."

The man, who had lost his air of self-confidence, seemed to be unable to decide what to do for the best. But Hylda Prout had risen, and he, too, stood up. He was compelled to follow her. Together they passed through the grounds toward the cliffs.

The same moonlight that saw them strolling there, saw at the same time Furneaux and Osborne racing in a trap along the road to Sedgecombe Junction to catch the late train on the main line. Furneaux was inclined to be chatty, but Osborne answered only in monosyllables, till his companion's talk turned upon the murder of the actress, when Osborne, with a sudden access of fury, assured him in very emphatic language that his ears were weary of that dreadful business, and prayed to be spared it. The old gentleman seemed to be shocked, but Osborne only glanced at his watch, muttering that they would have to be smart to catch the train; and as he put back the watch in its pocket, the other dropped his bag over the side of the vehicle.

There was nothing to be done but to stop, and the delinquent, with the stiffness and slowness of age, descended to pick it up. Thus some precious minutes were wasted. Furneaux, in fact, did not wish Osborne to start for London that night at that late hour, since he wanted to apprise Winter of Osborne's departure. Hence he had begged a seat in the conveyance, and had already lost time at the hotel. A little later, when Osborne again glanced at his watch, it was to say: "Oh, well, there is no use in going on," and he called to the driver to turn back. Indeed, the whistle of the departing train was heard at the station half a mile away.

"Well, yes," said Furneaux, curiously pertinacious, when the dog-cart was on the homeward road, "one is weary of hearing this murder discussed. I only spoke of it to express to you my feeling of disapproval of the lover— of the man Osborne. Is it credible to you that he was not even at her funeral? No doubt he was advised not to be— no doubt it was wise from a certain point of view. But *nothing* should have prevented him, if he had had any affection for her. But he had none—he was a liar. Talk of her deceiving him! It was he—it was *he*—who deceived her, I say!"

"Have a cigar," said Osborne, presenting his case; "these are rather good ones; you will find them soothing."

His hospitality was declined, but there was no more talk, and the trap trotted back into Tormouth.

Up at "St. Briavels" that same moment the same moonlight, shining on a balcony, illumined yet another scene in the network of events. Rosalind Marsh was sitting there alone, her head bent between her clenched hands. She had returned home early from the Abbey, and Mrs. Marsh, who had silently wondered, presently came out with the softness of a shadow upon her, and touched her shoulder.

"What is the matter?" she asked in a murmur of sympathy.

"My head aches a little, mother dear."

"I am sorry. You look tired."

"Well, yes, dear. There are moments of infinite weariness in life. One cannot avoid them."

"Did you dance?"

"Only a little."

"Weary of emotions, then?"

The old lady smiled faintly.

"Mother!" whispered Rosalind, and pressed her mother's hand to her forehead.

There was silence for a while. When Mrs. Marsh spoke again it was to change the subject.

"You have been too long at Tormouth this time. I think you need a change. Suppose we took a little of London now? Society might brighten you."

"Oh, yes! Let us go from this place!" said Rosalind under her breath, her fingers tightly clenched together.

"Well, then, the sooner the better," said Mrs. Marsh. "Let it be to-morrow."

Rosalind looked up with gratitude and the moonlight in her eyes.

"Thank you, dear one," she said. "You are always skilled in divining, and never fail in being right."

And so it was done. The next forenoon saw the mother and daughter driving in an open landau past the Swan to Tormouth station, and, as they rolled by in state, Hylda Prout, who was peeping from a window after the figure of Osborne on *his* way to the station, saw them.

A glitter came into her eyes, and the unspoken thought was voiced in eloquent gesture: "What, following him so soon?"—for she knew that they could only be going by the London train, which had but one stopping-place after Tormouth. At once she rushed in a frenzy of haste to prepare to travel by that very train.

Some wild ringing of bells and promise of reward brought chambermaid and "boots" to her aid.

In her descent to the office to pay her bill she was encountered by her new friend, the Italian, who, surprised at her haste, said to her, "What, you go?"—to which she, hardly stopping, answered: "Yes—we will meet when we said—in two days' time."

"But me, too, I go," he cried, and ran to get ready, the antics of the pair creating some stir of interest in the bar parlor.

At this time Furneaux was already at the station, awaiting the train, having already wired to Winter in London to meet him at Waterloo. And so the same train carried all their various thoughts and purposes and secrets in its different compartments on the Londonward journey.

Furneaux, who chose to sit in the compartment with Rosalind and Mrs. Marsh, listened to every sigh and syllable of Rosalind, and, with the privilege of the aged, addressed some remarks to his fellow-travelers. Hylda Prout and the Italian were together—a singular bond of intimacy having suddenly forged itself between these two. They were alone, and Hylda, who left Tormouth old and iron-gray, arrived at London red-headed and young, freckle-splashed and pretty. But as for Osborne, he traveled in the dull company of his black thoughts.

The first to alight at Waterloo, before the train stopped, was Furneaux. His searching eyes at once discovered Winter waiting on the platform. In a moment the Chief Inspector had a wizened old man at his ear, saying: "Winter—I'm here. Came with the crowd."

"Hallo," said Winter, and from old-time habit of friendship his hand half went out. Furneaux, however, seemed not to notice the action, and Winter's hand drew back.

"Osborne is in the train," whispered Furneaux. "I telegraphed because there is an object in his smaller bag that I want you to see—as a witness, instantly. There he comes; ask him into the first-class waiting-room. It is usually empty."

Furneaux himself went straight into the waiting-room and sat in a corner behind a newspaper. Soon in came

Winter, talking to Osborne with a marked deference:

"You will forgive me, I am sure, for this apparent lack of confidence, but in an affair of this sort one leaves no stone unturned."

"Do not mention it," said Osborne, who was rather pale. "I think I can guess what it is that you wish to see...."

A porter, who had followed them, put the two portmanteaux on a table, and went out. Osborne opened the smaller one, and Winter promptly had the blood-stained bit of lace in his hand.

"What is it, sir?" asked Winter.

"Heaven knows," came the weary answer. "It was not in my possession when I left London, and was put into one of my bags by someone at Tormouth. When I found it, I threw it out of the window, as that gentleman there can prove," for he had seen Furneaux, but was too jaded to give the least thought to his unaccountable presence. "Afterwards I ran down and recovered it. *He* was in the garden...."

The unhappy young man's glance wandered out of the door to see Rosalind and her mother go past towards a waiting cab. He cared not a jot if all Scotland Yard were dogging his footsteps now.

"Is that so, sir?" asked Winter of Furneaux.

"Exactly as Mr. Glyn says," answered Furneaux, looking at them furtively, and darting one very curious glance at Winter's face.

"And who, Mr.—Glyn, was about the place whom you could possibly suspect of having placed this object in your bag—someone with a wicked motive for throwing suspicion upon you?"

Winter's lips whitened and dwelt with venom upon the word "wicked."

"There was absolutely no one," answered Osborne. "The hotel was rather empty. Of course, there was this gentleman—"

"Yes," said Winter after him, "this gentleman."

"An elderly lady, a Mrs. Forbes, I believe, as I happened to read her name, a foreigner who probably never saw me before, an invalid girl and her sister—all absolutely unconnected with me."

Furneaux's eyes were now glued on Winter's face. They seemed to have a queer meaning in them, a meaning not wholly devoid of spite and malice.

"Well, Mr.—Glyn," said Winter, "let me tell you, if you do not know, that this bit of lace was certainly part of the dress in which Miss de Bercy was murdered. Therefore the man—or woman—who put it into your bag was there—on the spot—when the deed was done."

Osborne did then exhibit some perplexed interest in a strange discovery.

"How can you be certain that it was part of her dress?" he asked.

"Because a fragment of lace of this size was torn from the wrap she was wearing at the time of the murder—I noticed it at my first sight of the body. This piece would just fit into it. So, whoever put it into your bag—"

"In that case I may have put it in myself!" said Osborne with a nervous laugh, "since I may be the murderer."

Apparently the careless comment annoyed Winter.

"I don't think I need detain you any longer, sir," he said coldly. "As for the lace, I'll keep it. I feel very confident that this part of the mystery will not baffle me for more than a day or two."

And ever the eyes of Furneaux dwelt upon Winter's face with that queer meaning reveling in their underlook.

Osborne turned to go. He did not trouble to call another porter, but carried his own luggage. He was about to enter a cab when he caught sight of the back of a woman's head among the crowd hurrying to an exit, a head which seemed singularly familiar to him. The next moment it was gone from his sight, which was a pity, since the head belonged to Hylda Prout, who had not anticipated that Osborne would be delayed on the

platform, and had had to steal past the waiting-room door
at a rush, since she was no longer an old lady, but herself.
She could not wait in the train till he was well away, for
she thought it well to ascertain the whereabouts of
Rosalind Marsh in London, and wished to shadow her.

Mrs. Marsh and her daughter carried the usual
mountain of ladies' luggage, which demanded time and
care in stowing safely on the roof of a four-wheeler, so
Hylda Prout was in time to call a hansom and follow
them. After her went the Italian, who made off hastily
when the train arrived, but lurked about until he could
follow the girl unseen, for she had frightened him.

Now, at the station that day, keeping well in the
background, was a third detective beside Winter and
Furneaux.

Clarke, with his interest in Anarchists, knew that this
particular Italian was coming from Tormouth either that
day or the day after. Two nights before, while on a visit to
the Fraternal Club in Soho, he had overheard the
whispered word that "Antonio" would "be back" on the
Wednesday or the Thursday.

Clarke did not know Antonio's particular retreat in
London, and had strong reasons for wishing to know it.
He, therefore, followed in a cab the cab that followed
Rosalind's cab. In any other city in the world than
London such a procession would excite comment—if it
passed through street after street, that is. But not so in
cab-using London, where a string of a hundred taxis,
hansoms, and four-wheelers may all be going in the same
direction simultaneously.

As Clarke went westward down the Strand and across
Trafalgar Square, he was full of meditations.

"What is Antonio doing with Osborne's lady
secretary?" he asked himself. "For that is the young
woman he is after, I'll swear. By Jove, there's more in this
tangle than meets the eye. It's a case for keeping both
eyes, and a third, if I had it, wide, wide open!"

Rosalind's and Mrs. Marsh's cab drew up before a

house in Porchester Gardens. As they got out and went up the steps, the cabs containing Antonio and Hylda Prout almost stopped, but each went on again.

"Now, what in the world is the matter?" mused Clarke. "Why are those two shadowing a couple of ladies, and sneaking on each other as well?"

He told his own driver to pass the house slowly, as he wished to note its number, and the vehicle was exactly opposite the front door when it was opened by a girl with a cap on her head to let in Mrs. Marsh and Rosalind; Clarke's eye rested on her, and lit with a strange fire. A cry of discovery leapt to his lips, but was not uttered. A moment after the door had closed upon the two travelers, Clarke's hand was at the trap-door in the roof of the hansom, and, careless whether or not he was seen, he leaped out, ran up the steps, and rang.

A moment more and the door was opened to him by the same girl, whom he had recognized instantly as Pauline Dessaulx, the late lady's-maid of Rose de Bercy— a girl for whom he had ransacked London in vain. And not he alone, for Pauline had very effectively buried herself from the afternoon after the murder, when Clarke had seen her once, and she him, to this moment. And there now they stood, Clarke and Pauline, face to face.

He, for his part, never saw such a change in a human countenance as now took place in this girl's. Her pretty brown cheeks at once, as her eyes fell on him, assumed the whiteness of death itself. Her lips, the very rims of her eyelids even, looked ghastly. She seemed to be on the verge of collapse, and her whole frame trembled in an agony of fear. Why? What caused these deadly tremors? Instantly Clarke saw guilt in this excess of emotion, and by one of those inspirations vouchsafed sometimes even to men of his coarse fiber he did the cleverest act of his life.

Putting out his hand, he said quietly, but roughly:

"Come now, no nonsense! Give it to me!"

What "it" meant he himself had no more notion than

the man in the moon. His real motive was to set the terrified girl speaking, and thus lead her on to yield some chance clew on which his wits might work. But at once, like one hypnotized, Pauline Dessaulx, still keeping her eyes fixed on his face, slowly moved her right hand to a pocket, slowly drew out a little book, and slowly handed it to him.

"All right—you are wise," he said. "I'll see you again." The door slammed, and he ran down the steps, his blood tingling with the sense that he had blundered upon some tremendous discovery.

Nor was he far wrong. When in the cab he opened the book, he saw it was Rose de Bercy's diary. He did not know her handwriting, but he happened to open the book at the last written page, and the very first words his staring eyes devoured were these:

If I am killed this night, it will be by—or by C. E. F.

Where the blank occurred it was evident that some name had been written, and heavily scratched through with pen and ink.

But the alternative suggested by the initials! C. E. F.! How grotesque, how exquisitely ludicrous! Clarke, gazing at the enigma, was suddenly shaken with a spasm of hysterical laughter.

IX. The Letter

Two days later, not Britain alone, but no small part of the two hemispheres, was stirred to the depths by the adjourned inquest on the Feldisham Mansions crime. Nevertheless, though there were sensations in plenty, the public felt vaguely a sense of incompleteness in the process, and of dissatisfaction with the result. The police seemed to be both unready and unconvinced; no one was quite sincere in anything that was said; the authorities were swayed by some afterthought; in popular phrase, they appeared "to have something up their sleeve."

Furneaux, this time, figured for the police; but Winter, too, was there unobtrusively; and, behind, hidden away as a mere spectator, was Clarke, smiling the smile that knows more than all the world, his hard mouth set in fixed lines like carved wood.

As against Osborne the inquiry went hard. More and more the hearts of the witnesses and jury grew hot against him, and, by a kind of electric sympathy, the blood of the crowd which gathered outside the court caught the fever and became inflamed with its own rage, lashing itself to a fury with coarse jibes and bitter revilings.

Furneaux, bringing forth and marshaling evidence on evidence against Osborne, let his eye light often on Winter; then he would look away hastily as though he feared his face might betray his thoughts.

In that small head of his were working more, by far more, secret things, dark intents, unspoken mazy purposes, than in all the heads put together in the busy court. He was pale, too, but his pallor was nothing compared with the marble forehead of Winter, whose eyes were nailed to the ground, and whose forehead was knit in a frown grim and hard as rock.

It was rarely that he so much as glanced up from the reverie of pitch-black doubts weltering through his brain like some maelstrom drowned in midnight. Once he glanced keenly upon William Campbell, the taxicab driver, who kept twirling his motor-cap round and round on his finger until an irritated coroner protested; once again did he glance at Mrs. Bates, housekeeper, and at the fountain of tears that flowed from her eyes.

Campbell was asked to pick out the man whom he had driven from Berkeley Street to Feldisham Mansions, if he saw him in court. He pointed straight at Osborne.

"You will swear that that is the man?" he was asked.

"No, not swear," he said, and looked round defiantly, as if he knew that most of those present were almost disappointed with his non-committal answer.

"Just think—look at him well," said the Treasury representative, as Osborne stood up to confront the driver with his pale face.

"That gentleman is like him—very like him—that's all I'll swear to. His manner of dress, his stand, his height, yes, and his face, his mustache, the chin, the few hairs there between the eyebrows—remarkably like, sir—for I recollect the man well enough. It may have been his double, but I'm not here to swear positively it was Mr. Osborne, because I'm not sure."

"We will take it, then, that, assuming there were two men, the one was so much like the other that you swear it was either Mr. Osborne or his double?" the coroner said.

"Well, I'll go so far as that, sir," agreed Campbell, and, at this admission, Furneaux glanced at a veiled figure that sat among the witnesses at the back of the court.

He knew that Rosalind Marsh was present, and his expression softened a little. Then he looked at another veiled woman—Hylda Prout—and saw that her eyes were fastened, not on the witness, but ever on Rosalind Marsh, as though there was no object, no interest, in the room but that one black-clothed figure of Rosalind.

Campbell's memory of the drive was ransacked, and turned inside out, and thrashed and tormented by one and another to weariness; and then it was the turn of Hester Bates, all tears, to tell how she had seen someone like unto Osborne on the stairs at five to eight, whose feet seemed to reel like a drunken man's, and who afterwards impressed her, when she thought of it, as a shape rather of limbo and spirit-land than of Mayfair and everyday life.

Then the flint ax-head, or celt, was presented to the court, and Hylda Prout was called to give evidence against her employer. She told how she had missed an ax-head from the museum, and also a Saracen dagger, but whether this was the very ax-head that was missing she could not say. It was very like it—that was all—and even Osborne showed his amaze at her collectedness, her calm indifference to many eyes.

"May I not be allowed to examine it?" he asked his solicitor.

"Why not?" said the coroner, and there was a tense moment when the celt was handed him.

He bent over it two seconds, and then said quietly: "This is certainly one of my collection of flints!"

His solicitor, taken quite aback, muttered an angry protest, and a queer murmur made itself felt. Osborne heard both the lawyer's words and the subdued "Ah!" of the others echoing in his aching heart. By this time he was as inwardly sensitive to the opinion of the mob as a wretch in the hands of inquisitors to the whim and humors of his torturers.

"That evidence will be taken on oath in due course," said the coroner, dryly official, and the examination of Miss Prout went on after the incident.

"And now as to the dagger," resumed the Treasury solicitor, "tell us of that."

She described it, its shape, the blunt edges of the long and pointed blade, the handle, the label on it with the date. It was Saracen, and it, too, like the celt, had once been used, in all probability, in the hands of wild men in shedding blood.

"And you are sure of the date when you first missed it from its place in the museum?"

"It was on the third day after the murder"—and Hylda Prout's glance traveled for an instant to the veiled, bent head of Rosalind, as it seemed to droop lower after every answer that she gave.

"And you are unable to conceive how both the dagger and the celt could have vanished from their places about that time?"

"Yes, I conceive that they were stolen," she said— "unless Mr. Osborne made them a present to some friend, for I have known him to do that."

"'Stolen,' you say," the Treasury man remarked. "But you have no grounds for such a belief? You suggest no motive for a thief to steal these two objects and no other from the museum? You know of no one who entered the room during those days?"

"No, I know of no one—except Inspector Furneaux, who seems to have entered it about six o'clock on the evening of the murder."

The coroner looked up sharply from his notes. This was news to the court.

"Oh?" said the examiner. "Let us hear how that came about."

She explained that Furneaux had called to see Mr. Osborne, and, while awaiting his coming in the library, had apparently strolled into the museum. Jenkins, Mr. Osborne's valet, was her informant. It was not evidence, but the statement was out before the court well knew where it was leading. Winter's lip quivered with suppressed agitation, and over Clarke's face came a strange expression of amazement, a stare of utter wonderment widening his eyes, as when one has been violently struck, and knows not by what or whom.

When Hylda Prout stepped down, the coroner invited the officer in charge of the case to explain the curious bit of intelligence given by the last witness.

Furneaux, not one whit disturbed in manner, rose to give his evidence of the incident. Oddly enough, his eyes dwelt all the time, with a dull deadness of expression in them, upon the lowered face of Winter.

It was true, he told the court, that he had called upon Mr. Osborne that evening; it was true that he was asked to wait; and he seemed to remember now that he *had* wandered through a doorway into a room full of curios to have a look at them in those idle moments.

"So you knew Mr. Osborne *before* the murder?" inquired the court.

"Yes. I knew him very well by sight and repute, as a man about town, though not to speak to."

"And what was the nature of the business on which you called to see him?"

"It was a purely personal matter."

The coroner paused, with the air of a man who suddenly discovers a morass where he imagined there was a clear road.

"And did you see Mr. Osborne that evening?" he asked at length.

"No, sir. After I had waited some time the valet entered and told me that Mr. Osborne had just telephoned to say that he would not be home before dinner. So I came away."

"Have you spoken to Mr. Osborne *since* then about the matter on which you called to see him that evening?"

"No, sir."

"Why not?"

"Because after that evening there was no longer any need!"

Well, to the more experienced officials in court this explanation had an unusual sound, but to Winter, who slowly but surely was gathering the threads of the murder in the flat into his hands, it sounded like a sentence of death; and to Clarke, too, who had in his possession Rose de Bercy's diary taken from Pauline

Dessaulx, it sounded so amazing, that he could scarce believe his ears.

However, the coroner nodded to Furneaux, and Furneaux turned to Osborne's solicitor, who suddenly resolved to ask no questions, so the dapper little man seated himself again at the table—much to the relief of the jury, who were impatient of any red herring drawn across the trail of evidence that led unmistakably to the millionaire.

Then, at last, appeared six witnesses who spoke, no longer against, but for Osborne. Four were International polo-players, and two were waiters at the Ritz Hotel, and all were positive that at the hour when Mrs. Bates saw her employer at home, *they* saw him elsewhere—or some among them saw him, and the others, without seeing him, knew that he was elsewhere.

Against this unassailable testimony was the obviously honest cabman, and Osborne's own housekeeper: and the jury, level-headed men, fully inclined to be just, though perhaps, in this instance, passionate and prejudiced, weighed it in their hearts.

But Furneaux, to suit his own purposes, had contrived that the tag of lace should come last; and with its mute appeal for vengeance everything in favor of Osborne was swept out of the bosom of His Majesty's lieges, and only wrath and abhorrence raged there.

Why, if he had actually killed Rose de Bercy, Osborne should carry about that incriminating bit of lace in his bag, no one seemed to stop to ask; but when the dreadful thing was held up before his eyes, the twelve good men and true looked at it and at each other, and a sort of shuddering abhorrence pervaded the court.

Even the Italian Antonio, who had contrived to be present as representing some obscure paper in Paris—the very man who had put the lace into the bag— shook his head over Osborne's guilt, being, as it were, carried out of himself by the vigor and rush of the mental hurricane which swept around him!

When Osborne, put into the box, repeated that the "celt" was really his, this candor now won no sympathy. When he said solemnly that the bit of lace had been secreted among his belongings by some unknown hand, the small company of men present in court despised him for so childish a lie.

His spirit, as he stood in that box, exposed to the animus of so many spirits, felt as if it was being hurried by a kind of magnetic gale to destruction; his fingers, his knees shivered, his voice cracked in his throat; he could not keep his eyes from being wild, his skin from being white, and in his heart his own stupefied conscience accused him of the sin that his brothers charged him with.

Though the jury soon ascertained from the coroner's injunctions what their verdict had to be, they still took twenty minutes to think of it. However, they knew well that the coroner had spoken to them under the suggestion of the police, who, no doubt, would conduct their own business best; so in the end they came in with the verdict of "willful murder committed by some person or persons unknown."

And now it was the turn of the mob to have their say. The vast crowd was kept in leash until they were vouchsafed just a glimpse of Osborne, in the midst of a mass of police guarding him, as he emerged from the court to his automobile. Then suddenly, as it were, the hoarse bellow of the storm opened to roar him out of the universe—an overpowering load of sound for one frail heart to bear without quailing.

But if Osborne's heart quailed, there was one heart there that did not quail, one smooth forehead that suddenly flushed and frowned in opposition to a world's current, and dared to think and feel alone.

As the mob yelped its execration, Rosalind Marsh cried a protest of "Shame, oh, shame!"

For now her woman's bosom smote her with truth, and her compassion championed him, believed in him,

refused to admit that he could have been so base. If she
had been near him she would have raised her veil, and
gazed into his face with a steady smile!

As she was about to enter the carriage that awaited
her, someone said close behind her:

"Miss Marsh."

She looked round and saw a small man.

"You know me," he said—"Inspector Furneaux. We
have even met and spoken together before—you
remember the old man who traveled with you in the train
from Tormouth? That was myself in another aspect."

His eyes smiled, though his voice was respectful, but
Rosalind gave him the barest inch of condescension in a
nod.

"Now, I wish to speak to you," he muttered hurriedly.
"I cannot say when exactly—I am very occupied just
now—but soon.... To speak to you, I think, in your own
interests—if I may. But I do not know your address."

Very coldly, hardly caring to try and understand his
motive, she mentioned the house in Porchester Gardens.
In another moment she was in her carriage.

When she reached home she saw in her mother's face
just a shadow of inquiry as to where she had been driving
during the forenoon; but Rosalind said not a word of the
inquest. She was, indeed, very silent during the whole of
that day and the next. She was restless and woefully
uneasy. Through the night her head was full of strange
thoughts, and she slept but little, in fitful moments of
weariness. Her mother observed her with a quiet eye,
pondering this unwonted distress in her heart, but said
nothing.

On the third morning Rosalind was sitting in a
rocking-chair, her head laid on the back, her eyes closed;
and with a motion corresponding with the gentle to-and-
fro motion of the chair her head moved wearily from side
to side. This went on for some time; till suddenly she
brought her hand to her forehead in a rather excited
gesture, her eyes opened with the weak look of eyes

dazzled with light, and she said aloud:

"Oh, I *must!*..."

Now she sprang up in a hurry, hastened to an escritoire, and dashed off a letter in a very scamper of haste.

At last, then, the floods had broken their gates, for this is what she wrote:

My dear, my dear, I was brutal to you that night at the sun-dial. But it was necessary, if I was to maintain the severity which I felt that your lack of frankness to me deserved. Inwardly there was a terribly weak spot, of which I was afraid; and if you had come after me when I left you, and had commanded me, or prayed me, or touched me, no doubt it would have been all up with me. Forgive me, then, if I seemed over harsh where, I'm afraid, I am disposed to be rather too infinitely lenient. At present, you see, I quite lack the self-restraint to keep from telling you that I am sorry for you.... I was present at the inquest.... Pity is like lightning; it fills, it burns up, it enlightens ... see me here struck with it!... You are not without a friend, one who knows you, judges you, and acquits you.... If you want to come to me, come!... I once thought well of a Mr. Glyn, but, like a flirt, will forget him, if Osborne is of the same manner, speaks with the same voice.... My mother is usually good to me....

She enclosed it in a flurry of excitement, ran to the bell-rope, rang, and while waiting for a servant held the envelope in the manner of one who is on the very point of tearing a paper in two, but halts to see on which cheek the wind will hit. In the midst of this suspense of indecision the door opened; and now, straightway, she hastened to it, and got rid of the letter, saying rapidly in a dropped voice, confidentially:

"Pauline, put that in the pillar-box at once for me, will you?"

Another moment and she stood alone there, with a

shocked and beating heart, the deed done, past recall now.

As for Pauline Dessaulx, she was half-way down the stairs when she chanced to look at the envelope. "Rupert Osborne, Esq." She started! Everything connected with that name was of infinite interest to her! But she had not dreamt that Miss Marsh knew it, save as everyone else knew it now, from public gossip and the papers.

She had never seen Rosalind Marsh, or her mother, till the day of their arrival from the country. It was but ten days earlier that she had become the servant of a Mrs. Prawser, a friend of Mrs. Marsh's, who kept a private boarding-house, being in reduced circumstances. Then, after but an interval of peace and security, the Marshes had come, and as she let them in, and they were being embraced by Mrs. Prawser, Inspector Clarke had appeared at the door, nearly striking her dead with agitation, and demanding of her the diary, which she had handed him.

Luckily, luckily, she had been wise enough before that to scratch out with many thick scratches of the pen the name that had been written by the actress before the initials C. E. F. in that passage where the words appeared: "If I am killed this night it will be by — or by C. E. F." But suppose she had not shown such sense and daring, what then? She shivered at the thought.

And a new problem now tortured her. Was it somehow owing to the fact that Miss Marsh knew Osborne that Inspector Clarke had come upon her at the moment of the two ladies' arrival? What was the relation between Miss Marsh and Osborne? What was in this letter? It might be well to see....

Undecided, Pauline stood on the stairs some seconds, letter in hand, all the high color fled from lips and cheeks, her breast rising and falling, no mere housemaid now, but a figure of anguish fit for an artist to sketch there in her suspense, a well-molded girl of perfect curves and graceful poise.

Then it struck her that Miss Marsh might be looking out of the window to watch her hurrying with the letter to the pillar-box a little way down the street, and at this thought she ran downstairs and out, hurried to the pillar-box, raised her arm with the letter, inserted it in the slot, drew it out swiftly and hiddenly again, slipped it into her pocket, and sped back to the house.

In her rooms half an hour later she steamed the envelope open, and read the avowal of another woman's passion and sympathy. It appeared, then, that Miss Marsh was now in love with Osborne? Well, that did not specially interest or concern her, Pauline. It was a good thing that Osborne had so soon forgotten *cette salope*, Rose de Bercy. She, Pauline, had conceived a fondness for Miss Marsh: she had detested her mistress, the dead actress. At the first chance she crept afresh into the street, and posted the letter in grim earnest. But an hour had been lost, an hour that meant a great deal in the workings of this tragedy of real life and, as a minor happening, some of the gum was dissolved off the flap of the envelope.

Inspector Furneaux, as he had promised after the inquest, called upon Rosalind during the afternoon. They had an interview of some length in Mrs. Prawser's drawing-room, which was otherwise untenanted. Furneaux spoke of the picturesqueness of Tormouth, but Rosalind's downright questioning forced him to speak of himself in the part of the decrepit Mr. Pugh, and why he had been there as such. He had gone to have a look at Osborne.

"Is his every step, then, spied on in this fashion?" asked Rosalind.

"No," answered Furneaux. "The truth is that I had had reason to think that the man was again playing the lover in that quarter—"

"Ah, playing," said Rosalind with quick sarcasm. "It is an insipid phrase for so serious an occupation. But what reason had you for thinking that he was playing in that particular mood?"

"The reason is immaterial.... In fact, he had impressed on the back of a letter a name—I may tell you it was 'Rosalind'—and sent it off inadvertently—"

"Oh, poor fellow! Not so skilled a villain then, after all," she murmured.

"But the point was that, if this was so, it was clear to me that he could not be much good—I speak frankly—"

"Very, sir."

"And with a good meaning to *you*."

"Let us take it at that. It makes matters easier."

"Well, as I suspected, so I found. And—I was disgusted. I give you my assurance that he had professed to Mademoiselle de Bercy that he—loved her. He had, he had! And she, so pitifully handled, so butchered, was hardly yet cold in her grave. Even assuming his perfect innocence in that horrible drama, still, I must confess, I—I—was disgusted; I was put against the man forever. And I was more than disgusted with him, I was concerned for the lady whose inclinations such a weather-vane might win. I was concerned before I saw you; I was ten times more concerned afterwards. I travelled to town in the same compartment as you—I heard your voice—I enjoyed the privilege of breathing the same air as you and your charming mother. Hence—I am here."

Rosalind smiled. She found the detective's compliments almost nauseating, but she must ascertain his object.

"Why, precisely?" she asked.

"I want to warn you. I had warned you before: for I had given a certain girl whose love Mr. Osborne has inspired a hint of what was going on, and I felt sure that she would not fail to tell you who 'Mr. Glyn' was. Was I not right?"

Rosalind bent her head a little under this unexpected thrust.

"I received a note," she said. "Who, then, is this 'certain girl, whose love Mr. Osborne has inspired,' if one may ask?"

"I may tell you—in confidence. Her name is Prout. She is his secretary."

"He is—successful in that way," observed Rosalind coldly, looking down at a spray of flowers pinned to her breast.

"Too much so, Miss Marsh. Now, I felt confident that the warning given by Miss Prout would effectually quash any friendship between a lady of your pride and quality and Mr. Glyn—Osborne. But then, through your thick veil I noticed you at the inquest: and I said to myself, 'I am older than she is—I'll speak to her in the tone of an old and experienced man, if she will let me.'"

"You see, I let you. I even thank you. But then you notice that Mr. Osborne is just now vilified and friendless."

"Oh, there is his Miss Prout."

Rosalind's neck stiffened a little.

"That is indefinite," she said. "I know nothing of this lady, except that, as you tell me, she is ready to betray her employer to serve her own ends. Mr. Osborne is my friend: it is my duty to refuse to credit vague statements made against him. It is not possible—it cannot be—"

She stopped, rather in confusion. Furneaux believed he could guess what she meant to say.

"It *is* possible, believe me," he broke in earnestly. "Since it was possible, as you know, for him to turn his mind so easily from the dead, it is also possible—"

"Oh, the dead deceived him!" she protested with a lively flush. "The dead was unworthy of him. He never loved her."

"*He* deceived *her*," cried Furneaux also in an unaccountable heat—"he deceived her. No doubt she was as fully worthy of him as he of her—it was a pair of them. And he loved her as much as he can love anyone."

"Women are said to be the best judges in such matters, Inspector Furneaux."

"So, then, you will not be guided by me in this?"

Furneaux said, standing up.

"No. Nevertheless, I thank you for your apparent good intent," answered Rosalind.

He was silent a little while, looking down at her. On her part, she did not move, and kept her eyes studiously averted.

"Then, for your sake, and to spite him, I accuse him to you of the murder!" he almost hissed.

She smiled.

"That is very wrong of you, very unlike an officer of the law. You know that he is quite innocent of it."

"Great, indeed, is your faith!" came the taunt. "Well, then," he added suddenly, "again for your sake, and again to spite him, I will even let you into a police secret. Hear it—listen to it—yesterday, with a search-warrant, I raided Mr. Osborne's private apartments. And this is what I found—at the bottom of a trunk a suit of clothes, the very clothes which the driver of the taxicab described as those of the man whom he took from Berkeley Street to Feldisham Mansions on the night of the murder. And those clothes, now in the possession of the police, are all speckled and spotted with blood. Come, Miss Marsh— what do you say now? Is your trust weakened?"

Furneaux's eyes sparkled with a glint of real hatred of Osborne, but Rosalind saw nothing of that. She rose, took an unsteady step or two, and stared through the window out into the street. Then she heard the door of the room being opened. She turned at once. Before a word could escape her lips, Furneaux was gone.

One minute later, she was scribbling with furious speed:

> *Do not read my letter. I will call for it—unopened— in person.*
> *ROSALIND MARSH.*

She tugged at the bell-rope. When Pauline appeared, she whispered: "Quickly, Pauline, for my sake—this telegram." And as Pauline ran with it, she sank into a chair, and sat there with closed eyelids and trembling lips, sorely stricken in her pride, yet even more sorely in her heart.

Now, if her letter had gone by the post by which she had sent it, Osborne would have read it two hours or more before the telegram arrived. But it had been kept back by Pauline: and, as it was, the letter only arrived five minutes before the telegram.

At that moment Osborne was upstairs in his house. The letter was handed to Hylda Prout in the library. She looked at it, and knew the writing, for she had found in Osborne's room at Tormouth a note of invitation to luncheon from Rosalind to Osborne, and did not scruple to steal it. A flood of jealousy now stabbed her heart and inflamed her eyes. It was then near five in the afternoon, and she had on a silver tripod a kettle simmering for tea, for she was a woman of fads, and held that the servants of the establishment brewed poison. She quickly steamed open the letter—which had been already steamed open by Pauline—and, every second expecting Osborne to enter, ran her eye through it. Then she pressed down the flap of the envelope anew.

Two minutes afterwards Rupert made his appearance, and she handed him the letter.

He started! He stared at it, his face at one instant pale, at the next crimson. And as he so stood, flurried, glad, agitated, there entered Jenkins with a telegram on a salver.

"What is it?" muttered Osborne with a gesture of irritation, for he was not quite master of himself in these days. Nevertheless, to get the telegram off his mind at once before rushing upstairs to read the letter in solitude, he snatched at it, tore it open, and ran his eye over it.

"Do not read my letter. I will call for it *unopened....*"

He let his two hands drop in a palsy of anger, the letter in one, the telegram in the other—bitter disappointment in his heart, a wild longing, a mad temptation....

He lifted the letter to allow his gaze to linger futilely upon it, like Tantalus.... In spite of his agitation he could not fail to see that the envelope was actually open, for, as a matter of fact, the gum had nearly all been steamed away....

It was open! He had but to put in his finger and draw it out, and read, and revel, like the parched traveler at the solitary well in the desert. Would that be dishonest? Who could blame him for that? He had not opened the envelope....

"Miss Prout, just give me the gum-pot," he said, for he could see that the gum on the flap was too thin to be of any service.

Hylda Prout handed him a brush, and he pasted down the flap, but with fingers so agitated that he made daubs with the gum on the envelope, daubs which anyone must notice on examination.

Meantime, he had dropped the telegram upon the table, and Hylda Prout read it.

X. THE DIARY, AND ROSALIND

Strange as a process of nature is the way in which events, themselves unimportant, work into one another to produce some foredestined result that shall astonish the world.

The sudden appearance of Inspector Clarke before Pauline Dessaulx at the front door of Mrs. Marsh's lodgings produced by its shock a thorough upset in the girl's moral and physical being. And in Clarke himself that diary of Rose de Bercy which Pauline handed him produced a hilarity, an almost drunken levity of mind, the results of which levity and of Pauline's upset dovetailed one with the other to bring about an effect which lost none of its singularity because it was preordained.

To Clarke the diary was a revelation! Moreover, it was one of those sweet revelations which placed the fact of his own wit and wisdom in a clearer light than he had seen those admitted qualities before, for it showed that, though working in the dark, he had been guided aright by that special candle of understanding that must have been lit within him before his birth.

"Well, fancy that," cried he again and again in a kind of surprise. "I was right all the time!"

He sat late at night, coatless and collarless, at a table over the diary, Mrs. Clarke in the next room long since asleep, London asleep, the very night asleep from earth right up to heaven. Four days before a black cat had been adopted into the household. Surely it was *that* which had brought him the luck to get hold of the diary!—so easily, so unexpectedly. Pussie was now perched on the table, her purr the sole sound in the quietude, and Clarke, who would have scoffed at a hint of superstition, was stroking

her, as he read for the third time those last pages written
on the day of her death by the unhappy Frenchwoman.

*... I so seldom dream, that it has become the subject
of remark, and Dr. Naurocki of the Institute said once that
it is because I am such a "perfect animal." It is well to be a
perfect* something: *but that much I owe only to my father
and mother. I am afraid I am not a perfect anything else.
A perfect liar, perhaps; a perfect adventuress; using as
stepping-stones those whose fond hearts love me; shallow,
thin within; made of hollow-ringing tin from my skin to
the tissue of my liver. Oh, perhaps I might have done
better for myself! Suppose I had stayed with Marguerite
and* le père *Armaud on the farm, and helped to milk the
two cows, and met some rustic lover at the stile at dusk,
and married him in muslin? It might have been as well!
There is something in me that is famished and starved,
and decayed, something that pines and sighs because of
its utter thinness—I suppose it is what they call "the soul."
I have lied until I am become a lie, an unreality, a
Nothing. I seem to see myself clearly to-day; and if I could
repent now, I'd say "I will arise and go to my father, and
will say to him 'Father.'"*

*Too late now, I suppose. Marguerite would draw her
skirts away from touching me, though the cut of the skirt
would set me smiling; and, if the fatted calf was set before
me on a soiled table-cloth, I should be ill.*

*Too late! You can't turn back the clock's hands: the
clock stops. God help me, I feel horribly remorseful. Why
should I have dreamt it? I so seldom dream! and I have*
never, *I think, dreamt with such living vividness. I
thought I saw my father and Marguerite standing over my
dead body, staring at me. I saw them, and I saw myself,
and my face was all bruised and wounded; and
Marguerite said: "Well, she sought for it," and my father's
face twitched, and suddenly he sobbed out: "I wish to
Heaven I had died for her!" and my dead ears on the bed
heard, and my dead heart throbbed just once again at*

him, and then was dead for ever.

Clarke did not know that he was reading literature, but he did know that this was more exciting than any story he had ever set eyes on. He stopped, lit a pipe, and resumed.

I saw it, I heard it, though it was in a black world that it happened, a world all draped in crape; black, black. But what is the matter with me to-day? Is there any other woman so sad in this great city, I wonder? I have opened one of the bottles of Old Veuve, so there are only seven left now; and I have drunk two full glasses of it. But it has made no difference; and I have to dine with Lady Knox-Florestan, and go with her to the opera; and Osborne may be coming. They will think me a death's-head, and catch melancholy from me like a fever. I do not know why I dreamt it, and why I cannot forget. It seems rather strange. Is anything going to happen to me, really? Oh, inside this breast of mine there is a bell tolling, and a funeral moving to the tomb this afternoon. It is as if I had drunk of some lugubrious drug that turns the human bosom to wormwood. Is it my destiny to die suddenly, and lie in an early grave? No, not that! Let me be in rags, and shrunken, with old, old eyes and toothless gums, but give me life! Let me say I am still alive!

"By Jove!" growled Clarke, chewing his pipe, "that rings in my ears!"

Yet I have had curious tokens, hints, fancies, of late. Four nights ago, as I was driving down Pall Mall from Lady Sinclair's <u>diner dansant</u>—it was about eleven-thirty—I saw a man in the shadow at a corner who I could have sworn for a moment was F. I didn't see his face, for as the carriage approached him, he turned his back, and it was that turning of the back, I think, that made me observe him. Suppose all the time F. knows of me?—knows *who Rose de Bercy is! I never wanted to have that Academy portrait painted, and I must have been mad to consent in the end. If F. saw it? If he knows? What would he do? His nature is capable of ravaging flames of passion! Suppose he killed me? But could a poor woman be so unlucky? No, he doesn't know, he can't, fate is not so hard. Then there is that wretched Pauline—she shan't be in this house another week. My quarrel with her this morning was the third, and the most bitter of all. Really, that girl knows too much of me to permit of our living any longer under one roof; and, what is more, she has twice dropped hints lately which certainly seem to bear the interpretation that she knows of my work in Berlin for the Russian Government. Oh, but that must only be the madness of my fancy! Two persons, and two only, in the whole world know of it—how could she, possibly? Yet she said in her Friday passion: "You will not be a long liver, Madame, you have been too untrue to your dupes." Untrue to my dupes! Which dupes? My God, if she meant the Anarchists!*

Clarke's face was a study when he came to that word. It wore the beatific expression of the man who is justified in his own judgment.

Just suppose that she knows! For that she is mixed up with some of them to some uncertain extent I have guessed for two years. And if they knew that I have actually been a Government agent; they would do for me, oh, they would, I know, it would be all up with me. Three months ago Sauriac Paulus in the promenoire at Covent Garden, said to me: "By the way, do you know that you have been condemned to death?" I forget à propos of what he said it, and have never given it a thought from that day. He was bantering me, laughing in the lightest vein, but—God! it never struck me like this before!—Suppose there was earnest under the jest, deep-hidden under? He is a deep, deep, evil beast, that man. Those were his words—

I remember distinctly. "By the way, do you know that you have been condemned to death?" "By the way:" his heavy face shook with chuckling. And it never once till now entered my head!—Oh, but, after all, I must be horribly ill to be having such thoughts this day! The beast, of course, didn't mean anything. Think, though, of saying, "by the way?"—the terrible, evil beast. Oh, yes, I am ill. I have begun to die. This night, may be, my soul shall be required of me. I hear Marguerite saying again, "Well, she sought for it," and my father's bitter sobbing, "I wish to Heaven I had died for her!" But, if I am killed this day, it will be by ... or by C. E. F....

That last dash after the "F." was not, Clarke saw, meant as a dash, for it was a long curved line, as if her elbow had been struck, or she herself violently startled. She had probably intended, this time, to write the name in full, but the interruption stopped her.

At the spot of the first dash lay thick ink-marks—really made by Pauline Dessaulx—and Clarke, cute enough to see this, now commenced to scratch out the ink blot with a penknife, and after the black dust was scraped away, he used a damp sponge.

It was a delicate, slow operation, his idea being that, since under those layers of ink lay a written name, if he removed the layers with dainty care, then he would see the name beneath. And this was no doubt true in theory, but in practice no care was dainty enough to do the trick with much success. He did, however, manage to see the shape of some letters, and, partly with the aid of his magnifying glass, partly with the aid of his imagination, he seemed to make out the word "*Janoc.*"

The murder, then, was committed either by Janoc, or by C. E. F.—this, as the mantle of the night wore threadbare, and some gray was showing through it in the east, Clarke became certain of.

Who was C. E. F.? There was Furneaux, of course. Those were his initials, and as the name of Furneaux arose in his mind, Clarke's head dropped back over his chair-back, and a long, delicious spasm of laughter shook him. For the idea that it *might*, in very truth, be Furneaux who was meant never for one instant occurred to him. He assumed that it must needs be some French or Russian C. E. F., but the joke of the coincidence of the initials with Furneaux's, who had charge of the case, into whose hands the case had been given by Winter over his (Clarke's) head, was so rich, that he resolved to show the diary to Winter, and to try and keep from bursting out laughing, while he said:

"Look here, sir—this is your Furneaux!"

Clarke, indeed, had heard at the inquest how Furneaux had been seen on the evening of the murder in Osborne's museum, from which the "celt" and the dagger had vanished. Hearing this, his mind had instantly remembered the "C. E. F." of the diary, and had been amazed at such a coincidence. But his brain never sprang to grapple with the possibility that Rose de Bercy might, in truth, be afraid of Furneaux. So, whoever "C. E. F." might be, Clarke had no interest in him, never suspected him: his thoughts had too long been preoccupied with one idea—Anarchists, Janoc, Anarchists—to receive a new bent with real perspicacity and interest. And the diary confirmed him in this opinion: for she had actually been condemned to death as an agent of the Russian Government months before. At last he stood up, stretching his arms in weariness before tumbling into bed.

"Well! to think that I was right!" he said again, and again he laughed.

When he was going out in the morning, he put some more ink-marks over the "Janoc" in the diary—for he did not mean that any other than himself should lay his hand on the murderer of Rose de Bercy—and when he arrived at Scotland Yard, he showed the diary to the Chief Inspector.

Winter laid it on the desk before him, and as he read

where Clarke's finger pointed, his face went as colorless as the paper he was looking at.

A laugh broke out behind him.

"Furneaux!"

And Winter, glancing round, saw Clarke's face merry, like carved ivory in a state of gayety, showing a tooth or two lacking, and browned fangs. For a moment he stared at Clarke, without comprehension, till the absurd truth rushed in upon him that Clarke was really taking it in jest. Then he, too, laughed even more loudly.

"Ha! ha!—yes, Furneaux! 'Pon my honor, the funniest thing! Furneaux it is for sure!"

"Officer in charge of the case!"

"Ripping! By gad, I shall have to apply for a warrant!"

Finding his chief in this rare good humor, Clarke thought to obtain a little useful information.

"Do you know any of the Anarchist crowd with those initials, sir?" he asked.

"I think I do; yes, a Frenchman. Or it may be a German. There is no telling whom she means—no telling. But where on earth did you come across this diary?"

"You remember the lady's-maid, Pauline, the girl who couldn't be found to give evidence at the inquest? I was following the Anarchist Antonio, who seemed to be prowling after some ladies in a cab a day or two ago, and the door that was opened to the ladies when their cab stopped was opened by—Pauline."

Then he told how he had obtained the diary, and volunteered a theory as to the girl's possession of it.

"She must have picked it up in the flat on coming home from the Exhibition on the night of the murder, and kept it."

They discussed the circumstances fully, and Clarke went away, his conscience clear of having kept the matter dark from headquarters, yet confident that he had not put Winter on the track of his own special prey, Janoc. And as his footsteps became faint and fainter behind the closed door, Winter let his head fall low, almost upon the desk, and so he remained, hidden, as it were, from himself, a long while, until suddenly springing up with a face all fiery, he cried aloud in a rage:

"Oh, no more sentiment! By the Lord, I'm done with it. From this hour Inspector Furneaux is under the eye of the police."

Furneaux himself was then, for the second time that week, at Mrs. Marsh's lodgings in Porchester Gardens in secret and urgent talk with Rosalind.

"You will think that I am always hunting you down, Miss Marsh," he said genially on entering the room.

"You know best how to describe your profession," she murmured a little bitterly, for his parting shot at their last meeting had struck deep.

"But this time I come more definitely on business," he said, seating himself uninvited, which was a strange thing for Furneaux to do, since he was a gentleman by birth and in manners, "and as I am in a whirl of occupation just now, I will come at once to the point."

"To say 'I will come at once to the point' is to put off coming to it—for while you are saying it—"

"True. The world uses too many words—"

"It is a round world—hence its slowness in coming to a point."

"I take the hint. Yet you leave me rather breathless."

"Pray tell me why, Inspector Furneaux."

"For admiration of so quick and witty a lady. But I shall make you dumb by what I am going to suggest today. I want to turn you into a detective—"

"It *is* a point, then. You want me to be sharp?"

"You are already that. The question is, what effect did what I last said have upon your mind?"

"About your finding the blood-spotted clothes in Mr. Osborne's trunk?" she asked, looking down at his tired and worn face from her superior height, and suddenly moved to listen to him attentively. "Well, it was somewhat astounding at first. In fact, it sounded almost convincing. But then, I had already believed in Mr. Osborne's innocence in this matter. Nor am I over-easily shaken, I think, in my convictions. If he confessed his guilt to me, then I would believe—but not otherwise."

"Good," said Furneaux, "you have said that well, though I am sure he does not deserve it. Anyhow, since you persist in believing in his innocence, you must also believe that every new truth must be in his favor, and so may be willing to turn yourself into the detective I suggested.... You have, I think, a servant here named Pauline Dessaulx?"

This girl he had been seeking for some time, and had been gladly surprised to have her open the door to him on the day of his first visit to Rosalind. "She did not know me," he explained, "but *I* have twice seen her in the streets with her former mistress. Do you know who that mistress was? Rose de Bercy!"

Rosalind started as though a whip had cracked across her shoulders. She even turned round, looked at the door, tested it by the handle to see if it was closed, and stood with her back to it. Furneaux seemingly ignored her agitation.

"Now, you were at the inquest, Miss Marsh," he said. "You heard the description given by Miss Prout of the Saracen dagger missing from Mr Osborne's museum—the dagger with which the crime was probably committed. Well, I want to get that into my hands. It is lying in Pauline Dessaulx's trunk, and I ask you to secure it for me."

"In Pauline's trunk," Rosalind repeated after him, quite too dazed in her astonishment to realize the marvels that this queer little man was telling her.

"To be quite accurate," he continued, "I am not altogether sure of what I say. But that is where it *should* be, in her trunk, and with it you should find a second dagger, or knife, which I am also anxious to obtain, and if you happen to come across a little book, a diary, with a blue morocco cover, I shall be extremely pleased to lay my hand on it."

"How can you possibly know all this?" Rosalind asked, her eyes wide open with wonder now, and forgetful, for the moment, of the pain he had caused her.

"Going up and down in the earth, like Satan, and then sitting and thinking of it," he said, with a quick turn of mordant humor. "But is it a bargain, now? Of course, I could easily pounce upon the girl's trunk myself: but I want the objects to be *stolen* from her, since I don't wish to have her frightened—not quite yet."

"Do you, then, suspect this girl of having—of being— the guilty hand, Inspector Furneaux?" asked Rosalind, her very soul aghast at the notion.

"I have already intimated to you the person who is open to suspicion," answered Furneaux promptly, "a man, not a woman—though, if you find these objects in the girl's trunk, that *may* lighten the suspicion against the man."

A gleam appeared one instant in his eyes, and died out as quickly, but this time Rosalind saw it. She pulled a chair close to him and sat down, her fingers clasped tightly over her right knee—eager to serve, to help. But, then, to steal, to pry into a servant's boxes, that was not a nice action. And this Pauline Dessaulx was a girl who had interested her, had shown a singular liking for her.

She mentioned her qualms.

"At the bidding of the police," urged Furneaux—"in the interests of justice—to serve a possibly innocent man, who is also a friend—surely that is something."

"I might have been able to do it yesterday," murmured Rosalind, distraught, "but she is better to-day. I will tell you. For two days the girl has been ill—in a kind of hysteria or nervous collapse—a species of neurosis, I think—altogether abnormal and strange. I—you may as well know—wrote a letter to Mr. Osborne on the day you first came, a little before you came. I gave it her to post— she may have seen the address. Then you appeared. After you were gone, I sent him a telegram, also by Pauline's hand, telling him not to read my letter—"

"Ah, you see you did believe that what I told you proved his guilt—"

"Hear me.... No, I did not believe that. But—you had impressed me with the fact that Mr. Osborne has been, may have been, already sufficiently successful in attracting the sympathies of young ladies. I had been at the inquest—I had seen there in the box his exquisite secretary, of whose perfect ways of acting you gave me some knowledge that day, and I thought it might be rash of me to seem to be in rivalry with so charming a lady. Now you see my motive—I am often frank. So, when you were gone, I sent the telegram forbidding the reading of my letter; and the next morning I received a very brief note from Mr. Osborne saying that the letter was awaiting my wishes unopened."

"How did he know your address, if he did not open the letter?" asked Furneaux.

Rosalind started like a child caught in a fault. She was so agitated that she had not asked herself that question. As a matter of fact, it was Hylda Prout, having tracked Rosalind from Waterloo, who had given Osborne the address for her own reasons: Hylda had told Osborne, on hearing his fretful exclamation of annoyance, that she knew the address of a Miss Marsh from an old gentleman who had apparently come up from Tormouth with him and her, and had called to see Osborne when Osborne was out.

"He got the address from some source, I don't know what," Rosalind said, with a rather wondering gaze at Furneaux's face; "but the point is, that the girl, Pauline, saw my letter to him, and the telegram; and last night, coming home from an outing in quite a broken-down and enfeebled state, she said to me with tears in her eyes: 'Oh, he is innocent! Oh, do not judge him harshly, Miss Marsh! Oh, it was not he who did it!' and much more of that sort. Then she collapsed and began to scream and kick, was got to bed, and a doctor sent for, who said that she had an attack of neurasthenia due to mental strain. And I was sitting by her bedside quite a long while, so that I might then—if I had known—But I think she is better to-day."

"It is not too late, if she is still in bed," said Furneaux. "Sit with her again till she is asleep, and then see if the trunk is unlocked, or if you can find the key—"

"Only it doesn't seem quite fair to—"

"Oh, quite, in this case, I assure you," said Furneaux. "Whether this girl committed that murder with her own hand or not—"

"But how *could* she? She was at an Exhibition—!"

"Was she? Are you sure? I was saying that whether the girl committed the murder with her own hand or not—"

"If *she* did, it could not have been done by the person you said that you suspect!"

"No? Why speak so confidently? Have you not heard of such things as accomplices? She might have helped Osborne! *He* might have helped *her*! But I was saying— for the third time—that whether the girl committed the murder with her own hand or not, I am in a position to give you my assurance that she is not a lawful citizen, and that you needn't have the least compunction in doing anything whatever to her trunk or her—in the cause of truth."

"Well, if you say so—" Rosalind said, and Furneaux stood up to go.

It was then two o'clock in the afternoon. By five o'clock Rosalind had in her hand the Saracen dagger, and another dagger—though not, of course, the diary, which Clarke had carried off long ago.

At about three she had gone to sit by Pauline's bedside, and here, with the leather trunk strapped down, not two feet from her right hand, had remained over an hour. Pauline lay quiet, with a stare in her wide-open eyes, gazing up at the ceiling. Every now and again her body would twist into a gawky and awkward kind of position, a stupid expression would overspread her face, a vacant smile play on her lips; then, after some minutes, she would lie naturally again, staring at the ceiling.

Suddenly, about half-past four, she had had a kind of seizure; her body stiffened and curved, she uttered shrieks which chilled Rosalind's blood, and then her whole frame settled into a steady, strong agitation, which set the chamber all in a tremble, and could not be stilled by the two servants who had her wrists in their grip. When this was over, she dropped off into a deep sleep.

And now, as soon as Rosalind was again left alone with the invalid, she went to the trunk, unstrapped it, found it locked. But she was not long in discovering the key in the pocket of the gown which Pauline had had on when she fell ill. She opened the trunk, looking behind her at the closed eyes of the exhausted girl, and then, in feverish haste, she ransacked its contents. No daggers, however, and no diary were there. She then searched methodically through the room—an improvised wardrobe—a painted chest of drawers—kneaded and felt the bed, searched underneath—no daggers. She now stood in the middle of the room, her forehead knit, her eyes wandering round, all her woman's cunning at work in them. Then she walked straight, with decision, to a small shelf on the wall, full of cheap books; began to draw out each volume, and on drawing out the third, she saw that the daggers were lying there behind the row.

Her hand hovered during some seconds of hesitancy over the horrible blades, one of which had so lately been stained so vilely. Then she took them, and replaced the books. One of the daggers was evidently the Saracen weapon that she had heard described. The label was still on it; the other was thick-bladed, of an Italian type. She ran out with them, put them in a glove box, and, rather flurriedly, almost by stealth, got out of the house to take her trophies to Furneaux.

She drove to the address that he had given her, an eagerness in her, a gladness that the truth would now appear, and through *her*—most unexpectedly! Quite apart from her friendship for Osborne, she had an abstract interest in this matter of the murder, since from the first, before seeing Osborne, she had said that he was innocent, but her mother had seemed to lean to the opposite belief, and they were in hostile camps on the subject, like two good-natured people of different political convictions dwelling in the same house.

She bade her driver make haste to Furneaux's; but midway, seeing herself passing close to Mayfair, gave the man Osborne's address, thinking that she would go and get her unopened letter, and, if she saw Osborne himself, offer him a word of cheer—an "all will be well."

Her driver rapped for her at the house door, she sitting still in the cab, a hope in her that Osborne would come out. It seemed long since she had last seen his face, since she had heard that sob of his at the sun-dial at the Abbey. The message went inwards that Miss Marsh had called for a letter directed to Mr. Osborne by her; and her high spirits were damped when Jenkins reappeared at the door to say that the letter would be brought her, Mr. Osborne himself having just gone out.

In sober fact, Osborne had not stirred out of the house for days, lest her promised call "in person" should occur when he was absent, but at last, unable to bear it any longer, he had made a dash to see her, and was at that moment venturing to knock at her door.

However, though the news was damping, she had a store of high spirits that afternoon, which pushed her to leave a note scribbled with her gold pencil on the back of a letter—an act fraught with terrible sufferings for her in the sequel. This was her message:

> *I will write again. Meantime, do not lose hope! I have discovered that your purloined dagger has been in the possession of the late lady's-maid, Pauline. "A small thing, but mine own!" I am now taking it to Inspector Furneaux's.*

R. M.

"What *will* he think of '*I* have discovered'?" she asked herself, smiling, pleased; "he will say 'a witch'!"

She folded it crossways with a double bend so that it would not open, and leaning out of the cab, handed it to Jenkins.

As he disappeared with it, Hylda Prout stood in the doorway with Rosalind's letter to Osborne—Hylda's freckles showing strong against her rather pale face. She held the flap-side of the envelope forward from the first, to show the stains of gum on it.

As she approached the cab, Rosalind's neck stiffened a little. Their eyes met malignly, and dwelt together several seconds, in a stillness like that of somber skies before lightnings fly out. Truly, Rupert Osborne's millions were unable to buy him either happiness or luck, for it was the worst of ill-luck that he should not have been at home just then.

XI. ENTRAPPED!

When Rosalind's contemptuous eyes abandoned that silent interchange of looks, they fell upon the envelope in Hylda Prout's hand, nor could she help noticing that round the flap it was clumsily stained with gum. Yet Osborne had written her saying that it had been unopened....

The other woman stepped to the door of the cab.

"Miss Marsh?" she inquired, with an assumed lack of knowledge that was insolent in itself.

"Yes."

"Mr. Osborne left this for you, if you called."

"Thank you."

The business was ended, yet the lady-secretary still stood there, staring brazenly at Rosalind's face.

"Drive on—"

Rosalind raised her gloved hand to attract the driver's attention.

"One moment, Miss Marsh," said Hylda, also raising a hand to forbid him to move; "I want to tell you something—You are very anxious on poor Mr. Osborne's behalf, are you not?"

"I thought he was rich? You are not to say 'poor Mr. Osborne.'"

"Is that why you are so anxious, because he is rich?" and those golden-brown eyes suddenly blazed out outrageously.

"Driver, go on, please!" cried Rosalind again.

"Wait, cabman!" cried Hylda imperiously.... "Stay a little—Miss Marsh—one word—I cannot let you waste your sympathies as you do. You believe that Mr. Osborne is friendless; and you offer him your friendship—"

"*I!*"

Rosalind laughed a little, a laugh with a dangerous chuckle in it that might have carried a warning to one who knew her.

"Do you not say so in that letter? In it you tell him that since the night at the sun-dial, when you were *'brutal'* to him—"

"You know, then, my letter—by heart?" said Rosalind, her eyes sparkling and cheeks aflame. "That is quite charming of you! You have been at the pains to read it?"

"No, of course, Mr. Osborne wouldn't exactly *show* it to me, nor did I ask him. But I think you guess that I am in Mr. Osborne's confidence."

"Mr. Osborne, it would seem, has—read it? He even thought the contents of sufficient importance to repeat them to his typist? Is that so?"

"Mr. Osborne repeats many things to me, Miss Marsh—by habit. You being a stranger to him, do not know him well yet, but I have been with him some time, you see. As to his reading it, I know that you telegraphed him not to, and he received the telegram before the letter, I admit; but, the letter once in his hand, it became his private property, of course. He had a right to read it."

A stone in Rosalind's bosom where her heart had been ached like a wound; yet her lips smiled—a hard smile.

"But then, having read, to be at the pains to seal it down again!" she said. "It seems superfluous, a contemptible subterfuge."

"Oh, well," sneered Hylda, with a pouting laugh, "he is not George Washington—a little harmless deception."

"But you cry out all his secrets!"

"To you."

"Why to me?"

"I save you from troubling your head about him. He is not so friendless as you have imagined."

"Happy man! And was it you who wrote me the anonymous information that he was not Glyn but Osborne?"

"No, that was someone else."

And now Rosalind, blighting her with her icy smile, which no inward fires could melt, said contemplatively:

"I am afraid you are not speaking the truth. I shall tell Mr. Osborne to get rid of you."

The dart was well planted. The paid secretary's lips twitched and quivered.

"Try it! He'll laugh at you!" she retorted.

"No, I think he will do it—to please me!"

Sad to relate, our gracious Rosalind was deliberately adding oil to the fires of hate and rage that she saw devouring Hylda Prout; and when Hylda again spoke it was from a fiery soul that peered out of a ghost's face.

"Will he?—to please you?" she said low, hissingly, leaning forward. "He has a record in a diary of the girls he has kissed, and the number of days from the first sight to the first kiss. He only wanted to see in how few days he could secure you."

This vulgarity astonished its hearer. Rosalind shrank a little; her smile became forced and strained; she could only murmur:

"Oh, you needn't be so bourgeoise."

Hylda chuckled again maliciously.

"It's the mere truth."

"Still, I think I shall warn him against you, and have you dismissed,"—this with that feminine instinct of the dagger that plunged deepest, the lash that cut most bitterly.

"You try!" hissed Hylda sharply, as it were secretly, with a nod of menace. "I am not anybody! I am not some defenseless housemaid, the only rival you have experienced hitherto, perhaps. I am—at any rate, you try! You dare! Touch me, and I'll wither your arm—"

"Drive on!" cried Rosalind almost in a scream.

"Wait!" shrilled Hylda—"you *shall* hear me!"

"Cabman, please—!" wailed Rosalind despairingly.

And now at last the cab was off, Hylda Prout running with it to pant into it some final rancor; and when it left her, she remained there on the pavement a minute, unable to move, trembling from head to foot, watching the vehicle as it sped away from her.

When she re-entered the library the first thing that she saw was Rosalind's cross-folded note to Osborne, and, still burning inwardly, she snatched it up, tore it open, and read:

I will write again. Meantime, high hope! I have discovered that your purloined dagger has been in the possession of the late lady's-maid, Pauline. "A small thing but mine own." I am now taking it to Inspector Furneaux's.

R. M.

Hylda dashed the paper to the ground, put her foot on it, then catching it up, worried it in her hands to atoms which she threw into a waste-paper basket. Then she collapsed into a chair at her desk, her arms thrown heedlessly over some documents, and her face buried between them.

"I have gone too far, too far, too far—"

Now that her passion had burnt to ashes this was her thought. A crisis, it was clear, had come, and something had to be done, to be decided, now—that very day. Rosalind would surely tell Osborne what she, Hylda, had said, how she had acted, and then all would be up with Hylda, no hope left, her whole house in ruins about her, not one stone left standing on another. Either she must bind Osborne irrevocably to her at once, or her brain must devise some means of keeping Osborne and Rosalind from meeting—or both. But how achieve the apparently impossible? Osborne, she knew, was at that moment at Rosalind's residence, and if Rosalind was now going home ... they would meet! Hylda moved her buried head from side to side, woe-ridden, in the grip of a hundred fangs and agonies. She had boasted to Rosalind that she was not a whimpering housemaid, but of a better texture: and if that was an actual truth, the present moment must prove it. Yet she sat there with a buried head, weakly weeping....

Suddenly she thought of the words in Rosalind's note to Osborne, which she had thrown into the basket: "I have discovered that your purloined dagger has been in the possession of the late lady's-maid, Pauline.... I am now taking it to Inspector Furneaux's...."

That, then, was the person who had the dagger which had been so sought and speculated about—Pauline Dessaulx!

And at the recollection of the name, Hylda's racked brain, driven to invent, invented like lightning. Up she sprang, caught at her hat, and rushed away, pinning it on to her magnificent red hair in her flight, her eyes staring with haste. In the street she leapt into a motor-cab—to Soho.

She was soon there. As if pursued by furies she pelted up two foul staircases, and at a top back room, rapped pressingly, fiercely, with the clenched knuckles of both hands upon the panels. As a man in his shirt-sleeves, his braces dropped, smoking a cigarette, opened the door to her, she almost fell in on him, and the burning words burst from her tongue's tip:

"Antonio!—it's all up with Pauline—the dagger she did it with—has been found—by a woman—the same woman from Tormouth whom you and I tracked to Porchester Gardens—Pauline is in her employ probably— tell Janoc—he has wits—he may do something before it is too late—the woman has the dagger—in a motor-cab—in a long, narrow box—she is this instant taking it to Inspector Furneaux's house—if *she* lives, Pauline hangs— tell Janoc that, Antonio—don't stare—tell Janoc—it is *she* or Pauline—let him choose—"

"*Grand Dieu!*"

"Don't stare—don't stand—I'm gone."

She ran out; and almost as she was down the stair Antonio had thrown on a coat and was flying down behind her.

He ran down three narrow streets to Poland Street, darted up a stair, broke into a room; and there on the floor, stretched face downwards, lay the lank length of Janoc's body, a map of Europe spread before him, on which with an ivory pointer he was marking lines from town to town. He glanced at the intruder with a frowning brow, yet he was up like an acrobat, as the tidings leapt off Antonio's tongue.

"Found!" he whispered hoarsely, "Pauline found!"

"Yes, and the dagger found, too!"

"Found! dearest of my heart! my sweet sister!"

Janoc clasped to his bosom a phantom form, and kissed thrice at the air.

"Yes, and the dagger found that she did it with—"

"The dagger?"

"Yes, and the lady is this minute taking it to Inspector Furneaux—"

"Lady?—Oh, found! found! dear, sweet sister, why didst thou hide thyself from me?"

Janoc spread his arms with a face of rapture. He could only assimilate the one great fact in his joy.

"But Janoc—listen—the lady—"

"Lady?"

"The lady who has the dagger! Listen, my friend—she is on the way to Inspector Furneaux with Pauline's dagger—"

"*Mille diables!*"

"Janoc, what is to be done? O, arouse yourself, *pour l'amour de Dieu*— Pauline will be hanged—"

"Hanged? Yes! They hang women, I know, in England—the only country in Europe—this ugly nest of savages. Yes! they hang them by the neck on the gallows here—the gallant gentlemen! But they won't hang *her*, Antonio! Let them touch her, and *I,* I set all England dancing like a sandstorm of the Sahara! Furneaux's house No. 12?"

"Yes."

"And the lady's address?"

"Porchester Gardens—unfortunately I did not notice the number of the house."

"Pity: weak. What is she like, this lady?"

"Middle-size—plentiful brown hair—eyes blue—beautiful in the cold English way, elegant, too—yes, a pretty woman—I saw her in Tormouth—"

"Come with me"—and Janoc was in action, with a suddenness, a fury, a contrast with his previous stillness of listening that was very remarkable—as if he had waited for the instant of action to sound, and then said: "Here it is! I am ready!"

Out stretched his long leg, as he bent forward into running, catching at his cap and revolver with one sweep of his right arm, and at Antonio with a snatch of the left; and from that moment his motions were in the tone of the forced marches of Napoleon—not an instant lost in the business he was at.

He took Antonio in a cab to Furneaux's house in Sinclair Street. There he was nudged by Antonio, as they drove up, with a hysterical sob of "See! There she is!"

Rosalind was driving away at the moment. She had, then, seen Furneaux? told Furneaux? given Furneaux the dagger? In that case, the battle would lie between Furneaux and Janoc that day. Janoc's flesh was pale, but it was the paleness of iron, his eyes were full of fire. In his heart he was a hero, in brain and head an assassin!

He alighted at the detective's house, letting Rosalind go. But the landlady of the flat told him that Furneaux had not been at home for two hours, and was not expected for another hour. Rosalind, then, had not seen him; and the battle swung back to its first ground as between Rosalind and Janoc. Had the lady who had just called left any parcel, or any weapon for Mr. Furneaux? The answer was "No." He hurried down into his cab, to make for Rosalind's boarding-house.

But Antonio had not noted the number, and, to discover it, Janoc started off to Osborne's house, to ask it of Miss Prout.

Now, Rosalind was herself driving to the same place. On learning that Furneaux was not at home, she had paced his sitting-room a little while, undecided whether to wait, or to leave a message and go home. Then the new impulse had occurred in her to go to Osborne's in the meantime, and then return to Furneaux. Hylda Prout had contrived to put a lump in her throat and a firebrand in her bosom, an arrogance, a hot rancor. How much of what the hussy had said against Osborne might contain some truth she did not know; it had so scorched her, and inflamed her gorge, and kindled her eyes, that she had not had time to question its probability in her preoccupation with the gall and smart of it. But that Osborne should have opened the letter, and then written to say he had not—this was a vileness that the slightest reflection found to be incredible. The creature with the red hair certainly knew what was in the letter, but— might she not have opened it herself? And if any part of her statements were false, *all* might be false. An impatience to see Osborne instantly seized and transported Rosalind. He had honest eyes—had she not whispered it many a time to her heart? She hurried off to him.... And by accident Janoc went after her.

Osborne himself had arrived home some ten minutes before this, after a very cold reception from Mrs. Marsh at Porchester Gardens.

As he entered the library, he saw Hylda Prout standing in the middle of the room with a face of ecstasy which astonished him. She, lately arrived back from her visit to the Italian, had heard him come, and had leapt up to confront him, her heart galloping in her throat.

"Anything wrong?" he asked with a quick glance at her.

"Miss Marsh has been here."

"Ah?... Miss Marsh?"

She made a mad step toward him. The words that she uttered rasped harshly. She did not recognize her own voice.

"I told her straight out that it is not the slightest good her running after you."

"You told her *what?*"

Amazement struggled with indignation in his face. All the world seemed to have gone mad when the pale, studiously sedate secretary used such words of frenzy.

"I meant to stop—her pursuit of you.... Mr. Osborne—hear me—I—I...." Excessive emotion overpowered her. In attempting to say more she panted with distress.

"What is it all about, Miss Prout? Calm yourself, please—be quiet"—he said it with some effort to express both his resentment and his authority.

"Mr. Osborne—I warn you—I cannot endure—any rival—"

"Who can't? you speak of a *rival!*"

"Oh, Heaven, give me strength—words to explain. Ah!...."

She had been standing with her left hand resting on a table, shivering like a sail in the wind, and now the hand suddenly gave way under her, and she sank after it, falling to the ground in a faint, while her head struck the edge of the table in her descent.

"Well, if this isn't the limit," muttered Osborne, as he ran to her, calling loudly for Jenkins. He lifted her to a sofa, and, in his flurry, not knowing what else to do, wet her forehead with a little water from a carafe. Jenkins had not heard his call, and by the time he looked round for a bell to summon help, her eyes unclosed themselves, and she smiled at him.

"You are there...."

"You feel better now?" He sat on a chair at her head, looking down on her, wondering what inane words he should use to extricate both himself and her from an absurd position.

"It is all right.... I must have fainted. I have undergone a great strain, a dreadful strain. You should be sorry for me. Oh, I have loved—much."

"Miss Prout—"

"No, don't call me that, or you kill me. You should be sorry for me, if you have any pity, any shred of humanity in your heart. I have—passed through flames, and drunk of a cup of fire. Ten women, yes, ten—have hungered and wailed in me. I tell *you*—yet to whom should I tell it but to you?"

She smiled a ravished smile of pain; her hand fell upon his heavily; her restless head swung from side to side.

"Well, I am very sorry," said Osborne, forced to gentleness in spite of the anger that had consumed him earlier. "It is impossible not to believe you sincere. But, you will admit, all this is very singular and unexpected. I am afraid now that I shall have to send you on a trip to— Switzerland; or else go myself. Better you—it is chilling there, on the glaciers."

Yet the attempt at humor died when he looked at her face with its languishing, sick eyes, its expression of swooning luxury. She sighed deeply.

"No, you cannot escape me now, I think, or I you," she murmured. "There are powers too profound to be run from when once at work, like the suction of whirlpools. If you don't love me, my love is a force enough for two, for a thousand. It will draw and compel you. Yes, I think so. It will either warm you, or burn you to ashes—and myself, too. Oh, I swear to Heaven! It will, it shall! You shouldn't have pressed my hand that night."

"Pressed your hand! on which night?" asked Osborne, who had now turned quite pale, and wanted to run quickly out of the house but could not.

"What, have you *forgotten?*" she asked with tender reproach, gazing into his eyes; "the night I was going to see my brother nine months ago, and you went with me to Euston, and in saying good-by you—"

She suddenly covered her eyes with her fingers in a rapture at the memory.

Osborne stared blankly at her. He recalled the farewell at Euston, which was accidental, but he certainly had no memory of having pressed her hand.

"I loved you before," her lips just whispered in a pitiful assumption of confidence, "but timidly, not admitting it to myself. With that pressure of your hand, I was done with maidenhood, my soul rushed to you. After that, you were mine, and I was yours."

The words almost fainted on her bitten under lip, and in Osborne, too, a rush of soul, or of blood, took place, a little flush of his forehead. It was a bewitching woman who lay there before him, with that fair freckle-splashed face couched in its cloud of red hair.

"Come, now," he said, valiantly striving after the commonplace, "you are ill—you hardly know yet what you are saying."

She half sat up suddenly, bending eagerly toward him.

"Is it pity? Is it 'yes'?"

"Please, please, let us forget that this has ever—"

"It *would* be 'yes' instantly but for that Tormouth girl! Oh, drive her out of your mind! That cannot be—I could never, never permit it! For that reason alone—and besides, you are about to be arrested—"

"I!"

"Yes: listen—I know more of what is going on than you know. The man Furneaux, who, for his own reasons, hates you, and is eager to injure you, has even more proofs against you than you are aware of. *I* happen to know that in his search of your trunks he has discovered something or other which he considers conclusive against you. And there is that housemaid at Feldisham Mansions, who screamed out 'Mr. Osborne did it!'—Furneaux only pretended at the inquest that she was too ill to be present, because he did not want to produce the whole weight of his evidence just then. But he has her, too, safe up his sleeve, and *she* is willing to swear against you. And now he has got hold of your Saracen dagger. But don't you fear *him*: I shall know how to foil him at the last; I alone have knowledge that will surely make him look a fool. Trust in me! I tell you so. But I can't help your being arrested—that must happen. Believe me, for I know. And let that once take place, and that Tormouth girl will never look at you again. I understand her class, with its prides and prejudices—she will never marry you— innocent or guilty—if you have once stood in the dock at an assize court. Such as she does not know what love is. *I* would take you if you were a thousand times guilty—and I only can prove you innocent—even if you were guilty— because I am yours—your preordained wife—oh, I shall die of my love—yes, kiss me—yes—now—"

The torrent of words ended in a fierce fight for breath. Her eyes were glaring like two lakes of conflagration, her cheeks crimson, her forehead pale. Unexpectedly, eagerly, she caught him round the neck in an embrace from which there was no escape. She drew him almost to his knees, and pressed his lips to hers with a passion that frightened and repelled him.

And he was in the thick of this unhappy and ridiculous experience when he heard behind him an astonished "Oh!" from someone, while some other person seemed to laugh in angry embarrassment.

It was Jenkins who had uttered the "Oh!" and when the horrified Osborne glanced round he saw Rosalind's eyes peering over Jenkins's shoulder. She it was who had so lightly, so perplexedly, laughed.

Before he could free himself and spring up she was gone. She had murmured to Jenkins: "Some other time," and fled.

As she ran out blindly, and was springing into the cab, Janoc, in pursuit of her, drove up. In an instant he was looking in through the door of the cab.

"Miss Marsh?" he inquired.

"Yes."

His hands met, wringing in distress.

"You are the lady I am searching for, the mistress of the young girl Pauline Dessaulx, is it not? I am her brother. You see—you can see—the resemblance in our faces. She threatens this instant to commit the suicide—"

Rosalind was forced to forget her own sufferings in this new terror.

"Pauline!" she cried, "I am not her employer. Moreover, she is ill—in bed—"

"She has escaped to my lodging during your absence from home! Something dreadful has happened to her—she speaks of the loss of some weapon—one cannot understand her ravings! And unless she sees you—her hands cannot be kept from destroying herself—-Oh, lady! lady! Come to my sweet sister—"

Rosalind looked at him with the scared eyes of one who hears, yet not understands. There was a mad probability in all this, since Pauline *might* have discovered the loss of the daggers; and, in her present anguish of spirit, the thought that the man's story might only be a device to lure her into some trap never entered Rosalind's head. Indeed, in her weariness of everything, she regarded the mission of succor as a relief.

"Where do you live? I will go with you," she said.

"Lady! Lady! Thank God!" he exclaimed. "It is not far from here, in Soho."

"You must come in my cab," said Rosalind.

Janoc ran to pay his own cabman, came back instantly, and they started eastward, just as Osborne, with the wild face of a man falling down a precipice, rushed to his door, calling after them frantically: "Hi, there! Stop! Stop! For Heaven's sake—"

But the cab went on its way.

XII. The Saracen Dagger

Next morning, just as the clock was striking eight, Osborne was rising from his bed after a night of unrest when Jenkins rapped at the door and came in, deferential and calm.

"Mrs. Marsh below to see you, sir," he announced.

Osborne blinked and stared with the air of a man not thoroughly awake, though it was his mind, not his body, that was torpid.

"Mrs.," he said, "not Miss?"

"No, sir, Mrs."

"I'll be there in five minutes," he hissed with a fierce arousing of his faculties, and never before had he flung on his clothes in such a flurry of haste; in less than five minutes he was flying down the stairs.

"Forgive me!" broke from his lips, as he entered the drawing-room, and "Forgive me!" his visitor was saying to him in the same instant.

It was pitiful to see her—she, ever so enthroned in serenity, from whom such a thing as agitation had seemed so remote, was wildly agitated now. That pathetic pallor of the aged when their heart is in labor now underlay her skin. Her lips, her fingers, trembled; the tip of her nose, showing under her half-raised veil, was pinched.

"The early hour—it is so distressing—I beg your forgiveness—I am in most dreadful trouble—"

"Please sit down," he said, touching her hand, "and let me get you some breakfast."

"No, nothing—I couldn't eat—it is Rosalind—"

Now he, too, went a shade paler.

"What of Rosalind?"

"Do you by chance know anything of her

whereabouts?"

"No!"

"She has disappeared."

Her head bowed, and a sob broke from her bosom.

"Disappeared"—his lips breathed the word foolishly after her, while he looked at her almost stupidly.

Mrs. Marsh's hand dropped with a little nervous fling.

"She has not been at home all night. She left the house apparently between four and five yesterday—I was out; then I came in; then you called.... She has not come home—it is impossible to conceive...."

"Oh, she has slept with some friend," he said, feeling that the world reeled around him.

"No, she has never done that without letting me know.... She would surely have telegraphed me.... It is quite impossible even to imagine what dispensation of God—"

She stopped, her lips working; suddenly covering her eyes with her hand, as another sob gushed from her, she humbly muttered:

"Forgive me. I am nearly out of my senses."

He sprang up, touched a bell, and whispered to Jenkins, who instantly was with him: "Brandy—*quick*." Then, running to kneel at the old lady's chair, he touched her left hand, saying: "Take heart—trust in God's Providence—rely upon *me*."

"You believe, then, that you may find her—?"

"Surely: whatever else I may fail in, I could not fail now.... Just one sip of this to oblige me." Jenkins had stolen in, and she drank a little out of the glass that Osborne offered.

"You must think it odd," she said, "that I come to you. I could not give a reason—but I was so distracted and benumbed. I thought of you, and felt impelled—"

"You were right," he said. "I am the proper person to appeal to in this case. Besides, she was here yesterday—"

"Rosalind?"

"The fact is—"

"Oh, she was here? Well, that is something discovered! I did well to come. Yes—you were saying—"

"I will tell you everything. Three days ago she wrote me a letter—"

"Rosalind?"

"Are you astonished?"

"I understood—I thought—that your friendship with her had suffered some—check."

"That is so," said Osborne with a bent head. "You may remember the night of the dance at the Abbey down at Tormouth. That night, when I was full of hopes of her favor, she suddenly cast me off like a burr from her robe—I am not even now sure why—unless she had discovered that my name was not Glyn."

"If so, she no doubt considered that a sufficient reason, Mr. Osborne," said Mrs. Marsh, a chill in her tone. "One does not like the names of one's friends to be detachable labels."

"Don't think that I blame her one bit!" cried Osborne—"no more than I blame myself. I was ordered by—the police to take a name. There seemed to be good reason for it. I only blame my baleful fate. Anyway, so it was. She dropped me—into the Pit. But she was at the inquest—"

"Indeed? At the inquest. She was there. Singular."

"Deeply veiled. She didn't think, I suppose, that I should know. But I should feel her presence in the blackest— "

"Mr. Osborne—I must beg—do not make your declarations to *me*—"

"May I not? Be good—be pitiful. Here am I, charged with guilt, conscious of innocence—"

"Let us suppose all that, but are you a man free to make declarations of love? One would say that you are, as it were, married for some time to come to the lady who has lately been buried."

"True," said Osborne—"in the eyes of the world, in a formal way: but in the eyes of those near to me? Oh, I appeal to your indulgence, your friendship, your heart. Tell me that you forgive, that you understand me! and then I shall be so exuberantly gladsome that in the sweep of my exhilaration I shall go straight and find her, wherever she lies hidden.... Will you not say 'yes' on those terms?" He smiled wanly, with a hungry cajolery, looking into her face.

But she did not unbend.

"Let us first find her! and then other things may be discussed. But to find her! it is past all knowing—Oh, deep is the trouble of my soul to-day, Mr. Osborne!"

"Wait—hope—"

"But you were speaking of yesterday."

"Yes. She was at the inquest: and when I saw her— think how I felt! I said: 'She believes in me.' And three days after that she wrote to me—"

"My poor Rosalind!" murmured Mrs. Marsh. "She suffered more than I imagined. Her nature is more recondite than the well in which Truth dwells. What *could* she have written to you?"

"That I don't know."

"How—?"

"As I was about to open the letter, a telegram came from her. 'Don't read my letter: I will call for it unopened in person,' it said. Picture my agony then! And now I am going to tell you something that will move you to compassion for me, if you never had it before. Yesterday she called for the letter. I was with you at Porchester Gardens at that very hour. When I came home, an extraordinary scene awaited me with my secretary, a Miss Prout.... I tell you this as to a friend, a Mother, who will believe even the incredible. An extraordinary scene.... Without the least warning, the least encouragement that I know of, Miss Prout declared herself in love with me. While I stood astonished, she fainted. I bore her to a sofa. Soon after she opened her eyes, she—drew—me to her— no, I will say that I was *not* to blame; and I was in that situation, when the library door opened, and who should be there looking at me but—yes—*she*."

Mrs. Marsh's eyes fell. There was a little pressure of the lips that revealed scant sympathy with compromising situations. And suddenly a thought turned her skin to a ghastlier white. What if the sight of that scene accounted for Rosalind's disappearance? If Rosalind was dead—by her own act? The old lady had often to admit that she did not know the deepest deeps of her daughter's character. But she banished the half-thought hurriedly, contenting herself with saying aloud:

"That made the second time she came to you yesterday. Why a second time?"

"I have no idea!" was the dismayed reply. "She uttered not one word—just turned away, and hurried out to her waiting cab—and by the time I could wring myself free, and run after her, the cab was going off. I shouted—I ran at top speed—she would not stop. I think a man was in the cab with her—"

"A man, you say?"

"I think so. I just caught a glimpse of a face that looked out sideways—a dark man he seemed to me—I'm not sure."

"It becomes more and more mysterious!"

"Well, we must be making a move to do something—first, have you breakfasted?"

She had eaten nothing! Osborne persuaded her to join him in a hurried meal, during which his motor-car arrived, and soon they set off together. He was for going straight to the police, but she shrank from the notoriety of that final exposure until she had the clear assurance that it was absolutely necessary. So they drove from friend to friend of the Marshes who might possibly have some information; then drove home to Mrs. Prawser's to see if there was news. Osborne had luncheon there—a polite pretense at eating, since they were too full of wonder and woe to care for food. By this time Mrs. Marsh had unbent somewhat to Osborne, and humbly enough had said to him, "Oh, find her, and if she is alive, every

other consideration shall weigh less than my boundless
gratitude to you!"

After the luncheon they again drove about London,
making inquiries without hope wherever the least chance
of a clew lay; and finally, near six, they went to Scotland
Yard.

To Inspector Winter in his office the whole tale was
told; and, after sitting at his desk in a long silence,
frowning upon the story, he said at last:

"Well, there is, of course, a great deal more in this
than meets the eye." He spun round to Mrs. Marsh: "Has
your daughter undergone anything to upset her at home
lately?"

"Nothing," was the answer. "One of the servants in
the house has had a sort of hysteria: but that did not
trouble Rosalind beyond the mere exercise of womanly
sympathy."

"Any visitors? Any odd circumstance in that way?"

"No unusual visitors—except an Inspector Furneaux,
who—twice, I think—had interviews with her. She was
not very explicit in telling me the subject of them."

"Inspector Furneaux," muttered Winter. To himself he
said: "I thought somehow that this thing was connected
with Feldisham Mansions." And at once now, with a little
start, he asked: "What, by the way, is the name of the
servant who has had the hysteria?"

"Her name is Pauline," answered Mrs. Marsh—"a
French girl."

"Ah, Pauline!" said Winter—"just so."

The fewness of his words gave proof of the activity of
his brain. He knew how Clarke had obtained the diary of
Rose de Bercy from Pauline, and he felt that Pauline was
in some undetermined way connected with the murder.
He knew, too, that she was now to be found somewhere in
Porchester Gardens, and had intended looking her up for
general inquiries before two days had passed. That
Pauline might actually have had a hand in the crime had
never entered into his speculations—he was far too hot in

these days on the trail of Furneaux, who was being constantly watched by his instructions.

"I think I will see this Pauline to-night," he said. "Meantime, I can only recommend you to hope, Mrs. Marsh. These things generally have some simple explanation in the end, and turn out less black than they look. Expect me, then, at your residence within an hour."

But when Mrs. Marsh and Osborne were gone he was perplexed, remembering that this was Thursday evening, for he had promised himself on this very evening to be at a spot which he had been told by one of his men that Furneaux had visited on two previous Thursday evenings, a spot where he would see a sight that would interest him.

While he was on the horns of the dilemma as to going there, or going to Pauline, Inspector Clarke entered: and at once Winter shelved upon Clarke the business of sounding Pauline.

"You seem to have a lot of power over her—to make her give up the diary so promptly," he said to Clarke. "Go to her, then, get at the bottom of this business, and see if you cannot hit upon some connection between the disappearance of Miss Marsh and the murder of the actress."

Clarke stood up with alacrity, and started off. Presently Winter himself was in a cab, making for the Brompton Cemetery.

As for Clarke, the instant he was within sight of Porchester Gardens, his whole interest turned from Pauline Dessaulx and the vanished Rosalind to two men whom he saw in the street almost opposite the house in which Pauline lay. They were Janoc and the Italian, Antonio, and Antonio seemed to be reasoning and pleading with Janoc, who had the gestures of a man distracted.

Hanging about near them was a third man, whom Clarke hardly noticed—a loafer in a long coat of rags, a hat without any crown, and visible toes—a diminutive loafer—Furneaux, in fact, who, for his own reasons, was also interested in Janoc in these days.

Every now and again Janoc looked up at the windows of Mrs. Marsh's residence with frantic gestures, and a crying face—a thing which greatly struck Clarke; and anon the loafer passed by Janoc and Antonio, unobserved, peering into the gutter for the cast-aside ends of cigars and cigarettes.

Instantly Clarke stole down the opposite side of the square into which the house faced, looked about him, saw no one, climbed some railings, and then through the bushes stole near to the pavement where the foreigners stood. There, concealed in the shrubbery, he could clearly hear Janoc say:

"Am I never to see her? My little one! But I am about to see her! I will knock at that door, and clasp her in my arms."

"My friend, be reasonable!" pleaded Antonio, holding the arm of Janoc, who made more show of tearing himself free than he made real effort—with that melodramatic excess of gesture to which the Latin races are prone. "Be reasonable! Oh, she is wiser than you! She has hidden herself from you because she realizes the danger of being seen near you even in the dark. Be sure that she has longed to see you as keenly as you hunger to see her; but she feels that there must be no meeting with so many spying eyes in the world—"

"Let them spy! but they shall not keep me from the embrace of one whom I love, of one who has suffered," said Janoc, covering his face. "Oh, when I think of your cruelty—you who all the time knew where she was and did not tell me!"

"I confess it, but I acted for the best," said Antonio. "She wrote to me three days after the murder, so that she might have news of you. I met her, and received from her that bit of lace from the actress's dress which I put into Osborne's bag at Tormouth, to throw still more doubt upon him. But she implored me not to reveal to you where she was, lest, if you should be seen with her, suspicion of the murder should fall upon you—"

"Her heart's goodness! My sister! My little one!" exclaimed Janoc.

"Only be patient!" wooed Antonio—"do not go to her. Soon she will make her escape to France, and you also, and then you will embrace the one the other. And now you have no longer cause for much anxiety as to her capture, for the dagger cannot be found with her, since it lies safe in your room in your own keeping, and to-night you will drop it into the river, where it will be buried forever. Do not go to her—"

These were the last words of the dialogue that Clarke heard, for the tidings that "the dagger" was in Janoc's room sent him creeping away through the bushes. He was soon over the railings and in a cab, making for Soho; and behind him in another cab went Furneaux, whose driver, looking at his fare's attire, had said, "Pay first, and then I'll take you."

Clarke, for his part, had no difficulty in entering Janoc's room with his skeleton-keys—indeed, he had been there before! Nor was there any difficulty in finding the dagger. There it lay, with another, in the narrow cardboard box into which Rosalind had put both weapons on finding them behind the shelf of books in Pauline's room.

Clarke's eyes, as they fell at last upon that Saracen blade which he knew so well without ever having seen it, pored, gloated over it, with a glitter in them.

He relocked the trunk, relocked the door, and with the box held fast, ran down the three stairs to his cab—feeling himself a made man, a head taller than all Scotland Yard that night. He put his precious find on the interior front seat of the cab—a four-wheeler; for in his eagerness he had jumped into the first wheeled thing that he had seen, and, having lodged the box inside, being anxious to hide it, he made a step forward toward the driver, to tell him whither he had now to drive. Then he entered, shut the door, and, as the vehicle drove off, put out his hand to the box to feast his eyes on its contents again. But the box was gone—no daggers were there!

"Stop!" howled Clarke.

The cab stopped, but it was all in vain. The loafer, who had opened the other door of the cab with swift deftness while Clarke spoke to the driver, had long since turned a near corner with box and daggers, and was well away. Clarke, standing in the street, glanced up at the sky, down at the ground, and stared round about, like a man who does not know in which world he finds himself.

Meantime, Furneaux hailed another cab, again having to pay in advance, and started off on the drive to Brompton Cemetery—where Winter was already in hiding, awaiting his arrival.

Something like a storm of wind was tearing the night to pieces, and the trees of the place of graves gesticulated as if they were wrangling. The moon had moved up, all involved in heavy clouds whose grotesque shapes her glare struck into garish contrasts of black against silver. Furneaux bent his way against the gale, holding on his dilapidated hat, his rags fluttering fantastically behind him, till he came to the one grave he sought—the cheerless resting-place of Rose de Bercy. The very spirit of gloom and loneliness brooded here, in a nook almost inclosed with foliage. As yet no stone had been erected. The grave was just a narrow oblong of red marl and turf, which the driven rain now made soft and yielding. On it lay two withered wreaths.

Furneaux, standing by it, took off his hat, and the rain flecked his hair. Then from a breast-pocket of his rags he took out a little funnel of paper, out of which he cast some Parma violets upon the mound. This was Thursday—and Rose de Bercy had been murdered on a Thursday.

After that he stood there perhaps twenty minutes, his head bent in meditation.

Then he peered cautiously into the dark about him,

took a penknife with a good-sized blade from a pocket, and with it set to work to make a grave within the grave—a grave just big and deep enough to contain the box with the daggers. He buried his singular tribute and covered it over.

After this he waited silently, apparently lost in thought, for some ten minutes more.

Then, with that curious omniscience which sometimes seemed to belong to the man, he sent a strange cry into the gloom.

"Are you anywhere about, Winter?"

Nor was there anything aggressive in the call. It was subdued, sad, touched with solemnity, like the voice of a man who had wept, and dried his eyes.

There was little delay before Winter appeared out of the shadow of his ambush.

"I am!" he said; he was amazed beyond expression, yet his colleague had ever been incomprehensible in some things.

"Windy night," said Furneaux, in an absurd affectation of ease.

"And wet," said Winter, utterly at a loss how to take the other.

"Odd that we should both come to visit the poor thing's grave at the same hour," remarked Furneaux.

"It *may* be odd," agreed Winter.

There was a bitter silence.

Then Furneaux's cold voice was heard again.

"I dare say, now, it seems to you a suspicious thing that I should come to this grave at all."

"Why should it, Furneaux?" asked his chief bluntly.

"Yes, why?" said Furneaux. "I once knew her. I told you from the first that I knew her."

"I remember: you did."

"You asked no questions as to how I came to know her, or how long, or under what circumstances. Why did you not ask? Such questions occur among friends: and I— might have told you. But you did not ask."

"Tell me now."

"Winter, I'd see you hanged first!"

The words came in a sharp rasp—his first sign of anger.

"Hanged?" repeated Winter, flushing. "You'll see *me* hanged? *I* usually see the hanging, Furneaux!"

"Sometimes you do: sometimes you are not half smart enough!"

Furneaux barked the taunt like a dog at him.

Of the two, the big bluff man of Anglo-Saxon breed, mystified and saddened though he was, showed more self-control than the excitable little man more French than English.

"This is an occasion when I leave the smartness to you, Furneaux," he said bitterly, "though there is a sort of clever duplicity which ought to be drained out of the blood, even if it cost a limb, or a life."

"Ah, you prove yourself a trusty friend—loyal to the

backbone!"

"For Heaven's sake, make no appeal to our friendship!"

"What! Appeal? I? Oh, this is too much!"

"You are trying me beyond endurance. Can't you understand? Why keep up this farce of pretense?"

There was genuine emotion in Winter's voice, but Furneaux's harsh laugh mingled with the soughing of the laden branches that tossed in the wind.

"Farce, indeed!" he cried. "I refuse to continue it. Go, then, and be punished—you deserve it—you, whom I trusted more than a brother."

He turned on his heel, and made off, a weird figure in those wind-blown tatters, and Winter watched him with eyes that had in them some element of fear, almost of hope, for in that hour he could have forgiven Furneaux were he standing by his corpse.

But the instinct of duty soon came uppermost. He had seen his colleague bury something in the grave, and the briefest search brought to light the daggers in their cardboard coffin. Even in that overwhelming gloom of night and shivering yews he recognized one of the weapons. A groan broke from him, as it were, in protest.

"Mad!" he sighed, "stark, staring mad—to leave this here, where he knew I must find it. My poor Furneaux! Perhaps that is best. I must defer action for a few hours, if only to give him a last chance."

While the Chief Inspector was stumbling to the gate of the Cemetery—which was long since closed to all except those who could show an official permit—one of his subordinates was viewing the Feldisham Mansions crime in a far different light. Inspector Clarke, in whom elation at his discovery was chastened by chagrin at his loss, was walking towards Scotland Yard and saying to himself:

"I can prove, anyhow, that I took the rotten things from his trunk. So now, Monsieur Janoc, the next and main item is to arrest you!"

XIII. Osborne Makes A Vow

When Inspector Winter returned to his office from the
cemetery he sat at his desk, gazing at the two daggers
before him, and awaiting the coming of Clarke, from
whom he expected to receive a full report of an interview
with Pauline Dessaulx in connection with the
disappearance of Rosalind.

There lay that long sought-for Saracen dagger at last:
and Furneaux had it, had been caught burying it in the
grave of her who had been killed by it. Was not this fact,
added to the fact that Furneaux was seen in Osborne's
museum before the murder—was it not enough to
justify—indeed, enough to demand—Furneaux's arrest
straight away? And Furneaux had visited Rose de Bercy
that night—had been seen by Bertha Seward, the
actress's cook! And yet Winter hesitated.... What had
been Furneaux's motive? There was as yet no ray of light
as to that, though Winter had caused elaborate inquiries
to be made in Jersey as to Furneaux's earlier career
there. And there were *two* daggers buried, not one....

"Where does *this* come in, this *second* dagger...?"
wondered Winter, a maze of doubt and horror clouding
his brain.

Just then Clarke arrived, rather breathless, jubilant,
excited, but Winter had already hidden the daggers
instinctively—throwing them into a drawer of his
writing-desk.

"Well, what news of Miss Marsh?" he asked, with a
semblance of official calm he was far from feeling.

"The fact is, sir, I haven't been to Pauline Des—"

"What!"

"I was nearly at her door when I came across Gaston

Janoc—"

"Oh, Heavens!" muttered Winter in despair. "You and your eternal Janocs—"

The smiling Clarke looked at his chief in full confidence that he would not be reprimanded for having disobeyed orders. Suddenly making three steps on tiptoe, he said in Winter's ear:

"Don't be too startled—here's an amazing piece of information for you, sir—*it was Gaston Janoc* who committed the Feldisham Mansions murder!"

Winter stared at him without real comprehension. "Gaston Janoc!" his lips repeated.

"I want to apply to-morrow for a warrant for his arrest," crowed Clarke.

"But, man alive!—don't drive me distracted," cried out Winter; "what are you talking about?"

"Oh, I am not acting on any impulse," said Clarke, placidly satisfied, enthroned on facts; "I may tell you now that I have been working on the Feldisham Mansions affair from the first on my own account. I couldn't help it. I was drawn to it as a needle by a magnet, and I now have all the threads—ten distinct proofs—in my hands. It was Gaston Janoc did it! Just listen to this, sir—"

"Oh, do as you like about your wretched Anarchist, Clarke," said Winter pestered, waving him away; "I can't stop now. I sent you to do something, and you should have done it. Miss Marsh's mother is half dead with fright and grief; the thing is pressing, and I'll go myself."

With a snatch at his hat, he rushed out, Clarke following sullenly to go home, though on his way northward, by sheer force of habit, he strolled through Soho, looked up at Janoc's windows, and presently, catching sight of Janoc himself coming out of the restaurant on the ground floor, nodded after him, muttering to himself: "Soon now—" and went off.

But had he shadowed his Janoc just then, it might have been well! The Frenchman first went into a French shop labeled "Vins et Comestibles," where he bought slices of sausage and a bottle of cheap wine, from which he got the cork drawn—he already carried half a loaf of bread wrapped in paper, and with bread, sausage, and wine, bent his way through spitting rain and high wind, his coat collar turned up round his neck, to a house in Poland Street.

An unoccupied house: its window-glass thicker than itself with grime, broken in some of the panes, while in others were roughly daubed the words: "To Let." But he possessed a key, went in, picked up a candlestick in the passage, and lit the candle-end it contained.

At the end of the passage he went down a narrow staircase of wood, then down some stone steps, to the door of a back cellar: and this, too, he opened with a key.

Rosalind was crouching on the floor in the corner farthest from the door, her head bent down, her feet tucked under her skirt. She had been asleep: for the air in there was very heavy, the cellar hardly twelve feet square, no windows, and the slightest movement roused a cloud of dust. The walls were of rough stone, without break or feature, save three little vaulted caves like ovens in the wall facing the door, made to contain wine bottles and small barrels: in fact, one barrel and several empty bottles now lay about in the dust. Besides, there were sardine tins and a tin of mortadel, and relics of sausage and bread, with which Janoc had lately supplied his prisoner, with a bottle half full of wine, and one of water: all showing very dimly in the feeble rays of the candle.

She looked at him, without moving, just raising her scornful eyes and no more, and he, holding up the light, looked at her a good time.

"Lady," he said at last, "I have brought you some meat, wine, and bread."

She made no answer. He stepped forward, and laid them by her side; then walked back to the door, as if to go out, coughing at the dust; but stopped and leant his back on the wall near the door, his legs crossed, looking down at her.

"Lady," he said presently, "you still remain fixed in your obstinacy?"

No answer: only her wide-open reproving eyes dwelt on him with their steady accusation like a conscience, and her hand stuck and stuck many times with a hat-pin her hat which lay on her lap. Her gown appeared to be very frowsy and unkempt now; her hair was untidy, and quite gray with dust on one side, her face was begrimed and stained with the tracks of tears; but her lips were firm, and the wonderful eyes, chiding, disdainful, gave no sign of a drooping spirit.

"You will say nothing to me?" asked Janoc.

No answer.

"Is it that you think I may relent and let you free, lady, because my heart weakens at your suffering? Do not imagine such a thing of me! The more you are beautiful, the more you are sublime in your torture, the more I adore you, the more my heart pours out tears of blood for you, the more I am inflexible in my will. You do not know me—I am a man, I am not a wind; a mind, not an emotion. Oh, pity is strong in me, love is strong; but what is strongest of all is self-admiration, my worship of intelligence. And have I not made it impossible that you should be let free without conditions by my confession to you that it was my sister Pauline who killed the actress? I tell you again it was Pauline who killed her. It was not a murder! It was an assassination—a political assassination. Mademoiselle de Bercy had proved a traitress to the group of Internationals to which she belonged: she was condemned to death; the lot fell upon Pauline to execute the sentence; and on the day appointed she executed it, having first stolen from Mr. Osborne the 'celt' and the dagger, so as to cast the suspicion upon him. I tell you this of my sister—of one who to me is dearest on earth; and, having told you all this, is it any longer possible that I should set you free without conditions? You see, do you not, that it is impossible?"

No answer.

"I only ask you to promise—to give your simple word—not to say, or hint, to anyone that Pauline had the daggers. What a risk I take! What trust in you! I do not know you—I but trust blindly in the highly-evolved, that divine countenance which is yours; and since it was with the object of saving my sister that you came here with me, my gratitude to you deepens my trust. Give me, then, this promise, Miss Marsh!"

Now her lips opened a little to form the word "No," which he could just catch.

"Sublime!" he cried—"and I am no less sublime. If I was rich, if I had a fair name, and if I could dare to hope to win the love of a lady such as you, how favored of the gods I should be! But that is—a dream. Here, then, you will remain, until the day that Pauline is safely hidden in France: and on that day—since for myself I care little—I will open this door to you: never before. Meanwhile, tell me if you think of anything more that I can do for your comfort."

No answer.

"Good-night." He turned to go.

"You made me a promise," she said at the last moment.

"I have kept it," he said. "This afternoon, at great risk to myself, I wrote to your mother the words: 'Your daughter is alive and safe.' Are you satisfied?"

"Thank you," she said.

"Good-night," he murmured again.

Having locked the door, he waited five minutes outside silently, to hear if she sobbed or wailed in there in the utter dark: but no sound came to him. He went upstairs, put out the light, put down the candlestick in the passage, and was just drawing back the door latch, when he was aware of a strong step marching quickly along an almost deserted pavement.

After a little he peeped out and recognized the heavy figure of Inspector Winter. Even Janoc, the dreamer, whose dreams took such tragic shape, was surprised for an instant.

"How limited is the consciousness of men!" he muttered. "That so-called clever detective little guesses what he has just passed by."

But Winter, too, might have indulged in the same reflection: "How limited the consciousness of Janoc! He doesn't know where I am passing to—to visit and question his sister Pauline!"

Winter, a little further on, took a taxicab to Porchester Gardens, got out at the bottom of the street, and was walking on to Mrs. Marsh's temporary residence, when he saw Furneaux coming the opposite way.

Winter wished to pretend not to see him, but Furneaux spoke.

"Well, Providence throws us together somehow!"

"Ah! Why blame Providence?" said Winter, with rather a snarl.

"Not two hours ago there was our chance meeting by that graveside—"

The "chance" irritated Winter to the quick.

"You have all the faults of the French nature," he said bitterly, "without any of its merits: its levity without its industry, its pettiness without its minuteness—"

"And you the English frankness without its honesty. The chief thing about a Frenchman is his intelligence. At least you do not deny that I am intelligent?"

"I have thought you intelligent. I am damned if I think you so any longer."

"Oh, you will again—soon—when I wish it. We met just now at a grave, and there was more buried in that grave than the grave-diggers know: and we both stood looking at it: but I fancy there were more X-rays in my eye to see what was buried there than in yours!"

Driven beyond the bounds of patience, Winter threw out an arm in angry protest.

"Ha! ha! ha!" tittered Furneaux.

An important official at Scotland Yard must learn

early the value of self-control. Consumed with a certain sense of the monstrous in this display of untimely mirth, Winter only gnawed a bristle or two of his mustache. He looked strangely at Furneaux, and they lingered together, loath to part, having still something bitter and rankling to say, but not knowing quite what, since men who have been all in all to each other cannot quarrel without some childish tone of schoolboy spite mingling in the wrangle.

"I believe I know where you are going now!" jeered Furneaux.

"Ah, you were always good at guessing."

"Going to pump the Pauline girl about Miss Marsh."

"True, of course, but not a very profound analysis considering that I am just ten yards from the house."

"Don't you even know where Miss Rosalind Marsh is?" asked Furneaux, producing a broken cigar from a pocket and sniffing it, simply because he was well aware that the trick displeased his superior.

"No. Do you?" Winter jeered back at him.

"I do."

"Oh, the sheerest bluff!"

"No, no bluff. I know."

"Well, let me imagine that it is bluff, anyway: for brute as a man might be, I won't give you credit for being *such* a brute as to keep that poor old lady undergoing the torments of hell through a deliberate silence of yours."

"Didn't you say that I have all the bad qualities of the Latin temperament?" answered Furneaux. "Now, there is something cat-like in the Latin; a Spaniard, for example, can be infernally cruel at a bullfight; and I'll admit that *I* can, too. But 'torments of hell' is rather an exaggeration, nor will the 'torments' last mortally long, for to-morrow afternoon at about four—at the hour that I choose—in the hour that I am ready—Miss Marsh will drive up to that door there."

"Evidently you were not born in Jersey, but in Gascony," Winter said sourly.

"Wrong again! A Jersey man will bounce any Gascon

off his feet," said Furneaux. "And, just to pile up the agony, here is another sample for you, since you accuse me of bluffing. To-morrow afternoon, at that same hour—about four—I shall have that scoundrel Osborne in custody charged with the murder in Feldisham Mansions."

"Mr. Osborne?" whispered Winter, towering and frowning above his diminutive adversary. "Oh, Furneaux, you drive me to despair by your folly. If you are mad, which I hope you are, that explains, I suppose, your delusion that others are mad, too."

"Genius is closely allied with insanity," said Furneaux carelessly; "yet, you observe that I have never hinted any doubt as to your saneness. Wait, you'll see: my case against Osborne is now complete. A warrant can't be refused, not even by you, and to-morrow, as sure as you stand there, I lay my hand on your protégé's shoulder."

Winter nearly choked in his rage.

"All right! We'll see about that!" he said with a furious nod of menace. Furneaux chuckled; and now by a simultaneous impulse they walked apart, Furneaux whistling, in Winter a whirlwind of passion blowing the last shreds of pity from his soul.

He was soon sitting at the bedside of Pauline Dessaulx, now convalescent, though the coming of this strange man threw her afresh into a tumult of agitation. But Winter comforted her, smoothed her hand, assured her that there was no cause for alarm.

"I know that you took Mademoiselle de Bercy's diary," he said to her, "and it was very wrong of you not to give it up to the police, and to hide yourself as you did when your evidence was wanted. But, don't be frightened—I am here to-night to see if you can throw any light on the sad disappearance of Miss Marsh. The suspense is killing her mother, and I feel sure that it has some connection with the Feldisham Mansions affair. Now, can you help me? Think—tell me."

"Oh, I cannot!" She wrung her hands in a paroxysm of

distress—"If I could, I would. I cannot imagine—!"

"Well, then, that part of my inquiry is ended. Only, listen to this attentively. I want to ask you one other question: Why did you leave the Exhibition early on the night of the murder, and where did you go to?"

"*I—I—I*, sir!" she said, pointing to her guiltless breast with a gaping mouth; "I, poor me, I *left*—?"

"Oh, come now, don't delude yourself that the police are fools. You went to the Exhibition with the cook, Hester Se—"

"And she has said such a thing of me? She has declared that *I* left—?"

"Yes, she has. Why trouble to deny it? You did leave— By the way, have you a brother or any other relative in London—?"

"*I—I*, sir! A brother? Ah, mon Dieu! Oh, but, sir—!"

"Really you must calm yourself. You went away from the Exhibition at an early hour. There is no doubt about it, and you must have a brother or some person deeply interested in you, for some man afterwards got hold of the cook, Bertha Seward, and begged her for Heaven's sake not to mention your departure from the Exhibition that night. He gave her money—she told me so. And Inspector Clarke knows it, as well as I, for Hester Seward has told me that he went to question her—"

"M'sieur *Clarke*!"—at the name of "Clarke," which she whispered after him, the girl's face turned a more ghastly gray, for Clarke was the ogre, the griffon, the dragon of her recent life, at the mere mention of whom her heart leaped guiltily. Suddenly, abandoning the struggle, she fell back from her sitting posture, tried to hide her face in the bedclothes, and sobbed wildly:

"I didn't do it! I didn't do it!"

"Do what? Who said you had done anything?" asked Winter. "It isn't *you* that Mr. Clarke suspects, you silly child, it is a man named—"

She looked up with frenzied eyes to hear the name— but Winter stopped. In his hands the unhappy Pauline was a little hedge-bird in the talons of a hawk.

"Named?" she repeated.

"Never mind his name."

She buried her head afresh, giving out another heart-rending sob, and from her smothered lips came the words:

"It wasn't I—it was—it was—"

"It was who?" asked Winter.

She shivered through the whole of her delicate frame, and a low murmur came from her throat:

"You have seen the diary—it was Monsieur Furneaux."

Oddly enough, despite his own black conviction, this was not what Winter expected to hear.

He started, and said sharply:

"Oh, you are stupid. Why are you saying things that you know nothing of?"

"May Heaven forgive me for accusing anyone," she sobbed hoarsely. "But it was not anybody else. It could not be. You have seen the diary—it was Mr. Furneaux, or it was Mr. Osborne."

"Ah, two accusations now," cried Winter. "Furneaux or Osborne! You are trying to shield someone? What motive could Mr. Furneaux, or Mr. Osborne, have for such an act?"

"Was not Mr. Osborne her lover? And was not Mr. Furneaux her—husband?"

"Her—!"

In that awesome moment Winter hardly realized what he said. Half starting out of his chair, he glared in stupor at the shrinking figure on the bed, while every drop of blood fled away from his own face.

There was a long silence. Then Winter, bending over her, spoke almost in the whisper of those who share a shameful secret.

"You say that Mr. Furneaux was her husband? You know it?"

She trembled violently, but nerved herself to answer:

"Yes, I know it."

"Tell me everything. You must! Do you understand? I order you."

"She told me herself when we were friends. She was married to him in the church of St. Germain l'Auxerrois in Paris on the 7th of November in the year '98. But she soon left him, since he had not the means to support her. I have her marriage certificate in my trunk."

Winter sat some minutes spellbound, his big round eyes staring at the girl, but not seeing her, his forehead glistening. This, then, supplied the long-sought motive. The unfaithful wife was about to marry another. This was the key. An affrighting callousness possessed him. He became the cold, unbending official again.

"You must get up at once, and give me that certificate," he said in the tone of authority, and went out of the room. In a little while she placed the paper in his hands, and he went away with it. Were she not so distraught she might have seen that it shook in his fingers.

Now he, like Clarke, held all the threads of an amazing case.

The next afternoon Furneaux was to arrest Osborne—it was for him, Winter, then, to anticipate such an outrage by the swift arrest of Furneaux. But was he quite ready? He wished he could secure another day's grace to collate and systematize each link of his evidence, and he hurried to Osborne's house in order to give Osborne a hint to vanish again for a day or two. Nevertheless, when at the very door, he paused, refrained, thought that he would manage things differently, and went away.

On one of the blinds of the library as he passed he saw the shadow of a head—of Osborne's head in fact, who in that hour of despair was sitting there, bowed down, hopeless now of finding Rosalind, whom he believed to be dead.

Though Mrs. Marsh had that evening received a note from Janoc: "Your daughter is alive," as yet Osborne knew nothing of it. He was mourning his loss in solitude when a letter was brought to him by Jenkins. He tore it open. After an uncomprehending glare at the written words he suddenly grasped their meaning.

The writer believes that your ex-secretary, Miss Hylda Prout, could tell you where Miss Rosalind Marsh is imprisoned.

"Imprisoned!" That was the word that pierced the gloom and struck deepest. She was alive, then—that was joy. But a prisoner—in what hole of blackness? Subject to what risks? In whose power? In ten seconds he was rushing out of the house, and was gone.

During the enforced respite of a journey in a cab he looked again at the mysterious note. It was a man's hand; small, neat writing; no signature. Who could have written it? But his brain had no room for guessing. He looked out to cry to the driver: "A sovereign for a quick run."

To his woe, Hylda Prout was not in her lodgings when he arrived there. During the last few days he had known nothing of her movements. After that flare-up of passion in the library, the relation of master and servant had, of course, come to an end between them; and the lady of the house in Holland Park where Hylda rented two rooms told him that Miss Prout had gone to see her brother for the weekend, and was not expected back till noon on the following day.

And Osborne did not know where her brother lived! His night was dismal with a horror of sleeplessness.

Long before midday he was in Hylda's sitting-room, only to pace it to and fro in an agony of impatience till two o'clock—and then she came.

"Oh, I have waited hours—weary hours!" he cried with a reproach that seemed to sweep aside the need for explanations.

"I am so sorry!—sit here with me."

She touched his hand, leading him to a couch and sitting near him, her hat still on, a flush on her pale face.

"Hylda"—her heart leapt: he called her "Hylda"!—
"you know where Miss Marsh is."

She sprang to her feet in a passion.

"So it is to talk to me about another woman that you
have come? I who have humbled myself, lost my self-
respect—"

Osborne, too, stood up, stung to the quick by this
mood of hers, so foreign to the disease of impatience and
care in which he was being consumed.

"My good girl," he said, "are you going to be
reasonable?"

"Come, then," she retorted, "let us be reasonable." She
sat down again, her hands crossed on her lap, a
passionate vindictiveness in her pursed lips, but a mock
humility in her attitude.

"Tell me! tell me! Where shall I find her?" and he bent
in eager pleading.

"No. How is it possible that I should tell you?"

"But you do know! Somehow you do! I see and feel it.
Tell it me, Hylda! Where is she?"

She looked up at him with a smiling face which gave
no hint of the asp's nest of jealousy which the sight of his
agony and longing created in her bosom. And from those
calm lips furious words came out:

"Why, I horribly hate the woman—and since I happen
to know that she is suffering most vilely, do you think it
likely that I would tell you where she is?"

He groaned, as his heart sank, his head dropped, his
hope died. He moved slowly away to a window; then, with
a frantic rush was back to her, on his knees, telling her of
his wealth—it was more than she could measure!—and
he had a checkbook in his pocket—all, one might say, was
hers—she had only to name a sum—a hundred thousand,
two hundred—anything—luxury for life, mansions,
position—just for one little word, one little act of
womanly kindliness.

When he stopped for lack of breath, she covered her

eyes with the back of her hand, and began to cry; he saw her lips stretched in the tension of her emotion.

"Why do you cry?—that achieves nothing—listen—" he panted.

"To be offered money—to be so wounded—I who—" She could not go on.

"My God! Then I offer you—what you will—my friendship—my gratitude—my affection—only speak—"

"For another woman! Slave that you are to her! she is sweet to you, is she, in your heart? But she shall never have you—be sure of that—not while I draw the breath of life! If you want her free, I will sell myself for nothing less than yourself—you must marry me!"

Her astounding demand struck him dumb. He picked himself slowly up from her feet, walked again to the window, and stood with his back to her—a long time. Once she saw his head drop, heard him sob, heard the words: "Oh, no, not that"; and she sat, white and silent, watching him.

When he returned to her his eyes were calm, his face of a grim and stern pallor. He sat by her, took her hand, laid his lips on it.

"You speak of marriage," he said gently, "but just think what kind of a marriage that would be—forced, on one side—I full of resentment against you for the rest of my life—"

Thus did he try to reason with her, tried to show her a better way, offering to vow not to marry anyone for two years, during which he promised to see whether he could not acquire for her those feelings which a husband—

But she cut him short coldly. In two years she would be dead without him. She would kill herself. Life lived in pain was a thing of no value—a human life of no more value than a fly's. If he would marry her, she would tell him where Miss Marsh was: and, after the marriage, if he did not love her, she knew a way of setting him free— though, even in that case, Rosalind Marsh should never have him—she, Hylda, would see to that.

For the first time in his life Osborne knew what it was to hate. He, the man accused of murder, felt like a murderer, but he had grown strangely wise, and realized that this woman would die cheerfully rather than reveal her secret. He left her once more, stood ten minutes at the window—then laughed harshly.

"I agree," he said quite coolly, turning to her.

She, too, was outwardly cool, though heaven and hell fought together in her bosom. She held out to him a Bible. He kissed it.

"When?" she asked.

"This day week," he said.

She wrote on a piece of paper the address of a house in Poland Street; and handed it to him.

"Miss Marsh is there," she said, as though she were his secretary of former days, in the most business-like way.

He walked straight out without another word, without a bow to her.

When he was well out of the house he began to run madly, for there was no cab in sight. But he had not run far when he collided with Inspector Furneaux.

"Mr. Osborne," said Furneaux—"one word. I think you are interested in the disappearance of Miss Marsh? Well, I am happy to say that I am in a position to tell you where that lady is."

He looked with a glitter of really fiendish malice in his eyes at the unhappy man who leant against a friendly wall, his face white as death.

"Are you ill, sir?" asked Furneaux, with mock solicitude.

"Why, man, your information is a minute late," muttered Osborne; "I have it already—I have bought it." He held out the paper with the address in Poland Street.

Furneaux gazed at him steadily as he leant there, looking ready to drop; then suddenly, eagerly, he said:

"You say '*bought*': do you mean with money?"

"No, not with money—with my youth, with my life!"

Furneaux seemed to murmur to himself: "As I hoped!" And now the glitter of malice passed away from his softened eyes, his forehead flushed a little, out went his hand to Osborne, who, in a daze of misery, without in the least understanding why, mechanically shook it.

"Surely, Mr. Osborne," said Furneaux, "Miss Marsh would consider that a noble deed of you, if she knew it."

"She will never know it."

"Oh, never is a long time. One must be more or less hopeful. Unfortunately, I am compelled to inform you that I am here to arrest you—"

"Me? At last! For the murder?"

"It was to be, Mr. Osborne. But, come, you shall first have the joy of setting free Miss Marsh, to whom you have given so much—there's a cab—"

Osborne followed him into the cab with a reeling brain. Yet he smiled vacantly.

"I hope I shall be hanged," he said, in a sort of self-communing. "That will be better than marriage—better, too, than deserving to be hanged, which might have been true of me a few minutes ago. Why, I killed a woman in thought just now—killed her, with my hands. Yes, this is better. I should hate to have done that wretched thing, but now I am safe—safe from—myself."

XIV: THE ARRESTS

As Furneaux and Osborne were being driven rapidly to Poland Street, bent on the speedy release of Rosalind, Inspector Winter, for his part, was seeking for Furneaux in a fury of haste, eager to arrest his colleague before the latter could arrest Osborne. At the same time Clarke, determined to bring matters to a climax by arresting Janoc, was lurking about a corner of Old Compton Street, every moment expecting the passing of his quarry. Each man was acting without a warrant. The police are empowered to arrest "on suspicion," and each of the three could produce proof in plenty to convict his man.

As for Winter, he knew that where Osborne was Furneaux would not be far that day. Hence, when in the forenoon he received notice from one of his watchers that Furneaux had that morning deliberately fled from observation, he bade his man watch Osborne's steps with one eye, while the other searched the offing for the shadow of Furneaux, on the sound principle that "wheresoever the carcase is, there will the eagles be gathered together."

Thus Osborne's ride to Holland Park to see Hylda Prout had been followed; and, two hours afterwards, while he was still waiting for Hylda's arrival, Winter's spy from behind the frosted glass of a public-house bar had watched Furneaux's arrival and long wait on the pavement. He promptly telephoned the fact to Winter, and Winter was about to set out westward from Scotland Yard when the detective telephoned afresh to say that Mr. Osborne had appeared out of the house, and had been accosted by Furneaux. The watcher, quite a smart youngster from a suburban station, hastened from his hiding-place. Evidently, Furneaux was careless of espionage at that moment. He hailed a cab without so much as a glance at the man passing close to Osborne and himself on the pavement, and it was easy to overhear the address given to the driver—a house in Poland Street.

Why to Poland Street Winter could not conceive. At all events, the fact that the drive was not to a police-station inspired him with the hope that Osborne's arrest was for some reason not yet an accomplished fact, and he, too, set off for Poland Street, which happily lay much nearer Scotland Yard than Holland Park.

Meantime, Osborne and Furneaux were hastening eastward in silence, Osborne with his head bent between his clenched hands, and an expression of face as wrenched with pain as that of a man racked with neuralgia. It was now that he began to feel in reality the tremendousness of the vow he had just made to marry Hylda Prout, in order to set Rosalind free. Compared to that his impending arrest was too little a thing for him to care about. But as they were spinning along by Kensington Gardens, a twinge of curiosity prompted him to ask why he was to be arrested now, after being assured repeatedly that the police would not formulate any charge against him.

Furneaux looked straight in front of him, and when he answered, his voice was metallic.

"There was no escaping it, Mr. Osborne," he said. "But be thankful for small mercies. I was waiting there in the street for you, intending to pounce on you at once, but when I knew that you had sacrificed yourself for Miss Marsh, I thought, 'He deserves to be permitted to release her': for, to promise to marry Miss Prout—"

"What are you saying? How could you possibly know that I promised to marry Miss Prout?"

Osborne's brain was still seething, but some glimmer of his wonted clear judgment warned him of the exceeding oddity of the detective's remark.

"Well, you told me that you had 'bought' the knowledge of her whereabouts with 'your youth and your life'—so I assumed that there could be no other explanation."

"Still, that is singularly deep guessing—!"

"Well, if you demand greater accuracy, I foresaw exactly what would be the result of your interview with your late secretary, in case you really did care for Miss Marsh. Therefore, I brought about the interview because—"

"*You* brought it about?" cried Osborne in a crescendo of astonishment.

"Yes. You see I am candid. You are aware that I knew where Miss Marsh could be found, and I might have given you the information direct. But I preferred to write a note telling you that you must depend on Miss Prout for tidings."

"Ah! it was you, then, who sent that note! But how cruel, how savagely cruel! Could you not have told me yourself? Don't you realize that your detestable action has bound me for life to a woman whom—Oh, I hope, since you are about to arrest me, that you will prove me guilty, for if I live, life henceforth will hold nothing for me save Dead Sea fruit!"

He covered his eyes, but Furneaux, whose face was twitching curiously, laid a hand on his knee, and said in a low voice:

"Do not despair. You are not the only man in the world who suffers. I had reasons—and strong reasons—for acting in this manner. One reason was that I was uncertain of the depth of your affection for Miss Marsh, and I wished to be as certain as you have now made me."

"But how on earth could that concern you, the depth or shallowness of my affection for Miss Marsh?" asked Osborne in a white heat of anger and indignation.

"Nevertheless, it did concern me," answered Furneaux dryly; "I cannot, at present, explain everything to you. I had a suspicion that your affection for Miss Marsh was trivial: if it had been, you would then have shown a criminal forgetfulness of the dead woman whom so recently you said you loved. In that event, you would have found me continuing the part I have played in regard to you—anything but a friend. As matters stand, I say I may yet earn your gratitude for what to-day you call my cruelty."

Osborne passed his hands across his eyes wearily.

"I fear I can neither talk myself, nor quite understand what you mean by your words," he murmured. "My poor head is rather in a whirl. You see, I have given my promise—I have sworn on the Bible to that woman— nothing can ever alter that, or release me now. I am— done for—"

His chin dropped on his breast. He had the semblance of a man who had lost all—for whom death had no terrors.

"Nevertheless, I tell you that I forecasted the result of your interview with Hylda Prout," persisted Furneaux. "Even now I do not see your reason for despair. I knew that Miss Prout had an ardent attachment to you; I said to myself: 'She will surely seek to sell the information in her possession for what she most longs for, and the possibility is that Osborne may yield to her terms— always provided that his attachment to the other lady is profound. If it is not profound, I find out by this device; if it is profound, he becomes engaged to Miss Prout, which is a result that I greatly wish to bring about before his arrest.'"

"My God! why?" asked Osborne, looking up in a tense agony that might have moved a less sardonic spirit.

"For certain police reasons," said Furneaux, smiling with the smug air of one who has given an irrefutable answer.

"But what a price *I* pay for these police reasons! Is this fair, Inspector Furneaux? Now, in Heaven's name, is this fair? Life-long misery on the one hand, and some trick of officialism on the other!"

The detective seemed to think the conversation at an end, since he sat in silence and stared blankly out of the window.

Osborne shrank into his corner, quite drooping and pinched with misery, and brooded over his misfortunes. Presently he started, and asked furiously:

"In what possible way did Hylda Prout come to know where Miss Marsh was hidden, to use your own ridiculous word?"

"Miss Prout happens to be a really clever woman," answered Furneaux. "In the times of Richelieu she would have governed France from an *alcôve*. You had better ask her herself how she obtained her knowledge. Still, I don't mind telling you that Miss Marsh has been imprisoned in a wine-cellar by a certain Anarchist, a great man in his way, and that your former secretary has of late days developed quite an intimate acquaintance with Anarchist circles—"

"Anarchist?" gasped Osborne. "My Rosalind—imprisoned in a wine-cellar?"

"It is a tangled skein," purred Furneaux with a self-satisfied smirk; "I am afraid we haven't time now to go into it."

The cab crossed Oxford Circus—two minutes more and they were in Soho.

Winter at that moment was on the lookout for Furneaux at the corner of a shabby street which traverses Poland Street. As for Clarke, he had vanished from the nook in Compton Street where he was loitering in the belief that Janoc would soon pass. In order to understand exactly the amazing events that were now reaching their crisis it is necessary to go back half an hour and see how matters had fared with Clarke....

During his long vigil, he, in turn, had been watched most intently by the Italian, Antonio, who, quickly becoming suspicious, hastened to a barber's shop, kept by a compatriot, where Janoc was in hiding. Into this shop he pitched to pant a frenzied warning.

"Sauriac says that Inspector Clarke has been up your stairs—may have entered your rooms—and I myself have just seen him prowling round Old Compton Street!"

Agitation mastered Janoc; he, who so despised those bunglers, the police, now began to fear them. Out he pelted, careless of consequences, and Antonio after him.

He made straight for his third-floor back, and, losing a few seconds in his eagerness to unlock the door, rushed to the trunk in which he had left the two daggers, meaning to do away with them once and for all.

And now he knew how he had blundered in keeping them. He looked in the trunk and saw, not the daggers, but the gallows!

For the first time in his life he nearly fainted. Political desperadoes of his type are often neurotic—weak as women when the hour of trial is at hand, but strong as women when the spirit has subdued the flesh. During some moments of sheer despair he knelt there, broken, swaying, with clasped hands and livid face. Then he stood up slowly, with some degree of calmness, with no little dignity.

"They are gone," he said to Antonio, pointing tragically.

Antonio's hands tore at his hair, his black eyes glared out of their red rims with the look of a hunted animal that hears the hounds baying in close pursuit.

"This means the sure conviction either of her or me," went on Janoc. "My efforts have failed—I must confess to the murder."

"My friend!" cried Antonio.

"Set free Miss Marsh for me," said Janoc, and he walked down the stairs, without haste, yet briskly— Antonio following him at some distance behind, with awe, with reverence, as one follows a conqueror.

Janoc went unfalteringly to his doom. Clarke, seeing him come, chuckled and lunged toward him.

"It is for me you wait—yes?" said Janoc, pale, but strong.

"There may be something in *that*," said Clarke, though he was slightly taken aback by the question.

"You have the daggers—yes?"

This staggered him even more, but he managed to growl:

"You may be sure of that."

"Well, I confess! I did it!"

At last! The garish street suddenly assumed roseate tints in the detective's eyes.

"Oh, you do?" he cried thickly. "You confess that you killed Rose de Bercy on the night of the 3d of July at Feldisham Mansions?"

"Yes, I confess it."

Clarke laid a hand on Janoc's sleeve, and the two walked away.

As for Antonio, in an ecstasy of excitement he cast his eyes and his arms on high together, crying out, "*O Dio mio!*" and the next moment was rushing to find a cab to take him to Porchester Gardens. Arrived there, he rang, and the instant Pauline appeared, she being now sufficiently recovered to attend to her duties, his right hand went out in a warning clutch at her shoulder.

"Your brother is arrested!" he cried.

With her clenched fists drawn back, she glared crazily at him, and her face reddened for a little while, as if she were furious at the outrage and suddenness of his news. Then her cheeks whitened, she went faint, sank back into the shelter of the hall, and leant against an inner doorway, her eyes closed, her lips parted.

"Oh, Pauline, be brave!" said Antonio, and tears choked his voice.

After a time, without opening her eyes, she asked:

"What proofs have they?"

"They have found the daggers in his trunk."

"But *I* have the daggers!"

"No, that woman who lived here, your supposed friend, Miss Marsh, stole the daggers from you, and Janoc secured them from her."

She moaned, but did not weep. She, who had been timid as a mouse at sight of Clarke, was now braver than the man. Presently she whispered:

"Where have they taken him to?"

"He will have been taken to the Marlborough Street police-station."

After another silence she said:

"Thank you, Antonio; leave me."

Passionately he kissed her hand in silence, and went.

She was no sooner alone than she walked up to her room, dressed herself in clothes suited for an out-of-door mission, and went out, heedless and dumb when a wondering fellow-servant protested. She called a cab—for Marlborough Street; and now she was as calm and strong as had been her brother when he gave himself up to Clarke.

Her cab crossed Oxford Circus about ten minutes ahead of the vehicle which carried Furneaux and Osborne; and as she turned south to enter Marlborough Street, she saw Winter, who had lately visited her, standing at a corner awaiting the arrival of Furneaux.

"Stop!" Pauline cried to her driver: and she alighted.

"Well, you are better, I see," said Winter, who did not wish to be bothered by her at that moment.

"Sir," said Pauline solemnly in her stilted English, "I regret having been so unjust as to tell you that it was either Mr. Furneaux or Mr. Osborne who committed that murder, since it was I myself who did it."

"What!" roared Winter, stepping backward, and startled most effectually out of his official phlegm.

"Sir," said Pauline again, gravely, calmly, "it was not a murder, it was an assassination, done for political reasons. As I have no mercy to expect, so I have no pardon to ask, and no act to blush at. It was political. I give myself into your custody."

Winter stood aghast. His brain seemed suddenly to have curdled; everything in the world was topsy-turvy.

"So that was why you left the Exhibition—to kill that poor woman, Pauline Dessaulx?" he contrived to say.

"That is the truth, sir. I could bear to keep it secret no

longer, and was going now to the police-station to give myself up, when I saw you."

Still Winter made no move. He stood there, frowning in thought, staring at nothing.

"And all the proofs I have gathered against—against someone else—all these are false?" he muttered.

"I am afraid so, sir," said Pauline, "since it was I who did it with my own hands."

"And Mr. Osborne's dagger and flint—where do they come in?"

"It was I who stole them from Mr. Osborne's museum, sir, to throw suspicion upon him."

"Oh, come along," growled Winter. "I believe, I know, you are lying, but this must be inquired into."

Not unkindly, acting more like a man in a dream than an officer of the law, he took her arm, led her to the cab from which she had just descended, and the two drove away together to the police-station higher up the street.

Thus, and thus only, was Inspector Furneaux saved from arrest that day. Two minutes later he and Osborne passed the very spot where Pauline found Winter, and reached Poland Street without interference.

Furneaux produced a bunch of keys when he ran up the steps of the house. He unlocked the door at once, and the two men entered. Evidently Furneaux had been there before, for he hurried without hesitation down the kitchen stairs, put a key into the cellar door, flung it open, and Osborne, peering wildly over his shoulder, caught a glimpse of Rosalind sitting on the ground in a corner.

She did not look up when they entered—apparently she thought it was Janoc who had come, and with fixed, mournful eyes, like one gazing into profundities of vacancy, she continued to stare at the floor. Her face and air were so pitiable that the hearts of the men smote them into dumbness.

Then, half conscious of some new thing, she must have caught sight of two men instead of the usual one, for she looked up sharply; and in another moment was staggering to her feet, all hysterical laughter and sobbings, like a dying light that flickers wildly up and burns low alternately, trying at one instant to be herself and calm, when she laughed, and the next yielding to her distress, when she sobbed. She put out her hand to Osborne in a last effort to be graceful and usual; then she yielded the struggle, and fainted in his arms.

Furneaux produced a scent-bottle and a crushed cigar, such as it was his habit to smell, to present them to her nose....

But she did not revive, so Osborne took her in his arms, and carried her, as though she were a child, up the stone steps, and up the wooden, and out to the cab. Furneaux allowed him to drive alone with her, himself following behind in another cab, which was a most singular proceeding on the part of a detective who had arrested a man accused of an atrocious murder.

Half-way to Porchester Gardens Rosalind opened her eyes, and a wild, heartrending cry came from her parched lips.

"I will have no more wine nor water—let me die!"

"Try and keep still, just a few moments, my dear one!" he murmured, smiling a fond smile of pain, and clasping her more tightly in a protecting arm. "You are going home, to your mother. You will soon be there, safe, with her."

"Oh!"—Then she recognized him, though there was still an uncanny wildness in her eyes. "I am free—it is you."

She seemed to falter for words, but raised her hands instinctively to her hair, knowing it to be all rumpled and dusty. Instinctively, too, she caught her hat from her knee, and put it on hurriedly. She could not know what stabs of pain these little feminine anxieties caused her lover. No spoken words could have portrayed the sufferings she had endured like unto her pitiful efforts to conceal their ravages. At last she recovered sufficiently to ask if her mother expected her.

"I am not sure," said Osborne. "I am not your deliverer; Inspector Furneaux discovered where you were, and went to your rescue."

"But you are with him?" and an appealing note of love, of complete confidence, crept into her voice.

"I merely happen to be with him, because he is now taking me to a felon's cell. But he lets me come in the cab with you, because he trusts me not to run away."

His smile was very sad and humble, and he laid his disengaged hand on hers, yielding to a craving for sympathy in his forlornness. But memories were now thronging fast on her mind, and she drew herself away from both hand and arm. She recalled that her last sight of him was when in the embrace of Hylda Prout in his library; and, mixed with that vision of infamy, was a memory of her letter that had been opened, whose opening he had denied to her.

And that snatch of her hand as from a toad's touch, that shrinking from the pressure of his arm, froze him back into his loneliness of misery. They remained silent, each in a corner, a world between them, till the cab was nearly at the door in Porchester Gardens. Then he could not help saying from the depths of a heavy heart:

"Probably I shall never see you again! It is good-by now; and no more Rosalind."

The words were uttered in a tone of such heart-rending sadness that they touched some nerve of pity in her. But she could find nothing to say, other than a quite irrelevant comment.

"I will tell my mother of your consideration for me. At least, we shall thank you."

"If ever you hear anything—of me—that looks black—" he tried to tell her, thinking of his coming marriage with Hylda Prout, but the explanation choked in his throat; he only managed to gasp in a quick appeal of sorrow: "Oh, remember me a little!"

The cab was at the door. She put out her hand, and he shook it; but did not offer to escort her inside the house. It was Furneaux who led her up the steps, and Osborne heard from within a shrill outcry from Mrs. Marsh. Furneaux waited until the door was closed. Then he rejoined Osborne. They went, without exchanging a syllable of talk, to Marlborough Street police-station, where Janoc and his sister were already lodged. Arrived there, Furneaux formally arrested him, "on suspicion," charged with the murder of Rose de Bercy.

"But why *now*?" asked Osborne again. "What has happened to implicate me now more than before?"

"Oh, many things have happened, and will happen, that as yet you know nothing of," said Furneaux, smiling at the stolid station inspector, a man incapable of any emotion, even of surprise, and Osborne was led away to be searched for concealed weapons, or poison, before being placed in a cell.

Half an hour afterwards Furneaux walked into Winter's quarters. His chief, writing hard, hardly glanced up, and for some time Furneaux stood looking at his one-time friend with the eyes of a scientist who contemplates a new fossil.

"Well, I have Osborne safe," he said at last.

"You have, have you?" muttered Winter, scribbling rapidly; but a flush of anger rose on his forehead, and he added: "It will cost you your reputation, my good fellow!"

"Is that all?" cried Furneaux mockingly. "Why, I was looking out for worse things than that!"

Winter threw down his pen.

"You informed me last night," he snarled, "that by this hour Miss Marsh would have returned to her home. I need not ask—"

"I have just taken her there," remarked the other coolly.

Winter was thoroughly nonplused. Everybody, everything, seemed to be mad. He was staring at Furneaux when Clarke entered. The newcomer's hat was tilted a little backward, and there was an air of business-like haste in him from the creak of his boot soles to the drops of perspiration shining on his brow. He contrived to hold himself back just long enough to say, "Hello, Furneaux!" and then his burden of news broke from him:

"Well, I've got Janoc under lock and key all right."

"Oh, *you've* got somebody, too, have you?" groaned Winter. "And on what charge, pray, have you collared Janoc?"

"Why, what a question!" cried Clarke. "Didn't I tell you, sir——?"

"So true," said Winter; "I had almost forgotten. *You*'ve grabbed Janoc, and the genius of Mr. Furneaux is sated by arresting Mr. Osborne—"

Clarke slapped his thigh vigorously, doubling up in a paroxysm of laughter.

"Osborne! Oh, not Osborne at this time of day!" He leered at Furneaux in comic wonder—he, who had never dared question aught done by the little man, save in the safe privacy of his thoughts.

"And I have arrested Pauline," said Winter in grim irony.

"Who has?" asked Clarke, suddenly agape.

"I, I say. Pauline is *my* prize. *I* wouldn't be left out in the cold." And he added bitterly: "We've all got one!—*all* guilty!—a lovely story it will make for the newspapers. I suppose, to keep up the screaming farce, that we each ought to contrive to have our prisoner tried in a different court!"

Clarke's hands went akimbo. He swelled visibly, grew larger, taller, and looked down from his Olympus at the others.

"But *I* never dream at night," he cried. "When *I* arrest a man for murder he is going to be hanged. You see, *Janoc has confessed*—that's all: he has confessed!"

Winter leaped up.

"Confessed!" he hissed, unable to believe his ears.

"That's just it," said Clarke—"confessed!"

"But Pauline has confessed, too!" Winter almost screamed, confronting his subordinate like an adversary.

And while Clarke shrank, and gaped in dumb wonder, Furneaux, looking from one to the other, burst out laughing. Never a word he said, but turned in his quick way to leave the room. He was already in the corridor when Winter shouted:

"Come back, Furneaux!"

"Not I," was the defiant retort.

"Come back, or I shall have you brought back!"

Winter was in a white rage, but Furneaux pressed on daringly, whistling a tune, and never looking round. Clarke, momentarily expecting the roof of Scotland Yard to fall in, gazed from Furneaux to Winter and from Winter to Furneaux until the diminutive Jersey man had vanished round an angle of a long passage.

But nothing happened. Winter was beaten to his knees, and he knew it.

XV. Clearing The Air

Winter was far too strong a man to remain long buried in the pit of humiliation into which Furneaux, aided unwittingly by Clarke, had cast him. The sounds of Furneaux's jaunty footsteps had barely died away before he shoved aside the papers on which he had been engaged previously, and reached across the table for a box of cigars.

He took one, and shoved the box towards Clarke, whose face was still glistening in evidence of his rush from Marlborough Street police-station.

"Here, you crack-pate!" he said, "smoke; it may clear your silly head."

"But I can't repeat too often that Janoc has confessed—*confessed*!" and Clarke's voice rose almost to a squeal on that final word.

"So has his sister confessed. In an hour or two, when the silence and horror of a cell have done their work, we shall have Osborne confessing, too. Oh, man, man, can't you see that Furneaux has twisted each of us round his little finger?"

"But—sir—"

"Yes, I know," cried Winter, in a fume of wrath and smoke. "Believe these foreign idiots and we shall be hearing of a masked tribunal, glistening with daggers, a brace of revolvers in every belt—a dozen or more infuriated conspirators, cloaked in gaberdines, gathered in a West End flat, while a red-headed woman harangues them. Furneaux has fooled us, I tell you—deliberately brought the Yard into discredit—made us the laughing-stock of the public. Oh, I shall never—"

He pulled himself up, for Clarke was listening with the ears of a rabbit. Luckily, the detective's ideas were too self-concentrated to extract much food for thought from these disjointed outpourings.

"I don't wish to seem wanting in respect, sir," he said doggedly, "but have you forgotten the diary? Why, Rose de Bercy herself wrote that she would be killed either by C. E. F. or Janoc. Now—"

"Did she mention Janoc?" interrupted Winter sharply. "In what passage? I certainly *have* forgotten that."

Clarke, stubborn as a mule, stuck to his point, though he felt that he had committed himself.

"Perhaps I did wrong," he growled savagely, "but I couldn't help myself. You were against me all along, sir—now, weren't you?"

No answer. Winter waited, and did not even look at him.

"What was I to do?" he went on in desperation. "You took me off the job just as I was getting keen in it. Then I happened upon Janoc, and found his sister, and when I came across that blacked-out name in the diary I scraped it and sponged it until I could read what was written beneath. The name was Janoc!"

"Was it?" said Winter, gazing at him at last with a species of contempt. "And to throw dust in my eyes—in the eyes of your superior officer—you inked it out again?"

"You wouldn't believe," muttered Clarke. "Why, you don't know half this story. I haven't told you yet how I found the daggers—"

"You don't say," mocked Winter.

"But I do, I did," cried Clarke, beside himself with excitement. "I took them out of Janoc's lodgings, and put them in a cab. I would have them in my hands this minute if some d—d thing hadn't occurred, some trick of fate—"

Winter stooped and unlocked a drawer in his writing-desk.

"Are these your daggers?" he demanded, though Clarke was shrewd enough, if in possession of his usual senses,   to   have   caught   the   note   of   suppressed astonishment in the Chief Inspector's voice, since this was the first he had heard of Furneaux's deliberate pilfering of the weapons from his colleague.

But something was singing in Clarke's ears, and his eyes were glued on the blades resting there in the drawer. Denial was impossible. He recognized them instantly, and all his assurance fled from that moment.

"Well, there!" he murmured, in a curiously broken voice. "I give in! I'm done! I'm a baby at this game. Next thing, I suppose, I'll be asked to resign—me, who found 'em, and the diary, and the letter telling Janoc not to kill her—yet."

He was looking so fixedly at the two daggers that he failed to see the smile of relief that flitted over Winter's face. Now, more than ever, the Chief Inspector realized that he was dealing with one of the most complex and subtle crimes which had come within his twenty years of experience. He was well versed in Furneaux's sardonic humor, and the close friendship that had existed between them ever since the little Jersey man joined the Criminal Investigation Department had alone stopped him from resenting it. It was clear now to his quick intelligence that Furneaux had actually planned nearly every discovery which either he himself or Clarke had made. Why? He could not answer. He was moving through a fog, blind-folded, with hands tied behind his back. Search where he would, he could not find a motive, unless, indeed, Furneaux was impelled by that strangest of all motives, a desire to convict himself. At any rate, he did not want Clarke to tread on the delicate ground that must now be covered before Furneaux was arrested, and the happy accident which had unlocked Clarke's tongue with regard to the diary would serve admirably to keep him well under control.

"Now, look here, Inspector Clarke," said Winter severely, after a pause that left the other in wretched suspense, "you have erred badly in this matter. For once, I am willing to overlook it—because—because you fancied you had a grievance. But, remember this—never again! Lack of candor is fatal to the best interests of the service. It is for me to decide which cases you shall take up and which you shall leave alone. You know perfectly well that if, by chance, information reaches you with regard to any inquiry which may prove useful to the man in charge of it, it is your duty to tell him everything. I say no more now. You understand me fully, I have no doubt. You must take it from me, without question or protest, that neither Janoc nor his sister was responsible for that crime. They may have been mixed up in it—in some manner now hidden from me—but they had no share in it personally. Still, seeing that you have worked so hard, I don't object to your presence while I prove that I am right. Come with me now to Marlborough Street. Mr. Osborne must be set at liberty, of course, but I shall confront your Anarchist friends with one another, and then you will see for yourself my grounds for being so positive as to their innocence."

"But you yourself arrested Pauline, sir," Clarke ventured to say.

"Don't be an ass!" was the cool rejoinder. "Could I refuse to arrest her? Suppose you told me now that you had killed the Frenchwoman, wouldn't I be compelled to arrest *you?*"

"Ha!" laughed Clarke, in solemn mirth, "what about C. E. F.? Wouldn't it be funny if he owned up to it?"

Winter answered not a word. He was busy locking the drawer and rolling down the front of the desk. But Clarke did not really mean what he had said. His mind was dwelling on the inscrutable mystery of the daggers which he had last held in his hands in Soho and now knew to be reposing in a locked desk in Scotland Yard.

"Would you mind telling me, sir, how you managed to get hold of 'em?" he asked.

Winter did not pretend ignorance.

"You will be surprised to hear that I myself took them, disinterred them, from the poor creature's grave in

Kensal Green Cemetery," he said.

Clarke's jaw dropped in the most abject amazement. The thing had a supernatural sound. He felt himself bewitched.

"From her grave?" he repeated.

"Yes."

"But who put 'em there?"

"Ah," said the other with a new note of sternness in his voice, "who but the murderer? But come, we are wasting time—that unfortunate Osborne must be half-demented. I suppose the Marlborough Street people will let him out on my authority. If not, I must get an order from the Commissioner. By gad, there will be a fiendish rumpus about this business before it is all settled!"

Clarke shivered. He saw a certain well-belovèd detective inspector figuring prominently in that "rumpus," and he was in no mind to seek a new career after passing the best part of his life in the C. I. D.

But at Marlborough Street another shock awaited the Chief. He and Clarke were entering the street in a taxi when Furneaux crooked a finger at him from the pavement. Winter could not, nay, he dared not, ignore that demand for an interview.

"Stop here!" he said to Clarke. Then he sprang out, and approached Furneaux.

"Well?" he snapped, "have you made up your mind to end this tragic farce?"

"I am not its chief buffoon," sneered Furneaux. "In fact, I am mainly a looker-on, but I do appreciate its good points to the full."

Winter waved aside these absurdities.

"I have come to free Mr. Osborne," he said. "I was rather hoping that your own sense of fair dealing, if you have any left—"

"Exactly what I thought," broke in the other. "That is why *I* am here. I hate correcting your mistakes, because I fancy it does you good to discover them for yourself. Still, it is a pity to spoil a good cause. Mere professional pride forces me to warn you against liberating Osborne."

"Man alive, you try me beyond endurance. Do you believe I don't know the truth—that Rose de Bercy was your wife—that *you* were in that museum before the murder—that *you*.... Oh, Furneaux, you wring it from me. Get a pistol, man, before it is too late."

"You mean that?" cried Furneaux, his eyes gleaming with a new fire.

"Heaven knows I do!"

"You want to be my friend, then, after all?"

"Friend! If you realized half the torture—"

"Pity!" mused Furneaux aloud. "Why didn't you speak sooner? So you would rather I committed suicide than be in your hands a prisoner?"

Winter then awoke to the consciousness that this extraordinary conversation was taking place in a crowded thoroughfare, within a stone's throw of a police-station in which lay three people charged with having committed the very crime he was tacitly accusing Furneaux of, while Clarke's ferret eyes must be resting on them with a suspicion already half-formed.

"I can say no more," he muttered gruffly. "One must forego friendship when duty bars the way. But if you have a grain of humanity left in your soul, come with me and release that unhappy young man—"

Some gush of emotion wrung Furneaux's face as if with a spasm of physical pain. He held out his right hand.

"Winter, forgive me, I have misjudged you," he said.

"Is it good-by?" came the passionate question.

"No, not good-by. It is an alliance, Winter, a wiping of the slate. You don't understand, perhaps, that we are both to blame. But you can take my hand, old man. There is no stain of blood on it. I did not murder my wife. I am her avenger, her pitiless, implacable avenger—so pitiless, so implacable, that I may have erred in my harshness. For Heaven's sake, Winter, believe me, and take my hand!"

The man's magnetism was irresistible. Despite the

crushing weight of proof accumulated against him, the claims of old friendship were not to be ignored. Winter took the proffered hand and squeezed it with a vehemence that not only showed the tension of his feelings but also brought tears of real anguish to Furneaux's eyes.

"I only asked you for a friendly grip, Winter," he complained. "You have been more than kind. No matter what happens, don't offer to shake hands with me again for twelve months at least."

There was no comprehending him, and Winter abandoned the effort. Moreover, Clarke's puzzled brows were bent on them.

"An alliance implies confidence," he said, and the official mask fell on his bluff features. "If you can honestly—"

Furneaux laughed, with just a faint touch of that impish humor that the other knew so well.

"Not Winter, but Didymus!" he cried. "Well, then, let us proceed to the confounding of poor Clarke. *Peste!* he deserves a better fate, for he has worked like a Trojan. But leave Osborne to me. Have no fear—I shall explain, a little to him, all to you."

Clarke writhed with jealousy when Winter beckoned to him. While his chief was paying the cabman, he jeered at Furneaux.

"I had a notion—" he began, but the other caught his arm confidentially.

"I was just telling the guv'nor how much we owe to you in this Feldisham Mansions affair," he said. "You were on the right track all the time. You've the keenest nose in the Yard, Clarke. You can smell an Anarchist through the stoutest wall ever built. Now, not a word! You'll soon see how important your investigations have been."

Clarke was overwhelmed by a new flood. Never before had Furneaux praised him, unless in some ironic phrase that galled the more because he did not always extract its hidden meaning. He blinked with astonishment.

With a newborn trust, which he would have failed ignominiously to explain in words, Winter led his colleagues to Marlborough Street police-station. There, after a brief but earnest colloquy with the station inspector, he asked that Janoc and his sister should be brought to the inspector's office.

Janoc came first, pale, languid, high-strung, but evidently prepared to be led to his death that instant.

He looked at the four men, three in plain clothes and one in uniform, with a superb air of dignity, almost of superiority; in silence he awaited the inquisition which he supposed he would be compelled to undergo, but when no word was spoken—when even that phantom of evil, Clarke, paid no heed to him, he grew manifestly uneasy.

At last steps were heard, the door opened, and Pauline Dessaulx entered. Of course, this brother and sister were Gauls to the finger-tips. Each screamed, each flew to the other's arms; they raved; they wept, and laughed, and uttered incoherent words of utmost affection.

Winter indulged them a few seconds. Then he broke in on their transports.

"Now, Janoc," he said brusquely, "have done with this acting! Why have you given the police so much trouble?"

"Monsieur, I swear—"

"Oh, have done with your swearing! Your sister didn't kill Mademoiselle de Bercy. She wouldn't kill a fly. Come, Pauline, own up!"

"Monsieur," faltered the girl, "I—I—"

"You took the guilt on your shoulders in order to shield your brother?"

Wild-eyed, distraught, she looked from the face of the man who seemed to peer into her very soul to that other face so dear to her. She knew not what to say. Was this stern-visaged representative of the law merely torturing her with a false hope? Dared she say "Yes," or must she persist in self-accusation?

"Janoc," thundered Winter, "you ought to be ashamed of yourself. Don't you see how she is suffering for your sake? Tell her, then, that you are as innocent as she of this murder?"

The dreamer, the man who would reform an evil world by force, had the one great quality demanded of a leader—he knew a man when he met him. He turned now to Pauline.

"My sister," he said in French, "this gentleman can be trusted. He is no trickster. I had no hand in the slaying of the traitress, just though her death might be."

"Ah, *Dieu merci!*" she breathed, and fainted.

The police matron was summoned, and the Frenchwoman soon regained consciousness. Meanwhile, Janoc admitted readily enough that he did really believe in his sister's acceptance of the dread mission imposed on her by the revolutionary party in Russia.

"Rose de Bercy was condemned, and my sweet Pauline, alas! was deputed to be her executioner," he said. "We had waited long for the hour, and the dagger was ready, though I, too, distrusted my sister's courage. Then came an urgent letter from St. Petersburg that the traitress was respited until a certain list found among her papers was checked—"

"Found?" questioned Winter.

"By Pauline," said Janoc.

"Ah, stolen?"

Janoc brushed aside the substituted word as a quibble.

"Conceive my horror when I heard of the murder!" he cried with hands flung wide and eyes that rolled. "I was sure that Pauline had mistaken the instructions—"

"Where is the St. Petersburg letter?" broke in Furneaux.

"Sapristi! You will scarce credit. It was taken from me by a man—a Russian agent he must have been—one night in the Fraternal Club, Soho—"

"Clarke, produce it," said Furneaux, grinning.

Clarke flushed, grew white, nervously thumbed some papers in a pocketbook, and handed to Winter the letter which commenced: "St. Petersburg says ..." and ended: "You will see to it that she to whose hands vengeance has been intrusted shall fail on the 3d."

Winter read, and frowned. Furneaux, too, read.

"The 3d!" he muttered. "Just Heaven, what a fatal date to her!"

"What was I to think?" continued Janoc. "Antonio shared my view. He met Pauline at the Exhibition, and was ready, if necessary, to vouch for her presence there at the time Rose de Bercy went to her reckoning; but he is not in the inner—he had not heard of the Petersburg order."

"Yet he, and the rest of your gang, were prepared to let Mr. Osborne hang for this crime," said Winter, surveying the conspirator with a condemning eye. But his menace or scorn was alike to Janoc, who threw out his arms again.

"*Cré nom!*" he cried, "why not? Is he not a rich bourgeois like the rest? He and his class have crushed us without mercy for many a century. What matter if he were hanged by mistake? He could be spared—my Pauline could not. He is merely a rich one, my Pauline is a martyr to the cause!"

"Listen to me, Janoc," said Winter fiercely. "Spout what rubbish you please in your rotten club, but if ever you dare again to plot—even to plot, mind you—any sort of crime against life or property in this free country, I shall crush you like a beetle—like a beetle, do you hear, you wretched—insect! Now, get out!"

"Monsieur, my sister?"

"Wait outside there till she comes. Then leave England, the pair of you, or you will try what hard labor in a British prison can do for your theories."

Janoc bowed.

"Monsieur," he said, "a prison has made me what I am."

Pauline was candid as her brother. She had, in truth, misunderstood the respite given to her mistress, and meant to kill her on the night of the 3d. The visit to the Exhibition was of her own contriving. She had got rid of her English acquaintance, the cook, very easily after meeting Antonio by appointment. Then she left him, without giving a reason, and hurried back to the mansions, where, owing to her intimate knowledge of the internal arrangements, she counted on entering and leaving the flat unseen. She did actually succeed in her mission, but found Rose de Bercy lying dead.

On the floor, close to the body, was a dagger, and she had no doubt whatever that her brother had acted in her stead, so she picked up the weapon, secreted it with the dagger given her in readiness for the crime, and took the first opportunity of hiding herself, lest the mere fact that Janoc was seen in her company should draw suspicion towards him.

"Ah, but the lace? What of the piece of blood-stained lace?" demanded Furneaux.

"I wished to make sure, monsieur," was the astounding reply. "Had she not been dead, but merely wounded, I—*Eh, bien!* I tore her dress open, in order to feel if her heart was beating, and the bit of lace remained in my hand. I was so excited that I hardly knew what I was doing. I took it away. Afterwards, when Antonio said that the police were cooling in their chase of Osborne, I gave it to him; he told me he could use it to good effect."

"Phew!" breathed Winter, "you're a pretty lot of cutthroats, I must say. Why did you keep the daggers and the diary, sweet maid?"

"The knife that rid us of a traitress was sacred. I thought the diary might be useful to the—to our friends."

"Yet you gave it to Mr. Clarke without any demur?"

The girl shot a look at Clarke in which fright was mingled with hatred.

"He—he—I was afraid of him," she stammered.

Winter opened the door.

"There is your brother," he said. "Be off, both of you. Take my advice and leave England to-night."

They went forth, hand in hand, in no wise cast down by the loathing they had inspired. Clarke looked far more miserable than they, for by their going he had lost the prize of his life.

"Now for Osborne," whispered Furneaux. "Leave him to me, Winter. Trust me implicitly for five minutes—that is all."

Osborne was brought in by the station inspector, that human ledger who would record without an unnecessary word the name of the Prime Minister or the Archbishop of Canterbury on any charge preferred against either by a responsible member of the force. The young American was calm now, completely self-possessed, disdainful of any ignominy that might be inflicted on him. He did not even glance at Furneaux, but nodded to Winter.

"Your assurances are seemingly of little value," he said coldly.

"Mr. Winter is quite blameless," snapped Furneaux, obviously nettled by the implied reproof. "Please attend to me, Mr. Osborne—this affair rests wholly between you and me. Learn now, for the first time, I imagine, that Rose de Bercy was my wife."

Osborne did truly start at hearing that remarkable statement. Clarke's mouth literally fell open; even the uniformed inspector was stirred, and began to pare a quill pen with a phenomenally sharp knife, this being the only sign of excitement he had ever been known to exhibit.

"Yes, unhappily for her and me, we were married in Paris soon after she ran away from home," said Furneaux. "I—I thought—we should be happy. She had rare qualities, Mr. Osborne; perhaps you discovered some of them, and they fascinated you as they fascinated me. But—she had others, which *I* learnt to my sorrow, while *you* were spared. I cannot explain further at this moment.

I have only to say that you are as free from the guilt of her death—as *I* am!"

Winter alone was conscious of a queer note in the little man's voice as he dwelt on the comparison. He seemed to be searching for some simile of wildest improbability, and to have hit upon himself as supplying it. But Osborne was in no mood for bewilderment. He cared absolutely nothing about present or future while the horrible past still held the pall it had thrown on his prospects of bliss with Rosalind.

"In that event, one might ask why I am here," he said quietly. "Not that I am concerned in the solving of the riddle. You have done your worst, Mr. Furneaux. You can inflict no deeper injury on me. If you have any other vile purpose to serve by telling me these things, by all means go right ahead."

Furneaux's eyes glinted, and his wizened cheeks showed some token of color, but he kept his voice marvelously under control.

"In time you will come to thank me, Mr. Osborne," he said. "To-day you are bitter, and I am not surprised at it, but you could never have been happy in your marriage with Miss Rosalind Marsh while the shadow of suspicion clung to you. Please do not forget that the world believes you killed Rose de Bercy. If you walked forth now into Regent Street, and the word went around that you were there, a thousand people would mob you in a minute, while ten thousand would be prepared to lynch you within ten minutes. I have played with you, I admit— with others, too, and now I am sorry—to a certain extent. But in this case, I was at once detective, and judge, and executioner. If you wantonly transferred your love from the dead woman to the living one, I cared not a straw what you suffered or how heavily you were punished. That phase has passed. To-day you have justified yourself. Within twenty-four hours you will be free to marry Rosalind Marsh, because your name will have lost the smirch now placed on it, while your promise to Hylda

Prout will be dissolved. But for twenty-four hours you must remain here, apparently a prisoner, in reality as much at liberty as any man in London. Yes, I vouch for my words—" for at last wonder and hope were dawning in Osborne's eyes—"my chief, Mr. Winter, will tell you that I have never spoken in this manner without making good what I have said—never, I repeat. If I could spare you the necessity of passing a night in a cell I would do so; but I cannot. You are the decoy duck for the wild creature that I mean to lay hands on before another day has closed. Make yourself as comfortable as possible—the inspector will see to that—but I *must* keep you here, a prisoner in all outward semblance. Are you willing?"

"For Heaven's sake—" began Osborne.

"For Rosalind's sake, too," said Furneaux gravely. "No, I can answer no questions. She has more to bear than you. She does not know what to believe, whom to trust, whereas you have my solemn assurance that all will soon be well with both you and her. You see, I am not craving your forgiveness—yet. It suffices that I have forgiven *you*, since your tribulation will end quickly, whereas mine remains for the rest of my days. I *did* love Rose de Bercy: you did not.... Ah, bah! I am growing sentimental. Winter, have you ever seen me weep? No; then gag me if you hear me talking in this strain again. Come, I have much to tell you. Good-day, Mr. Osborne. The hours will soon fly; by this time to-morrow you will be gay, light-hearted, ready to shout your joy from the housetops—ready even to admit that a detective may be bothered with that useless incubus—a heart."

Osborne took a step towards him, but Furneaux sprang out and banged the door. Winter caught the millionaire by the shoulder.

"I am as thoroughly in the dark as you," he said. "Perhaps not, though. I have a glimmer of light; you, too, will begin to see dimly when you have collected your thoughts. But you must let Furneaux have his way. It may not be your way—it certainly is not mine—but he never fails when he promises, and, at any rate, you must now be sure that no manner of doubt rests in the minds of the police where you are concerned. It is possible, after Furneaux and I have gone into this thing fully, that you may be released to-night—"

"Mr. Winter," cried Osborne, in whose veins the blood was coursing tumultuously, "let that strange man justify his words concerning Miss Marsh, and I shall remain here a month if that will help."

XVI. Wherein Two Women Take The Field

Some tears, some tea, a bath, a change of clothing—where is the woman who will not vie with the Phoenix under such conditions, especially if she be sound in mind and limb? An hour after her arrival at Porchester Gardens, Rosalind was herself again, a somewhat pale and thin Rosalind, to be sure, but each moment regaining vigor, each moment taking huge strides back to the normal.

Of course, her ordered thoughts dwelt more and more with Osborne, but with clear thinking came a species of confusion that threatened to overwhelm her anew in a mass of contradictions. If ever a man loved a woman then Osborne loved her, yet she had seen him in the arms of that dreadful creature, Hylda Prout. If ever a man had shown devotion by word and look, then Osborne was devoted to her, yet he had taken leave of her with the manner of one who was going to his doom. Ah, he spoke of "a felon's cell." Was that it? Was it true what the world was saying—that he had really killed Rose de Bercy? No, that infamy she would never believe. Yet Furneaux had arrested him—Furneaux, the strange little man who seemed ever to say with his lip what his heart did not credit.

During those weary hours in Poland Street, when she was not dozing or faint with anxiety, she had often recalled Furneaux's queer way of conducting an inquiry. She knew little or nothing of police methods, yet she was sure that British detectives did not badger witnesses with denunciations of the suspected person. In newspaper reports, too, she had read of clever lawyers who defended those charged with the commission of a crime; why, then, was Osborne undefended; what had become of the solicitor who appeared in his behalf at the inquest? Unfortunately, she had no friend of ripe experience to whom she could appeal in London, but she determined, before that day closed, to seek those two, the solicitor and Furneaux, bidding the one protect Osborne's interests, and demanding of the other an explanation of his gross failure to safeguard her when she was actually carrying out his behests.

Mrs. Marsh, far more feeble and unstrung than her daughter, was greatly alarmed when Rosalind announced her intention.

"My dear one," she sobbed, "I shall lose you again. How can you dream of running fresh risk of meeting those terrible beings who have already wreaked their vengeance on you?"

"But, mother darling, you shall come with me—there are lives at stake—"

"Of what avail are two women against creatures like these Anarchists?"

"We shall go to Scotland Yard and obtain police protection. Failing that, we shall hire men armed with guns to act as our escort. Mother, I did not die in that den of misery, but I shall die now of impotent wrath if I remain here inactive and let Mr. Osborne lie in prison for my sake."

"For your sake? Rosalind? After what you have told me?"

"Oh, it is true, true! I feel it here," and an eager hand pressed close to her heart. "My brain says, 'You are foolish—why not believe your eyes, your ears?' but my heart bids me be up and doing, for the night cometh when no man can work, and I shall dream of death and the grave if I sleep this day without striking one blow for the man that loves me."

"Yet he said—"

"Bear with me, mother dear! I cannot explain, I can

only feel. A woman's intuition may sometimes be trusted when logic points inexorably to the exact opposite of her beliefs. And this is a matter that calls for a woman's wit. See how inextricably women are tangled in the net which has caught Osborne in its meshes. A woman was killed, a woman found the poor thing's body, a woman gave the worst evidence against Osborne, a woman has sacrificed all womanliness to snatch him from me. Ah, where is Pauline Dessaulx? She, too, is mixed up in it. Has she discovered the loss of the daggers? Has she fled?"

Rosalind rose to her feet like one inspired, and Mrs. Marsh, fearing for her reason, stammered brokenly her willingness to go anywhere and do anything that might relieve the strain. When her daughter began to talk of "daggers" she was really alarmed. The girl had alluded to them more than once, but poor Mrs. Marsh's troubled brain associated "daggers" with Anarchists. That any such murderous-sounding weapons should be secreted in a servant's bedroom at Porchester Gardens, be found there by Rosalind, and carried by her all over London in a cab, never entered her mind. Perhaps the sight of Pauline would in itself have a soothing effect, since one could not persist in such delusions when the demure Frenchwoman, in the cap and apron of respectable domestic service, came in answer to the bell. So Mrs. Marsh rang: and another housemaid appeared.

"Please send Pauline here," said the white-faced mother.

"Pauline is out, ma'm," came the answer.

"Will she return soon?"

"I don't know, ma'm—I—I think she has run away."

"Run away!"

Two voices repeated those sinister words. To Rosalind they brought a dim memory of something said by Janoc, to Mrs. Marsh dismay. The three were gazing blankly at each other when the clang of a distant bell was heard.

"That's the front door," exclaimed the maid. "Perhaps Pauline has come back."

She hurried away, and returned, breathless.

"It isn't Pauline, ma'm, but a lady to see Miss Rosalind."

"What lady?"

"She wouldn't give a name, miss; she says she wants to see you perticular."

"Send her here.... Now, mother, don't be alarmed. This is not Soho. If you wish it, I shall get someone to wait in the hall until we learn our mysterious visitor's business."

Most certainly, the well-dressed and elegant woman whom the servant ushered into the room was not of a type calculated to cause a pang of distrust in any household in Porchester Gardens. She was dressed quietly but expensively, and, notwithstanding the heat of summer, so heavily veiled that her features were not recognizable until she raised her veil. Then a pair of golden-brown eyes flashed triumphantly at the startled Rosalind, and Hylda Prout said:

"May I have a few words in private with you, Miss Marsh?"

"You can have nothing to say to me that my mother may not hear," said Rosalind curtly.

The visitor smiled, and looked graciously at Mrs. Marsh.

"Ah, I am pleased to have this opportunity of meeting you," she said. "You may have heard of me. I am Hylda Prout." ... Then, seeing the older woman's perplexity, she added: "Since you do not seem to know me by name, let me explain that Mr. Rupert Osborne, of whom you must have heard a good deal, is my promised husband."

Mrs. Marsh might be ill and worried; but she was a well-bred lady to the marrow, and she realized instantly that the stranger's politeness covered a studied insult to her daughter.

"Has Mr. Osborne sent you as his ambassador?" she asked.

"No, he could not: he is in prison. But your daughter and I have met under conditions that compel me to ask her now not to interfere in the efforts I shall make to secure his release."

"Please go!" broke in Rosalind, and she moved as if to summon a servant.

"I am not here from choice," sneered Hylda. "I have really come to plead for Mr. Osborne. If you care for him as you say you do I want you to understand two things: first, that your pursuit is in vain, since he has given his word to marry me within a week, and, secondly, that any further interference in his affairs on your part may prove disastrous to him. You cannot pretend that I have not warned you. Had you taken my advice the other day, Rupert would not now be under arrest."

Mrs. Marsh was sallow with indignation, but Rosalind, though tingling in every fiber, controlled herself sufficiently to utter a dignified protest.

"You had something else in your mind than Mr. Osborne's safety in coming here today: I do not believe one word you have said," she cried.

"Oh, but you shall believe. Wait one short week—"

"I shall not wait one short hour. Mr. Osborne's arrest is a monstrous blunder, and I am going this instant to demand his release."

"He has not taken you into his confidence, it would seem. Were it not for his promise to me you would still be locked in your den at Poland Street."

"Some things may be purchased at a price so degrading that a man pays and remains silent. If Mr. Osborne won my liberty by the loss of his self-respect I am truly sorry for him, but the fact, if it is a fact, only strengthens my resolution to appeal to the authorities in his behalf."

"You can achieve nothing, absolutely nothing," shrilled Hylda vindictively.

"I shall try to do much, and accomplish far more, perhaps, than you imagine."

"You will only succeed in injuring him."

"At any rate, I shall have obeyed the dictates of my

conscience, whereas your vile purposes have ever been directed by malice. How dare you talk of serving him! Since that poor woman was struck dead by some unknown hand you have been his worst enemy. In the guise of innocent friendship you supplied the police with the only real evidence they possess against him. Probably you are responsible now for his arrest, which could not have happened had I been at liberty during the past two days. Go, and vent your spite as you will—no word of yours can deter me from raising such a storm as shall compel Mr. Osborne's release!"

For a second or two those golden-brown eyes blazed with a fire that might well have appalled Rosalind could she have read its hidden significance. During a tick of the clock she was in mortal peril of her life, but Hylda Prout, though partially insane, was not yet in that trance of the wounded tiger which recks not of consequences so that it gluts its rage.

Mrs. Marsh, really frightened, rushed to the electric bell, and the jar of its summons, faintly audible, seemed to banish the grim specter that had entered the room, though unseen by other eyes than those of the woman who dreamed of death even while she glowered at her rival. Her bitter tongue managed to outstrip her murderous thoughts in the race back to ordered thought.

"You are powerless," she taunted Rosalind, "but, like every other discarded lover, you cling to delusions. Now I shall prove to you how my strength compares with your weakness. You speak of appealing to the authorities. That means Scotland Yard, I suppose. Very well. I, too, shall go there, in your very company, if you choose, and it will then be seen which of us two can best help Mr. Osborne."

The housemaid appeared.

"Please show this person out," said Rosalind.

"My carriage is waiting—Rupert's carriage," said Hylda.

"After she has gone, Lizzie," said Rosalind to the maid, "kindly get me a taxicab."

Porchester Gardens is well out to the west, so the taxicab, entered in a fever of haste by Rosalind and her mother, raced ahead of Osborne's bays in the flight to Westminster. Hylda Prout had experienced no difficulty in securing the use of the millionaire's carriage. She went to his Mayfair flat, paralyzed Jenkins by telling him of his master's arrest, assured him, in the same breath, that she alone could prove Osborne's innocence, and asked that all the resources of the household should be placed at her disposal, since Mr. Osborne meant to marry her within a few days. Now, Jenkins had seen things that brought this concluding statement inside the bounds of credibility, so he became her willing slave in all that concerned Osborne.

Winter was sitting in his office, with Furneaux straddled across a chair in one corner, when Johnson, the young policeman who was always at the Chief Inspector's beck and call, entered.

"Two ladies to see you, sir," he said.

Furneaux's eyes sparkled, but Winter took the two cards and read: "Mrs. Marsh; Miss Rosalind Marsh."

"Bring them here," he said.

"I rather expected the other one first," grinned Furneaux, who was now evidently on the best of terms with his Chief.

"Perhaps she won't show up. She must be deep, crafty as a fox, or she could never have humbugged me in the way you describe."

"My dear Winter, coincidence is the best dramatist yet evolved. You were beaten by coincidence."

"But you were not," and the complaint fell querulously from the lips of one who was almost unrivaled in the detection of crime.

"You forget that *I* supplied the coincidence. Clarke, too, blundered with positive genius. I assure you that, in your shoes, I must have acted with—with inconceivable folly."

"Thank you," said Winter grimly.

Rosalind and her mother came in. Both ladies had been weeping, but the girl's eyes shone with another light than that of tears when she cried vehemently:

"You are the responsible official here, I understand. I have no word for *that* man," and she transfixed Furneaux with a tragic finger, "but I do appeal to someone who may have a sense of decency—"

"You have come to see me about Mr. Osborne?" broke in Winter, for Rosalind's utterance was choked by a sob.

"Yes, of course. Are you aware—"

"I am aware of everything, Miss Marsh. Please be seated; and you, too, Mrs. Marsh. Mr. Osborne is in no danger whatsoever. I cannot explain, but you must trust the police in this matter."

"Ah, so *he* said," and Rosalind shot a fiery glance at the unabashed Furneaux.

"Seen anybody?" he asked, with an amiable smirk.

"What do you mean?"

"Has anybody been gloating over Mr. Osborne's arrest?"

For the life of her, Rosalind could not conceal the surprise caused by this question. She even smothered her resentment in her eagerness.

"Mr. Osborne's typist, a woman named Hylda Prout, has been to see me," she cried.

"Excellent! What did she say?"

"Everything that a mean heart could suggest. But you will soon hear her statements. She is coming here herself, or, at least, so she said."

"Great Scott!"

Furneaux sprang up, and ran to the bell. For some reason which neither Mrs. Marsh nor her daughter could fathom, the mercurial little Jersey man was wild with excitement; even Winter seemed to be disturbed beyond expression. Johnson came, and Furneaux literally leaped at him.

"Ring up that number, quick! You know exactly what to say—and do!"

Johnson saluted and vanished again; Winter had chosen him for his special duties because he never uttered a needless word. Still, these tokens of activity in the police headquarters did not long repress the tumult in Rosalind's breast.

"If, as you tell me, Mr. Osborne is in no danger—" she began; but Winter held up an impressive hand.

"You are here in order to help him," he said gravely. "Pray believe that we appreciate your feelings most fully. If this girl, Hylda Prout, is really on her way here we have not a moment to lose. No more appeals, I beg of you, Miss Marsh. Tell us every word that passed between you and her. You can speak all the more frankly if I assure you that Mr. Furneaux, my colleague, has acted throughout in Mr. Osborne's interests. Were it not for him this young gentleman, who, I understand, will soon become your husband, would never have been cleared of the stigma of a dreadful crime.... No, pardon me, not a syllable on that subject.... What did Hylda Prout say? Why is she coming to Scotland Yard?"

Impressed in spite of herself, Rosalind gave a literal account of the interview at Porchester Gardens. She was burning to deliver her soul on matters that appeared to be so much more important, such as the finding and loss of the daggers, the strange behavior of Pauline Dessaulx, the statement, now fiery bright in her mind, made by Janoc when he spoke of his sister's guilt—but, somehow, the tense interest displayed by the two detectives in Hylda Prout's assertions overbore all else, and Rosalind proved herself a splendid witness, one able to interpret moods and glances as well as to record the spoken word.

Even while she spoke a lurid fancy flashed through her brain.

"Oh, gracious Heaven!" she cried. "Can it be—"

Winter rose and placed a hand on her shoulder.

"You have endured much, Miss Marsh," he said in a voice of grave sympathy. "Now, I trust to your intelligence and power of self-command. No matter what suspicions you may have formed, you must hide them. Possibly, Mr. Furneaux or I may speak or act within the next half-hour in a manner that you deem prejudicial to Mr. Osborne. I want you to express your resentment in any way you may determine, short of leaving us. Do you understand? We shall act as on the stage; you must do the same. You need no cue from us. Defend Mr. Osborne; urge his innocence; threaten us with pains and penalties; do anything, in short, that will goad Hylda Prout into action in his behalf for fear lest you may prevail where she has failed."

A knock was heard at the door. He sank back into his seat.

"Do you promise?" he muttered.

"Yes," she breathed.

"Come in!" cried Winter, and the imperturbable Johnson ushered in Hylda Prout. Even in the storm and stress of contending emotions Rosalind knew that there was a vital difference between the reception accorded to the newcomer and that given to her mother and herself. They had been announced, their names scrutinized in advance, as it were, whereas Hylda Prout's arrival was expected, provided for; in a word, the policeman on guard had his orders and was obeying them.

"Well, this *is* a surprise, Miss Prout," exclaimed Furneaux before anyone else could utter a word.

"Is it?" she asked, smiling scornfully at Rosalind.

"Quite. Miss Marsh told us, of course, of your visit, and I suppose that your appearance here is inspired by the same motive as hers. My chief, Mr. Winter, has just been telling her that the law brooks no interference, yet she persists in demanding Mr. Osborne's release. She cannot succeed in obtaining it, unless she brings a positive order from the Home Secretary—"

"I shall get it," vowed Rosalind, to whom it seemed that Furneaux's dropped voice carried a subtle hint.

"Try, by all means," said Furneaux blandly. "Nevertheless, I strongly advise you ladies, all three, to go home and let matters take their course."

"Never!" cried Rosalind valiantly. "You must either free Mr. Osborne to-night or I drive straight from this office to the House of Commons. I have friends there who will secure me a hearing by the Home Secretary."

Furneaux glanced inquiringly at Winter, whose hand was stroking his chin as if in doubt. Hylda Prout took a step nearer the Chief Inspector. Her dress brushed against the drawer which contained the daggers, and one of those grewsome blades had pierced Rose de Bercy's brain through the eye.

"The Home Secretary is merely an official like the rest of you," she said bitingly. "Miss Marsh may appeal to whom she thinks fit, but the charge against Mr. Osborne will keep him in custody until it is heard by a magistrate. Nothing can prevent that—nothing—unless—" and her gaze dwelt warily on Furneaux for a fraction of an instant—"unless the police themselves are convinced that the evidence on which they rely is so flimsy that they run the risk of public ridicule by bringing it forward."

"Ha! ha!" laughed Furneaux knowingly.

"I think I am wasting time here," cried Rosalind, half rising.

"One moment, I pray you," put in Winter. "There is some force in Miss Prout's remarks, but I am betraying no secret in saying that Mr. Osborne's apparently unshakable alibi can be upset, while we have the positive identification of at least three people who saw him on the night of the crime."

"Meaning the housekeeper, the driver of the taxicab, and the housemaid at Feldisham Mansions?" said Hylda coolly, and quite ignoring Rosalind's outburst.

"At least those," admitted Winter.

"Are there others, then?"

"Really, Miss Prout, this is most irregular. We are not trying Mr. Osborne in this room."

"I see there is nothing for it but to carry my plea for justice to the Home Secretary," cried Rosalind, acting as she thought best in obedience to a lightning glance from

Furneaux. "Come, mother, we shall soon prove to these legal-minded persons that they cannot juggle away a man's liberty to gratify their pride—and spite."

Hylda's eyes took fire at that last word.

"Go to your Home Secretary," she said with measured venom. "Much good may it do you! While *you* are being dismissed with platitudes *I* shall have rescued my affianced husband from jail."

"Dear me! this is most embarrassing. Your affianced husband?"

Furneaux cackled out each sentence, and looked alternately at Hylda and Rosalind. There was no mistaking his meaning. He implied that the one woman was callously appropriating a man who was the acknowledged suitor of the other.

Hylda laughed shrilly.

"That is news to you, Mr. Furneaux," she cried. "Yet I thought you were so clever as to be almost omniscient. Come now with me, and I shall prove to you that the so-called identification of Mr. Osborne by Hester Bates and Campbell, the chauffeur, is a myth. The hysterical housemaid I leave to you."

Winter leaned back in his chair and waved an expostulating hand.

"'Pon my honor, this would be amusing if it were not so terribly serious for Osborne," he vowed.

"If that is all, I prefer to depend on the Home Secretary," said Rosalind.

"Let her go," purred Hylda contemptuously. "I can make good my boast, but she cannot."

"Boasting is of no avail in defeating a charge of murder," said Furneaux. "Before we even begin to take you seriously, Miss Prout, we must know what you actually mean by your words."

"I mean this—that I, myself, will appear before Hester Bates in such guise that she will swear it was me, and not Mr. Osborne, whom she saw on the stairs that night. If that does not suffice, I shall meet Campbell at the corner

of Berkeley Street, if you can arrange for his presence
there, and tell him to drive me to Feldisham Mansions,
and he will swear that it was I, and not Mr. Osborne, who
gave him that same order on the night of the third of
July. Surely, if I accomplish so much, you will set Rupert
at liberty. Believe me, I am not afraid that you will
commit the crowning blunder of arresting *me* for the
murder, after having arrested Janoc, and his sister, *and*
Rupert."

Winter positively started. So did Furneaux. Evidently
they were perturbed by the extent of her information.
Hylda saw the concern depicted on their faces; she
laughed low, musically, full-throated.

"Well, is it a bargain?" she taunted them.

"Of course—" began Winter, and stopped.

"There is no denying the weakness of our position if
you can do all that," said Furneaux suavely.

"Pray do not let me detain you from visiting the House
of Commons," murmured Hylda to Rosalind.

"Perhaps, in the circumstances, you had better wait
till to-morrow," said Winter, rising and looking hard at
Rosalind.

This man had won her confidence, and she felt that
she was in the presence of a tragedy, yet it was hard to
yield in the presence of her rival. Tears filled her eyes,
and she bowed her head to conceal them.

"Come, mother," she said brokenly. "We are powerless
here, it would seem."

"Allow me to show you the way out," said Winter, and
he bustled forward.

In the corridor, when the door was closed, he caught
an arm of each and bent in a whisper.

"Furneaux was sure she would try some desperate
move," he breathed. "Rest content now, Miss Marsh. If all
goes well, your ill-used friend will be with you to-night.
Treat him well. He deserves it. He did not open your
letter. He sacrificed himself in every way for your sake.
He even promised to marry that woman, that arch-fiend,

in order to rescue you from Janoc. So, believe him, for he is a true man, the soul of honor, and tell him from me that he owes some share of the restitution of his good name in the eyes of the public to your splendid devotion during the past few minutes."

Not often did the Chief Inspector unbend in this fashion. There was no ambiguity in his advice. He meant what he said, and said it so convincingly that Rosalind was radiantly hopeful when she drove away with her mother.

XVII. The Closing Scene

It was a scared and worried-looking Jenkins who admitted Hylda Prout and the two detectives to Osborne's flat in Clarges Street, Mayfair. These comings and goings of police officers were disconcerting, to put it mildly, and an event had happened but a few minutes earlier which had sorely ruffled his usually placid acceptance of life as it presented itself. Still, the one dominant thought in his mind was anxiety in his master's behalf, and, faithful to its promptings, he behaved like an automaton.

Hylda carried herself with the regal air of one who was virtual mistress of the house. She had invited the two men to share her carriage, and there was an assured authority in her voice when she now directed the gray-headed butler to show them into the library while she went upstairs to Mr. Osborne's dressing-room.

"And, by the way, Jenkins," she added, "tell Mrs. Bates to come to these gentlemen. They wish to ask her a few questions."

"Yes, bring Mrs. Bates," said Furneaux softly. "Don't let her come alone. She might be frightened, and snivel, being a believer in ghosts, whereas we wish her to remain calm."

Jenkins thought he understood, but said nothing. Hylda Prout sped lightly up the stairs, and when Jenkins came with the housekeeper, Furneaux crept close to him, pointed to a screened doorway leading to the kitchen quarters, and murmured the one word:

"There!"

At once he turned to Mrs. Bates and engaged her in animated chatter, going so far as to warn her that the police were trying an experiment which might definitely set at rest all doubts as to Mr. Osborne's innocence, so she must be prepared to see someone descend the stairs who might greatly resemble the person she saw ascending them on the night of the murder.

The maisonette rented by the young millionaire was not constructed on the lines associated with the modern self-contained flat. It consisted of the ground floor, and first story of a mid-Victorian mansion, while the kitchen was in a basement. As it happened to be the property of a peer who lived next door—a sociable person who entertained largely—these lower stories were completely shut off from the three upper ones, which were thrown into the neighboring house, thus supplying the landlord with several bedrooms and bathrooms that Osborne did not need. As a consequence, the entrance hall and main staircase were spacious, and the staircase in particular was elaborate, climbing to a transverse corridor in two fine flights, of which the lower one sprang from the center of the hall and the upper led at a right angle from a broad half-landing.

Anyone coming down this upper half of the stairs could be seen full face from the screened door used by the servants: but when descending the lower half, the view from the same point would be in profile.

At present, however, the curtains were drawn tightly across the passage, and the only occupants of the hall and library were the two detectives, Jenkins, and Mrs. Bates.

Hylda Prout did not hurry. If she were engaged in a masquerade which should achieve its object she evidently meant to leave nothing to chance, and a woman cannot exchange her costume for a man's without experiencing difficulty with her hair, especially when she is endowed by nature with a magnificent chevelure.

Jenkins returned from the mission imposed by Furneaux's monosyllable,—insensibly the four deserted the brilliantly lighted library and gathered in the somewhat somber hall, whose old oak wainscoting and Grinling Gibbons fireplace forbade the use of garish lamps. Insensibly, too, their voices lowered. The butler and housekeeper hardly knew what to expect, and were creepy and ill at ease, but the two police officers realized that they were about to witness a scene of unparalleled effrontery, which, in its outcome, might have results vastly different from those anticipated.

They were sure now that Hylda Prout had killed Rose de Bercy. Furneaux had known that terrible fact since his first meeting with Osborne's secretary, whereas Winter had only begun to surmise it when he and Furneaux were reconciled on the very threshold of Marlborough Street police-station. Now he was as certain of it as Furneaux. Page by page, chapter by chapter, his colleague had unfolded a most convincing theory of the crime. But theories will not suffice for a judge and jury—there must be circumstantial evidence as well—and not only was such evidence scanty as against Hylda Prout, but it existed in piles against Osborne, against Pauline Dessaulx, and against Furneaux himself. Indeed, Winter had been compelled to recall his permission to Janoc and his sister to leave England that day. He foresaw that Hylda Prout, if brought to trial, would use her knowledge of Rose de Bercy's dealings with the Anarchist movement to throw the gravest suspicion on its votaries in London, and it would require no great expert in criminal law to break up the theoretical case put forward by the police by demonstrating the circumstantial one that existed in regard to Pauline Dessaulx.

This line of defense, already strong, would become impregnable if neither Janoc nor Pauline were forthcoming as witnesses. So Clarke, greatly to his delight, was told off again to supervise their movements, after they had been warned not to quit Soho until Winter gave them his written permission.

Some of the difficulties ahead, a whole troupe of fantastic imageries from the past, crowded in on Winter's mind as he stood there in the hall with Furneaux. What a story it would make if published as he could tell it! What a romance! It began eight years ago at a *fête champêtre* in

Jersey. Then came a brief delirium of wedded life for
Furneaux, followed by his wife's flight and reappearance
as a notable actress. Osborne came on the scene, and
quickly fell a victim to her beauty and charm of manner.
It was only when marriage was spoken of that Furneaux
decided to interfere, and he had actually gone to
Osborne's residence in order to tell him the truth as to his
promised wife on the very day she was killed. Failing to
meet him, after a long wait in the library and museum,
during which he had noted the absence of both the
Saracen dagger and the celt, already purloined for their
dread purposes, he had gone to Feldisham Mansions.

During a heart-breaking scene with his wife he had
forced from her a solemn promise to tell Osborne why she
could not marry him, and then to leave England. The
unhappy woman was writing the last word in her diary
when Furneaux was announced! No wonder she canceled
an engagement for dinner and the theater. She was sick
at heart. A vain creature, the wealth and position she
craved for had been snatched from her grasp on the very
moment they seemed most sure.

The murder followed his departure within half an
hour. Planned and executed by a woman whom none
would dream of, it was almost worthy to figure as the
crime of the century. Hylda Prout had counted on no
other suspect than the man she loved. She knew he was
safe—she assured herself, in the first place, that he could
offer the most positive proof of his innocence—but she
reckoned on popular indignation alleging his guilt, while
she alone would stand by him through every pang of
obloquy and despair. She was well prepared, guarded
from every risk. Her open-hearted employer had no
secrets from her. She meant to imperil him, to cast him
into the furnace, and pluck him forth to her own arms.

But fate could plot more deviously and strangely than
Hylda Prout. It could bring about the meeting of Osborne
and Rosalind, the mutual despair and self-sacrifice of
Janoc and Pauline, the insensate quarrel between Winter

and Furneaux, and the jealous prying of Clarke, while scene after scene of tragic force unfolded itself at Tormouth, in the Fraternal Club, in the dismal cemetery, in Porchester Gardens, and in the dens of Soho.

Winter sighed deeply at the marvel of it all, and Furneaux heard him.

"She will be here soon," he said coolly. "She is just putting on Osborne's boots."

Winter started at the apparent callousness of the man.

"This is rather Frenchified," he whispered. "Reminds one of the 'reconstructed crime' method of the *juge d'instruction*. I wish we had more good, sound, British evidence."

"There is nothing good, or sound, or British about this affair," said Furneaux. "It is French from beginning to end—a passionate crime as they say—but I shall be glad when it is ended, and I am free."

"Free?"

"Yes. When she is safely dealt with," and he nodded in the direction of the dressing-room, "I shall resign, clear off, betake my whims and my weaknesses to some other clime."

"Don't be an ass, Furneaux!"

"Can't help it, dear boy. I'm a bit French, too, you know. No Englishman could have hounded down Osborne as I have done, merely to gratify my own notions of what was due to the memory of my dead wife. And I have played with this maniac upstairs as a cat plays with a mouse. I wouldn't have done that, though, if she hadn't smashed Mirabel's face. She ought to have spared that. Therein she was a tiger rather than a woman. Poor Mirabel!"

Not Rose, but Mirabel! His thoughts had bridged the years. He murmured the words in a curiously unemotional tone, but Winter was no longer deceived. It would be many a day, if ever, before Furneaux became his cheery, impish, mercurial self again.

And now there was an opening of a door, and Winter shot one warning glance at the curtains which shrouded the passage to the kitchen. A man's figure appeared beyond the rails of the upper landing, a man attired in a gray frock-coat suit and wearing a silk hat. Mrs. Bates uttered a slight scream.

"Well, I never!" she squeaked.

"But you did, once," urged Furneaux, instantly alert. "You see now that you might be mistaken when you said you saw Mr. Osborne on that evening?"

"Oh, yes, sir; if that is Miss Prout she's the very image—Now, who would have believed it?"

"You did," prompted Furneaux again. "But this time you must be more careful. Tell us now who it was you saw on the stair, your master, or his secretary made up to represent him?"

Mrs. Bates began to cry.

"I wouldn't have said such a thing for a mint of money, sir. It was cruel to deceive a poor woman so, real cruel I call it. Of course, it was Miss Prout I saw. Well, there! What a horrid creature to behave in that way—"

"No comments, please," said Furneaux sternly.

Throughout he was gazing at Hylda Prout with eyes that scintillated. She was standing now on the half-landing, and her face had lost some of its striking semblance to Osborne's because of the expression of mocking triumph that gleamed through its make-up.

"That will do, thank you, Miss Prout," he said. "Now, will you kindly walk slowly up again, reeling somewhat, as if you were on the verge of collapse after undergoing a tremendous strain?"

A choked cry, or groan, followed by a scuffle, came from the curtained doorway, and Hylda turned sharply.

"Who is there?" she demanded, in a sort of quick alarm that contrasted oddly with her previous air of complete self-assurance.

"Jenkins," growled Winter, "just go there and see that none of the servants are peeping. That door should have been closed. Slam it now!"

The butler hurried with steps that creaked on the parquet floor. Hylda leaned over the balusters and watched him. He fumbled with the curtains.

"It is all right, sir," he said thickly.

"Some one is there," she cried. "Who is it? I am not here to be made a show of, even to please some stupid policemen."

Winter strode noisily across the hall, talking the while, vowing official vengeance on eavesdroppers. He, too, reached the doorway, glanced within, and drew back the curtains.

"Some kitchen-maid, I suppose," he said off-handedly. "Anyhow, she has run away. You need not wait any longer, Miss Prout. Kindly change your clothing as quickly as possible and come with us. You have beaten us. Mr. Osborne must be released forthwith."

"Ah!"

Her sudden spasm of fear was dispelled by hearing that promise. She forgot to "reel" as she ran upstairs, but Furneaux did not remind her. He exchanged glances with Winter, and the latter motioned Jenkins to take Mrs. Bates to her own part of the establishment.

"At Vine Street, I think," muttered Winter in Furneaux's ear.

"No, here, I insist; we must strike now. She must realize that we have a case. Give her time to gather her energies and we shall never secure a conviction."

Winter loathed the necessity of terrifying a woman, but he yielded, since he saw no help for it. This time they had not long to wait. Soon they heard a rapid, confident tread on the stairs, and Hylda Prout was with them in the library. Both men, who had been seated, rose when she entered.

"Well," she said jauntily, "are you convinced?"

"Fully," said Winter.

She turned to Furneaux.

"But you, little man, what do *you* say?"

"I have never needed to be convinced," he answered. "I have known the truth since the day when we first met."

Something in his manner seemed to trouble her, but those golden brown eyes dwelt on him in a species of scornful surprise.

"Why, then, have you liberated Janoc and his sister?" she demanded.

"Because they are innocent."

She laughed, a nervous, unmirthful laugh.

"But there only remains Mr. Osborne," she protested.

"There is one other, the murderess," he said. Even while she gazed at him in wonder he had come quite near. His right hand shot out and grasped her arm.

"I arrest you, Hylda Prout," he said. "I charge you with the murder of Mirabel Furneaux, otherwise known as Rose de Bercy, at Feldisham Mansions, on the night of July 3d."

She looked at him in a panic to which she tried vainly to give a semblance of incredulity. Even in that moment of terror a new thought throbbed in her dazed brain.

"Mirabel Furneaux!" she managed to gasp.

"Yes, my wife. You committed a needless crime, Hylda Prout. She had never done, nor ever could have done, you any injury. But it is my duty to warn you that everything you now say will be taken down in writing, and may be used in evidence against you."

She tried to wrest herself free, but his fingers clung to her like a steel trap. Winter, too, approached, as if to show the folly of resistance.

"Let go my arm!" she shrieked, and her eyes blazed redly though the color had fled from her cheeks.

"I cannot. I dare not," said Furneaux. "I have reason to believe that you carry a weapon, perhaps poison, concealed in your clothing."

"Idiot!" she screamed, now beside herself with rage, "what evidence can you produce against me? You will be the laughing stock of London, you and your arrests."

"Mrs. Bates knows now who it was she saw on the

stairs," said Furneaux patiently. "Campbell, the driver of the taxicab, has recognized you as the person he drove to and from Feldisham Mansions. Mary Dean, the housemaid there, can say at last why she fancied that Mr. Osborne killed her mistress. But you'll hear these things in due course. At present you must come with me."

"Where to?"

"To Vine Street police-station."

"Shall I not be permitted to see Rupert?"

"No."

A tremor convulsed her lithe body. Then, and not till then, did she really understand that the apparently impossible had happened. Still, her extraordinary power of self-reliance came to her aid. She ceased to struggle, and appealed to Winter.

"This man is acting like a lunatic," she cried. "He says his wife was killed, and if that be true he is no fit person to conduct an inquiry into the innocence or guilt of those on whom he wreaks his vengeance. You know why I came here to-night—merely to prove how you had blundered in the past—yet you dare to turn my harmless acting into a justification of my arrest. Where are these people, Campbell and the woman, whose testimony you bring against me?"

Now, in putting that impassioned question, she was wiser than she knew. Furneaux was ever ready to take risks in applying criminal procedure that Winter fought shy of. He had seen more than one human vampire slip from his grasp because of some alleged unfairness on the part of the police, of which a clever counsel had made ingenious use during the defense. If Hylda Prout had been identified by others than Mrs. Bates, of whose presence alone she was aware, she had every right to be confronted with them. He turned aside and told the horrified Jenkins to bring the witnesses from the room in which they had taken refuge. As a matter of fact, Campbell and Mary Dean, in charge of Police Constable Johnson, had been concealed behind the curtains that draped the servants' passage, and Johnson had scarce been able to stifle the scream that rose to the housemaid's lips when she saw on the stairs the living embodiment of her mistress's murderer.

But Furneaux did not mean to allow Hylda Prout to regain the marvelous self-possession which had been imperiled by the events of the past minute.

"While we are waiting for Campbell and the girl you may as well learn the really material thing that condemns you," he said, whispering in her ear with quiet menace. "You ought to have destroyed that gray suit which you purchased from a second-hand clothes dealer. It was a deadly mistake to keep those blood-stained garments. The clothes Osborne wore have been produced long since. They were soiled by you two days after the murder, a fact which I can prove by half a dozen witnesses. Those which you wore to-night, *which you are wearing now*, are spotted with your victim's blood. I know, because I have seen them in your lodgings, and they can be identified beyond dispute by the man who sold them to you."

Suddenly he raised his voice.

"Winter! Quick! She has the strength of ten women!"

For Hylda Prout, hearing those fateful words, was seized with a fury of despair. She had peered into Furneaux's eyes and seen there the pitiless purpose which had filled his every waking moment since his wife's untimely death. Love and hate had conspired to wreck her life. They had mastered her at last. From being their votary she had become their victim. An agonizing sigh came from her straining breast. She was fighting like a catamount, while Winter held her shoulders and Furneaux her wrists; then she collapsed between them, and a thin red stream issued from her lips.

They carried her to the sofa on which she had lain when for the first and only time in her life those same red lips had met Rupert Osborne's.

Winter hurried to the door, and sent Campbell,

coming on tiptoe across the hall, flying in his taxi for a doctor. But Furneaux did not move from her side. He gazed down at her with something of the judge, something of the executioner, in his waxen features.

"All heart!" he muttered, "all heart, controlled by a warped brain!"

"She has broken a blood vessel," said Winter.

"No; she has broken her heart," said Furneaux, hearing, though apparently not heeding him.

"A physical impossibility," growled the Chief Inspector, to whom the sight of a woman's suffering was peculiarly distressing.

"Her heart has dilated beyond belief. It is twice the normal size. This is the end, Winter! She is dying!"

The flow of blood stopped abruptly. She opened her eyes, those magnificent eyes which were no longer golden brown but a pathetic yellow.

"Oh, forgive!" she muttered. "I—I—loved you, Rupert—with all my soul!"

She seemed to sink a little, to shrink, to pass from a struggle to peace. The lines of despair fled from her face. She lay there in white beauty, a lily whiteness but little marred by traces of the make-up hurriedly wiped off her cheeks and forehead.

"May the Lord be merciful to her!" said Furneaux, and without another word, he hurried from the room and out of the house.

Winter, having secured some degree of order in a distracted household, raced off to Marlborough Street; but Furneaux had been there before him, and Osborne, knowing nothing of Hylda Prout's death, had flown to Porchester Gardens and Rosalind.

The hour was not so late that the thousand eyes of Scotland Yard could not search every nook in which Furneaux might have taken refuge, but in vain. Winter, grieving for his friend, fearing the worst, remained all night in his office, receiving reports of failure by telephone and messenger. At last, when the sun rose, he went wearily to his home, and was lying, fully dressed, on his bed, in the state of half-sleep, half-exhaustion, which is nature's way of healing the bruised spirit, when he seemed to hear Furneaux's voice sobbing:

"My Mirabel, why did you leave me, you whom I loved!"

Instantly he sprang up in a frenzy of action, and ran out into the street. At that early hour, soon after six o'clock, there was no vehicle to be found except a battered cab which had prowled London during the night, but he woke the heavy-witted driver with a promise of double fare, and the horse ambled over the slow miles to the yews and laurels of Kensal Green Cemetery.

There he found him, kneeling by the side of that one little mound of earth, after having walked in solitude through the long hours till the gates were opened for the day's digging of graves. Winter said nothing. He led his friend away, and had him cared for.

Slowly the cloud lifted. At last, when a heedless public had forgotten the crime and its dramatic sequel, there came a day when Furneaux appeared at Scotland Yard.

"Hello, Winter," he said, coming in as though the world had grown young again.

"Hello, Furneaux, glad to see you," said Winter, pushing the cigar-box across the table.

"Had my letter?"

"Yes."

"Who has taken my place—Clarke?"

"No, not Clarke."

"Who, then?"

"Nobody, yet. The fact is, Furneaux—"

"I've resigned—that is the material fact."

"Yes, I know. But you don't mind giving me your advice."

"No, of course not—just for the sake of old times."

"Well, there is this affair of Lady Harringay's disappearance. It is a ticklish business. Seen anything about it in the paper?"

"A line or two."

"I'm at my wits' end to find time myself to deal with it. And I've not a man I can give it to—"

"Look here, Winter, I'm out of the force."

"But, to oblige me."

"I would do a great deal on that score."

"Get after her, then, without a moment's delay."

"But there's my resignation."

Winter picked a letter from a bundle, struck a match, set fire to the paper, and lighted a cigar with it.

"There goes your resignation!" he said.

*   *   *   *   *

During the following summer Rosalind Marsh and Rupert Osborne were married at Tormouth. It was a quiet wedding, and since that day they have led quiet lives, so it is to be presumed that they have settled satisfactorily the problem of how to be happy though rich.

THE END

Resurrected Press books in A. E. Fielding's *The Chief Inspector Pointer Mystery* Series

The Eames-Erskine Case (1924)
The Charteris Mystery (1925)
The Footsteps that Stopped (1926)
The Clifford Affair (1927)
The Cluny Problem (1928)
The Net Around Joan Ingilby (1928)
The Murder at the Nook (1929)
The Mysterious Partner (1929)
The Craig Poisoning Mystery (1930)
The Wedding Chest Mystery (1930)
The Upfold Farm Mystery (1931)
Death of John Tait (1932)
The Westwood Mystery (1932)
The Tall House Mystery (1933)
The Cautley Conundrum (1934)
The Paper-Chase (1934)
The Case of the Missing Diary (1935)
Tragedy at Beechcroft (1935)
The Case of the Two Pearl Necklaces (1935)
Mystery at the Rectory (1936)
Black Cats Are Lucky (1937)
Scarecrow (1937)
Pointer to a Crime (1944)

Resurrected Press Books in H. Ashbook's *Detective Spike Tracy Mystery* Series

The Murder of Cicely Thane (1930)

The Murder of Stephen Kester (1931)

The Murder of Sigurd Sharon (1933)

A Most Immoral Murder (1935)

Murder Makes Murder (1937)

Murder Comes Back (1940)

Murder on Friday (1941)

RESURRECTED PRESS BOOKS FROM *THE ETHEL THOMAS DETECTIVE STORY* SERIES BY CORTLAND FITZSIMMON'S

The Whispering Window

The Moving Finger

Mystery at Hidden Harbor

The Evil Men Do

AVAILABLE FROM RESURRECTED PRESS!

THE EDWARDIAN DETECTIVES
LITERARY SLEUTHS OF THE EDWARDIAN ERA

The exploits of the great Victorian Detectives, Poe's C. Auguste Dupin, Gaboriau's Lecoq, and most famously, Arthur Conan Doyle's Sherlock Holmes, are well known. But what of those fictional detectives that came after, those of the Edwardian Age? The period between the death of Queen Victoria and the First World War had been called the Golden Age of the detective short story, but how familiar is the modern reader with the sleuths of this era? And such an extraordinary group they were, including in their numbers an unassuming English priest, a blind man, a master of disguises, a lecturer in medical jurisprudence, a noble woman working for Scotland Yard, and a savant so brilliant he was known as "The Thinking Machine."

To introduce readers to these detectives, Resurrected Press has assembled a collection of stories featuring these and other remarkable sleuths in The Edwardian Detectives.

- The Case of Laker, Absconded by Arthur Morrison
- The Fenchurch Street Mystery by Baroness Orczy
- The Crime of the French Café by Nick Carter
- The Man with Nailed Shoes by R Austin Freeman
- The Blue Cross by G. K. Chesterton
- The Case of the Pocket Diary Found in the Snow by Augusta Groner
- The Ninescore Mystery by Baroness Orczy
- The Riddle of the Ninth Finger by Thomas W. Hanshew
- The Knight's Cross Signal Problem by Ernest Bramah

- The Problem of Cell 13 by Jacques Futrelle
- The Conundrum of the Golf Links by Percy James Brebner
- The Silkworms of Florence by Clifford Ashdown
- The Gateway of the Monster by William Hope Hodgson
- The Affair at the Semiramis Hotel by A. E. W. Mason
- The Affair of the Avalanche Bicycle & Tyre Co., LTD by Arthur Morrison

RESURRECTED PRESS CLASSIC MYSTERY CATALOGUE

Journeys into Mystery
Travel and Mystery in a More Elegant Time

The Edwardian Detectives
Literary Sleuths of the Edwardian Era

Gems of Mystery
Lost Jewels from a More Elegant Age

E. C. Bentley
Trent's Last Case: The Woman in Black

Ernest Bramah
Max Carrados Resurrected:
The Detective Stories of Max Carrados

Agatha Christie
The Secret Adversary
The Mysterious Affair at Styles

Octavus Roy Cohen
Midnight

Freeman Wills Croft
The Ponson Case
The Pit Prop Syndicate

J. S. Fletcher
The Herapath Property
The Rayner-Slade Amalgamation
The Chestermarke Instinct
The Paradise Mystery
Dead Men's Money

The Middle of Things
Ravensdene Court
Scarhaven Keep
The Orange-Yellow Diamond
The Middle Temple Murder
The Tallyrand Maxim
The Borough Treasurer
In the Mayor's Parlour
The Saftey Pin

R. Austin Freeman
The Mystery of 31 New Inn from the Dr. Thorndyke Series
John Thorndyke's Cases from the Dr. Thorndyke Series
The Red Thumb Mark from The Dr. Thorndyke Series
The Eye of Osiris from The Dr. Thorndyke Series
A Silent Witness from the Dr. John Thorndyke Series
The Cat's Eye from the Dr. John Thorndyke Series
Helen Vardon's Confession: A Dr. John Thorndyke Story
As a Thief in the Night: A Dr. John Thorndyke Story
Mr. Pottermack's Oversight: A Dr. John Thorndyke Story
Dr. Thorndyke Intervenes: A Dr. John Thorndyke Story
The Singing Bone: The Adventures of Dr. Thorndyke
The Stoneware Monkey: A Dr. John Thorndyke Story
The Great Portrait Mystery, and Other Stories: A Collection of Dr. John Thorndyke and Other Stories
The Penrose Mystery: A Dr. John Thorndyke Story
The Uttermost Farthing: A Savant's Vendetta

Arthur Griffiths
The Passenger From Calais
The Rome Express

Fergus Hume
The Mystery of a Hansom Cab
The Green Mummy
The Silent House
The Secret Passage

Edgar Jepson
The Loudwater Mystery

A. E. W. Mason
At the Villa Rose

A. A. Milne
The Red House Mystery
Baroness Emma Orczy
The Old Man in the Corner

Edgar Allan Poe
The Detective Stories of Edgar Allan Poe

Arthur J. Rees
The Hampstead Mystery
The Shrieking Pit
The Hand In The Dark
The Moon Rock
The Mystery of the Downs

Mary Roberts Rinehart
Sight Unseen and The Confession

Dorothy L. Sayers
Whose Body?

Sir William Magnay
The Hunt Ball Mystery

Mabel and Paul Thorne
The Sheridan Road Mystery

Louis Tracy
The Strange Case of Mortimer Fenley
The Albert Gate Mystery
The Bartlett Mystery
The Postmaster's Daughter
The House of Peril
The Sandling Case: What Would You Have Done?
Charles Edmonds Walk
The Paternoster Ruby

John R. Watson
The Mystery of the Downs
The Hampstead Mystery

Edgar Wallace
The Daffodil Mystery
The Crimson Circle

Carolyn Wells
Vicky Van
The Man Who Fell Through the Earth
In the Onyx Lobby
Raspberry Jam
The Clue
The Room with the Tassels
The Vanishing of Betty Varian
The Mystery Girl
The White Alley
The Curved Blades
Anybody but Anne
The Bride of a Moment
Faulkner's Folly
The Diamond Pin
The Gold Bag
The Mystery of the Sycamore
The Come Backy

Raoul Whitfield
Death in a Bowl

And much more!
Visit ResurrectedPress.com
for our complete catalogue

About Resurrected Press

A division of Intrepid Ink, LLC, Resurrected Press is dedicated to bringing high quality, vintage books back into publication. See our entire catalogue and find out more at www.ResurrectedPress.com.

About Intrepid Ink, LLC

Intrepid Ink, LLC provides full publishing services to authors of fiction and non-fiction books, eBooks and websites. From editing to formatting, from publishing to marketing, Intrepid Ink gets your creative works into the hands of the people who want to read them. Find out more at www.IntrepidInk.com.

www.ingramcontent.com/pod-product-compliance
Lightning Source LLC
Chambersburg PA
CBHW070844250626
47159CB00003B/928